The Madness of Captain Mills

Bryan Kesselman

RIVERSONG
BOOKS

An Imprint of Sulis International Press
Los Angeles | Dallas | London

ISBN (print): 978-1-946849-89-2
ISBN (eBook): 978-1-946849-91-5

Published by Riversong Books
An Imprint of Sulis International
Los Angeles | Dallas | London
www.sulisinternational.com

Contents

PART ONE

Captain Mills and the Scandal of the

Song: Bound for Australia

I have not seen my home for many a day,
I've left it behind and I'm sailing away,
To come on this voyage I spent all my pay,
Now we're bound for Australia.

Here up on deck, when the sun's shining bright,
Hopeful and happy, though land's out of sight,
We forget all our cares till the cold of the night,
While we're bound for Australia.

I was down on my luck with nothing to do,
Had not a potato to put in a stew,
A babe on the way: in three months it's due,
So we're bound for Australia.

Here up on deck &c.

1
Dr Gover's Introduction

There are no pictures of Captain John Powell Mills of the Merchant Navy. Perhaps, though, we can imagine him in his prime—a head of reddish, unkempt hair (inherited from his Irish mother), the full beard sported by sailors, a pipe in his mouth, a mouth which churned out rough-and-ready talk— that is when he chose to speak, for he was, as a young man at least, constitutionally taciturn. Brought up by his widowed mother, he (and his siblings) had roamed free, until, with that foresight granted only to mothers, he was entered into a school for children of mariners. His father, John Mills senior, had been a sea-faring man, and, though John junior was nearly six when that parent died, father had rarely seen son being oft at sea for much of those early years.

The son's life was at times fraught with difficulties, often of his own making. His is not a personality which lends itself easily to liking. He was a rogue and a scoundrel, one who would chance his arm on any adventure which might bring profit, but whose apparent incompetence may be enough to explain his lack of success in his early ventures. On the other hand, he would find himself praised as a hero and thanked for his cool-headedness in times of danger. However, his behaviour, as the years passed, became self-obsessed and unacceptable.

But more of that later. After an education over which discipline loomed large, he went to sea.

2
Northallerton Prison, February 1867

I had not intended to follow his story, being engaged on a completely different matter, but, in February 1867, I was sent to investigate overcrowding at Her Majesty's Prison Northallerton in North Yorkshire.

My name is Robert Mundy Gover, Member of the Royal College of Physicians, and Medical Inspector of Her Majesty's Prisons. I was thirty-four at the time of my visit to Northallerton. I had been Resident Surgeon at Millbank Prison in London since 1860, and since 1865 in full charge of medical matters there, so I was not best pleased at being given this assignment which, at the time, I felt to be beneath my dignity. I arrived late at night, after a most tedious journey. The air was cold enough to freeze the lungs; the town was dark and silent. I was met by the ex-postmaster, one Marmaduke Sedgwick who had agreed to give me hospitality: a grizzled man with a hoary coat.

It was a short walk to Tutins Yard and his house. He lived there with his wife, their five children, and his wife's mother. All were asleep when we arrived.

'Come this way, sir, welcome to my poor home.'

It was poor, indeed. The man had evidently fallen on hard times.

'Bankrupt, sir; I am bankrupt. No money at all, save what you will give me for this night's lodging. 'Tis my mother-in-law's house—times are hard.'

He held out his hand, and I counted the coins into it.

I spent an uncomfortable night sleeping in what usually passed for a parlour. The house was cold, my bed was hard and the blankets were thin. In the morning, my host was nowhere to be seen. The house was empty but for me, and when, upon foraging in the kitchen for some breakfast, I found nothing to eat, I wrapped myself up in my coat, and made my way to the prison, stopping on my way to buy a hot pie from a stall in the Market Square.

Upon my arrival, I was shown into the presence of the governor, an imposing figure of a man with a lop-sided mouth. He was taking morning tea with the prison chaplain. The room was not spartan, exactly, but was gloomy and cold. The sad fire that burned in the grate gave no warmth, and the two men who stood to greet me both seemed to wish that they were elsewhere.

'Mr Gover, is it? Allow me to introduce you to our chaplain, Mr Nethercliffe, who was just telling me how he intends to improve the pastoral care we give the prisoners.'

I doubted this 'care' was taken vey seriously. Some of the reports I had read went back to 1833, when prisons were first inspected, and they left me in little doubt that the needs of prison inmates were largely ignored.

Nethercliffe smiled wanly, and addressed his superior, 'Thank-you for your time, Mr Gardner, I should be getting back to my duties.'

'Nonsense,' replied the Governor, 'I will need you to show Mr Gover how we do things here. Really,' addressing me, 'he is the most self-conscious fellow I know, always needs bucking up. Have some more tea,' this to Nethercliffe. 'I am sure Mr Gover would like some as well. Dear me, the pot is cold. I'll call for more. Not in a hurry, are you, Gover?' Mr Gardner rang a bell.

I had hardly uttered a word the whole time. The proceedings reminded me of a double act I had seen once in the music hall —Two Gloomy Men. These two were just as unfunny.

A fresh pot was brought in by a prisoner.

'Leave it there, Mills,' said Gardner. The prisoner did as he was told, and then made his escape from The Presence. Gardner continued: 'You know, Nethercliffe, Mills may be just the lad to show our friend around. What do you say?'

'Well… I, er…'

'Exactly! Arrange it, will you, Nethercliffe!' Then to me: 'Interesting lad, that Mills. Bound apprentice to one ship for five years, jumped ship to join another, in and out of trouble ever since. Don't believe everything he says, mind you, he's the smoothest liar you'll hear this side of next Christmas.'

So it was that I met John Powell Mills, not the captain with the red beard, but his eldest son, currently a prisoner at Northallerton. Although I was not there to delve into his life, there was something pleasing about the lad with his rough London accent, and I couldn't help but listen to him chatter about himself. Later that day, in Sedgwick's icy house, by the light of a candle (my own) I wrote down from memory some of the things he said; here is a sample:

'You may very well ask how I came to this pretty pass. Imprisoned as the result of a jape, a prank that went wrong. Look, I'm only here for three months, all I took was a rug, a blanket, two pairs of stockings and a f***ing cloth cap, hardly the crown jewels, it was a lark, that's all. The judge called me a juvenile delinquent. I'm nearly nineteen and this is the first time I have been in trouble to tell you the truth. Honestly, I only took the stuff for fun, don't know what Bob made such a fuss for. Bob, Robert White, that is, it was his stuff: he left it in his bunk. Our ships were laid abreast of each other on the east side of Whitby Harbour, and I sneaked on board the *Belle* and grabbed it all. Well, it was cold on the *Norma*. yes, it was probably cold on the *Belle* too… A Sunday afternoon it was… Later on, I put the blanket and the rug back on the *Belle*—our mate made me when he saw they were in my bag. Couldn't get them back to Bob's bunk just laid them down in the forecastle. Next day, noon it was, I was on the *Norma* with the other men, when a policeman comes on board and charges me with stealing. Didn't believe me when I said I hadn't taken the stockings or the cap... must've been because he made me pull up my trousers and saw I was wearing the stockings... Told him I'd bought them in Hartlepool: hard to keep to that story when he could see that I'd tried to pick out the threads which Bob had used to mark his name. The cap was still in my bag; Bob was angry when he saw the peak had been torn off... All right, it wasn't for fun; I took them to keep warm. I won't forget that policeman in a hurry, you bet! Constable Tom Bowson, young chap in his twenties.

'My mother doesn't know I'm here, thank God; I won't be telling her, you bet. My father?... Oh, yes! My father... Something of a rogue himself. What a rascal! Let me tell you something of him, he died last year... You mean you don't know about him. In that case, listen to this...

'December 1847, and my father, Captain John Powell Mills of the Merchant Navy, stood on the deck of the *Subraon*. My mother was not pleased with him: off gallivanting about again. She's never been one to hold back when she's angry. I don't blame him really; he never answered her back. His way of escaping her sharp tongue was by escaping her company completely. Mind you, he was always glad to get back to her at the end of a long voyage—I'd like to say that that's how I came to be born. But my mother was not the faithful type, maybe that's another reason he liked to get away from her. The *Subraon* left London on the 10th of December with him on board, and I was born on the following 8th of October; you do the sums if you like! She named me after him, though, and I never knew any father but him.

'Look, I didn't hang around him too much. Used to get a good walloping with a belt from him if I didn't look out. I was the oldest, but, soon as I could, I took to the Merchant Navy myself—just to get away. If you're interested you need to talk to my sister Rachel or my brother Masterman. They're both younger than what I am, but he liked them better. Masterman, he's apprentice to a plumber… I've decided to give the Merchant Navy up and be a blacksmith.'

He was very loquacious, and I learned much about him as we walked, including the confusing fact that his full name was Masterman John Powell Mills and his brother was John Masterman Mills, but that he was known as John and his brother as Masterman. He entertained me by impersonating some of the other prisoners as we walked, but my tour was too soon at an end. The results of my investigation submitted, but never acted upon, I was soon busy with other tasks.

*

Four years after the events which I related above, I was browsing through a bookstall in one of the run-down shops near Cheapside, when I came across a tatty leather-bound notebook. Several pages were missing, but the name Acret was written inside the cover. On flicking through the pages, I found a reference to the *Subraon*, and, intrigued, I bought the book for a few pennies and took it home. You will read some of the entries yourself later on—Acret had been the ship's surgeon. I was reminded of my prison guide, and dug out my old notes from my visit to Northallerton. On reading them through, I was almost surprised at how much I had written about him. Young Mills, I had written, had been born in Deptford not far from the London docks where his family had all been based. He had told me that his father had been mentioned in newspapers, and I decided to visit the offices of *The Times*. My own father is a friend of the editor, and I was allowed to look through old copies. And I did indeed find mention of Captain Mills of the *Subraon*.

I discovered that he had been caught up in more than one scandal over the years, and though some facts were reported in the press, all inquiries into his actions seemed to have been since forgotten or perhaps smothered aborning. So I determined to find more about Captain Mills and his strange career.

I found plenty, and some of it not very nice. I'll try to put it in chronological order for you and tell it as it should be told. I interviewed several of the participants in this tale, and managed to discover the whereabouts of some journals. What follows is an amalgamation of the information I found. In order to avoid any confusion, let me at once iterate that there were three men called John Mills. The eldest John Mills was the father of the subject of our tale. Then there was his son John Powell Mills, and *his* son John Powell Mills who I saw in Northallerton Prison.

*

From my own diary:

'December 1871—Another discovery.

'I placed an advertisement in *The Times* for information. My mother always said that if there was any mystery to be fathomed, any information to be found, any lost article to find, then I was the one to uncover the truth. She said that I had inherited that ability from her side of the family, the Mundys. It is true that, as a child, I had an uncanny knack of finding missing items. Moreover, I had an inquiring mind and also a retentive memory. Perhaps I missed my calling, and should have been a detective. I have just discovered the diary of Emma Smith, an Irish girl who had emigrated to Australia on the *Subraon*. It was in the keeping of a sailor who read my advertisement and brought it to me: another item to add to my collection of evidence.'

*

June 1872. One Monday morning, my landlady, Mrs Latchford, came bustling to my door with the post: five letters, all bills, and a dirty package measuring about seven by nine inches. Inside was a much-weathered leather-bound book. There was no other enclosure or covering note. Upon opening it I found something I had long wished to see, for, after much searching and letter writing, finally I was in possession of that most sort-after primary source—the journal of Captain Mills himself while he was Master of the *Subraon*. What mysteries might I unlock? What puzzles might I solve? I trembled as I began to read, wanting to know all instantaneously without having the trouble of reading.

The book itself may, when new, have been a well-produced item, but now its pages were grimy, and the cover soiled with hard use. The word '*Subraon*' was inscribed on the first page, and beneath it the name 'JP Mills, Master'. Many pages had been ripped out, and on those left, the text was mostly illegible due to water damage. The entries were undated, and, as I read, I realised that what I had before me seemed merely to be a collection of thoughts and aphorisms invented by the writer. Though this may at first sight seem disappointing, and I was disappointed, I have nevertheless included a little of Captain Mills's thoughts in the description of events which took place on the *Subraon*.

3

The Early Life of Captain John Powell Mills

In order to give sufficient background to this tale, we must step back in time. John Powell Mills (our hero—known to the friends of his childhood as JP) was born in Swansea, Wales on the 22nd of July 1816 to parents who lived a wandering kind of life. His mother, Frances Mills (née Powell) had grown up in Cove, County Cork, Ireland. She, from an early age, could not abide the thought of spending all her days in such a small, dull place as Cove, and yearned for adventures such as her own mother had told her as a child at bedtime. Essex born John Mills, seaman, whose ship, H.M.S. *Brisk*, was anchored one summer in Cork harbour was very taken with the small but fiery Irish colleen. Full of himself, he often told her how he would take her away from Ireland so that they could make their fortune together. How she longed to go with him and share his life! (Her parents were not best pleased with the idea.) They married in her hometown early in December 1811, and he whisked her away with him to the romantic haven that was Swansea. She was soon disillusioned with her new life: a hard time of it she had. He was often away, and their children came while he was not there to be of any use.

Soon after JP was born, his father appeared again, this time to move his entire family to London, that great heaving metropolis. Frances's hopes were raised—only to be dashed yet again when the beautiful house she had pictured for herself

11

turned out to be a dilapidated dwelling in Rotherhithe, Surrey almost on the south bank of the Thames. Mills senior thought it grand to be so near to the docks; he was immune, perhaps, to the foul smells of the place and to the fog which came rolling in from the east: a grey thickness which turned brown as it passed through London itself on its westward journey. He was happy to be near to his two aunts—Margaret, his late father's married sister, and Martha, widow of his father's uncle.

By this time, he happily made it known to all that he was a ship's master, though he had until not long before been a ship's *quarter*master, a worthy profession, but hardly the same thing. Quartermasters are given charge of food and drink—a position of trust. Nine years he spent as quartermaster of the *Brisk*, an 18 gun sloop and the second of His Majesty's ships to bear that name. The *Brisk* visited Cork a number of times, before Mills left the Navy in 1815 so that, finally, he could realise his ambition of being a ship's master, if not in the Royal Navy, then in the Merchant Navy. His uncle, William Mellish, who owned more than one ship, had promised him command of the *Minerva*, built in Bombay. The *Minerva* had been chartered by the East India Company to undertake six voyages to India. Mills was delighted; the *Minerva* was only three years old, and he looked forward to a long association with her. Mellish was later sued for breach of contract by the *Minerva's* previous master, Captain George Richardson, to whom he had promised captaincy of another vessel in exchange for giving up the *Minerva*, Mellish having failed in that promise. Mills had nothing but scorn for Richardson, and Richardson had nothing but scorn for Mills whom he regarded as an upstart; the two kept out each other's way by sailing in opposite directions. Richardson had the better of it becoming Captain of H.M.S. *Semiramis*, a frigate of the Royal Navy.

And so, John Mills and family bumped along the merry pathway of life, he away for weeks on end, Mrs Mills glad for the peace obtained when he was not there to abuse his children or her. But seamen are not, and have never been, known for their temperate ways, and it should be no surprise to learn that he did not live to a ripe old age. Indeed, he died in 1822 on board the *Minerva* while making a fourth return journey from India, leaving his wife expecting yet another baby. His oldest surviving child, the subject of our story, was not quite six.

Mills senior left a will which makes interesting reading both for what was written there, and what was not written there.

*

I, John Mills of Woodford in the County of Essex, Master Mariner, being of sound and disposing Mind Memory and Understanding, do hereby make and publish my last Will and Testament in manner following: I give devise and bequeath all and singular my property, house, Effects and things real and personal whatsoever and wheresoever, and especially a freehold house Messuage or Tenement situate and being in Mile End Road, now in the occupation of my Aunt Martha Mills Widow, and which will become my property at her decease, unto my Aunt Margaret Mellish, Wife of William Mellish of Shadwell dock in the County of Middlesex, Merchant, to her sole use and benefit, to be by her disposal of as she may think fit, free from the debts and control of her said husband. And I do hereby appoint my said Aunt Margaret Mellish Executrix of this my Will, revoking all former and other wills by me heretofore made in witness whereof I have hereunto set my Hand and Seal the ninth day of April One thousand eight hundred and twenty-one.

*

From which it can be seen that he did not leave his possessions to his wife and children, though the reason for this seems obscure. Frances Mills was therefore left with a son, a daughter, another child on the way, and little means to support herself. She had never enjoyed the company of her husband's aunts, which is to say that they had no intention of offering her any assistance in the bringing up of her children. Her husband's friends, those who had witnessed the will, were all sea-faring fellows—all great men in their own estimation. John Thurgar, George Scott and J. Edge had no interest in the widow of their friend, but only in his wake at which his memory was toasted many times and into the early hours of the morning, when the tavern keeper turned them out, and they all staggered back to their various berths on board ship.

Frances worked hard to turn her infant sons, John and Joseph, into well-behaved boys. Their home at 8 West Lane, Rotherhithe was kept as clean as she could make it, while she herself took in laundry. Her daughter helped her, but her sons did not, and it was hard to pay for the upkeep of herself and her three hungry children; their appetites did not grow smaller with time. And then she discovered that sons of seamen of her husband's rank and above were entitled to train for the navy, though certain conditions had to be met.

John Powell Mills was baptised on the 13th of February 1825 at St. Mary, Rotherhithe when he was nearly nine together with his brother Joseph who was nearly two. Of their sister, the middle child, there is no mention.

Joseph was too young to raise serious objection to the process, except by turning bright pink during the ceremony and wailing at the top of his voice, for the gloomy atmosphere in the church was not to his liking. His older brother, though, was fully able to give voice to his opinions, and made it known in no uncertain terms that he was not happy with the arrangement. His objections were largely founded on the shoes that his mother had borrowed for him to wear since they were too tight. The objections were overruled by his mother. And so he had suffered the indignity of walking painfully along Paradise Street, past the houses where his friends lived, dressed in clothes that disgusted him for their so-called 'finery', while his mother made a great show of her pride.

When they reached the church, his anger had been bottled up for so long a time that he was ready to burst, but he could only manage a strangulated whisper: 'Mother, must we do this?'

'Yes,' came the response, followed after a pause with, 'It's for your own good, John—and for heaven's sake stop fiddling with those buttons, they took an age to sew on!'

'But it's too tight!' he gasped while wrestling manfully with the jacket she had made him wear.

'Stop it at once!' This last from the Reverend Thomas Hardwicke M.A. the Curate of St. Mary's who was to perform the ceremony. Four years he had been installed there, and the misbehaviour of his parishioners' children never ceased to amaze him, for his own children were always (always) well-behaved. The party proceeded into the church.

*

On the 11th of August 1825, John Powell Mills was entered by his mother for training at the Royal Naval Asylum, Greenwich, whose regulations stated that certificates of birth and baptism must be produced before entry could be permitted, and since his baptismal certificate was included in the application she made on his behalf, it would appear that the baptism had been carried out with the specific purpose of allowing him to train there.

His mother produced in addition a reference for her late husband from Lieutenant Peter Blake, late of the *Brisk*, stating that Mills had conducted himself with diligence, sobriety and obedience to command. It is hard to imagine how she managed to persuade Lieut. Blake to testify to her husband's good qualities, knowing, as they both did, what he was really like.

There were other requirements which had to be met in order to satisfy the board. It was deemed necessary that two should sponsor entrants. One of her husband's old shipmates, William Henry Taylor of the barque *Europa*, agreed to act in that capacity.

And so young John Powell Mills, aged nine, with his life set fair before him and with the world to conquer, joined the ranks of boys and girls at the Royal Naval Asylum, to start his formal education. At fourteen boys would be sent to sea, and girls put to trade or household services.

The younger boys disdained to have any contact with the girls, and the younger girls had no interest in the boys. Nevertheless, they were rigorously kept apart—that at least was the intention. The older boys and girls had other ideas. Eight hundred boys were taught reading, writing and cyphering. The girls were taught reading, writing, needlework and household industry. During hours of relaxation the boys deemed suitable were supposed to be undergoing instruction in navigation, rope-and-sail-making, and the rudiments of naval discipline. A small number of those boys, however, found greater pleasure in plotting ways to tease the girls surreptitiously.

JP was one of that number. Capable as he was, and quick, he found that the lessons bored him. Feeling time dragging, and aware of his ability to find correct answers to problems without the need to study, he became ringleader of a foursome whose every intention was to make the lives of their chosen victims miserable. So, it was that there were occasions when a girl might rise from where she had been sitting to discover that the seat of her chair had previously been covered with wet ink, resulting in tears and a scolding from a teacher for having a dirty dress; or, at other times, books might be hidden from their owners, or doors might be jammed shut.

The boys were rarely discovered in any wrong-doings; JP's time there reached its nadir when he was caught passing a packet containing sweets to one of the girls, a crime strictly forbidden, but not the worst act of which he had been guilty. He was beaten, then duly hauled off to see the Governor of the Royal Naval Asylum, Captain George McKinley, a grand gentleman nearly seventy years of age. JP's fate might have been dismissal, were it not for the fact that the crusty old gentleman, a veteran of the Battle of Copenhagen, had already discovered a liking for the boy's mischievous ways.

'Mills, sir.'

'Ah, Mills, come in, lad. Stand up straight, and keep your eyes forward.'

'Yes, sir.'

'What is this they've been telling me about you talking to one of the girls, hey?'

'Well, sir…'

'Don't hedge, lad! Out with it, or it will be the worse for you.'

'I thought she might like… some refreshment, sir.'

'Oh, you did, did you? Well, if I ever hear of you doing such a thing again, you'll get another lashing, and be out of here before you can blink an eye.'

'Yes, sir.'

'Mind—I said if I ever, ever, hear of such a thing… Now, go!'

And it can be said that Captain McKinley never did hear of JP misbehaving in that way again. Though it cannot be said that JP modified his ways in any manner except insofar as to be more careful that he was not caught again.

The masters were hard on him, and he was regularly beaten for sloppy work, but they did not expel him, seeing some promise in the lad.

And so six years passed. His lack of diligence at his studies meant that, despite his natural talent, the boys who worked hard, though they were less able, surpassed him in knowledge. They were found apprenticeships with the Royal Navy, but JP remained at his studies for an extra year, till all were thoroughly fed up with the sight of him.

It was not till August 1831 when he was fifteen that he found himself apprenticed for the first time—but to a ship of the Merchant Navy. The *London Packett* was a brigantine built in 1790 at Liverpool. Forty-one years old the ship had seen hard use in the cork trade. The dirt and smells on board had been something that young John had been looking forward to, but now that he was there, reality gave a firm check to his eagerness. Not only was he expected to keep the deck clean, an onerous and dull task in itself, but he was the only member of the crew given the duty of keeping the ship's head clean. This, he felt, was the last straw: for cleaning latrines used by others on a bouncing ship was famed as being the worst (and most degrading) job on board, and despite the importance of this task the others mocked him for it. The language he acquired, and used, on that first ship was of the saltiest kind. The crew seemed to delight in hearing one so young swear in so enthusiastic a manner. Disappointment in his situation manifested itself in acts of petty disobedience, and he lasted there only three months. In November, the captain was glad to return him to the Royal Naval Asylum. Since he was now too old to remain there, he would have to be returned to his family unless another apprenticeship could be found for him. Once again, his mother's connections were brought into play. She, greatly troubled by the thought that she might have her son on her hands again, visited her late husband's uncle, William Mellish. Mellish was on the verge of selling his ships and retiring, but offered an apprenticeship. JP was indentured to the *Thames*, another ship of the Merchant Navy, master: Captain J.G. Dunn, to serve his apprenticeship for a period of five years. The *Thames* was bound for Jamaica for trade in the West Indies. JP's spirits soared as he contemplated adventure on the high seas, something he and his school friends had spoken about incessantly.

4
From Apprentice to Chief Mate

It soon became apparent to JP that he would not be able to take advantage of his family relationship with the owner of the *Thames*, as the ship was very soon sold to James Thomson and Co. of 6 Billiter Square, a large concern. Captain Dunn, who remained master, let it be known to his crew that he would not be standing any nonsense while he was in charge. The hull had been sheathed with copper to protect it from the salt water; the *Thames* was a first class vessel, and Dunn made certain that his crew knew it. JP's first on-board use of bad language was in the presence of Captain Dunn, and he was soundly berated for it.

'Mind your tongue in the future, or I'll make every second on this ship a living hell for you,' was Dunn's final word on the matter before stalking off. This, despite Dunn's reputation for being able to hold forth with abominable curses of the worst description for five minutes without once repeating himself. Well, that reputation may have been exaggerated somewhat; nevertheless, his hoarse voice, when heard, was enough to silence the conversation of others on board the *Thames*.

JP spent much of his time scrubbing and swabbing the deck. All the way outbound and all the way inbound, he saw more of the wood beneath his feet than the sea and the sky. The sweat poured into his eyes as he worked, and his back ached: thus the life of a new ship's apprentice. When he thought of the five years that stretched before him as he worked he longed to be back on land, and yet, when lying in his hammock for the short hours he was allowed to sleep, his dreams were of standing on the quarter deck, staring ahead: a ship's captain obeyed by all, leaving port with a cargo of expensive stuffs, while, from the land, bevies of beautiful girls waved their handkerchiefs at him in loving and tearful farewells. Oh, the shock of those waking moments, hearing the groans of the men in their own hammocks nearby, willing time to go more slowly so that he could snatch one more breath of sleep before having to swing himself down and start work. Blindly, he would drag on his trousers and stagger out onto the deck where the boatswain, stood glaring at each man as he appeared.

'Hurry, insect!'

The boatswain's hoarse roar shattered any traces of sleep. A hurried breakfast of ship's biscuit and water would be followed by more work with scrubbing brush and bucket. Sometimes, when the work made him too hot, he would splash himself with the dirty water, but it didn't help much.

*

On the second voyage, there was a new apprentice who took over the menial scrubbing. JP was delighted to be given other duties, which, though just as physically taxing, were far more rewarding. Captain Dunn, who had hardly seemed to notice him since his telling off months earlier, watched him through narrow eyes. Head never turning, Dunn's eyes, mobile through the narrow slits between the lids, saw everything that moved. Tiger-like, he was ready to pounce on anything or anybody out of place. The *Thames* was successful in her ventures, but only because of Dunn's attention to detail and an obsessive mathematical approach to everything connected with the business in hand. He was a large man with a nose fit for a Roman emperor and a mouth like a line drawn with a pencil. His fleshy chin and low brow, though, seemed to contradict any pretensions to nobility of mien, while his swarthy complexion, tanned by hot sun and rough winds gave him a barbaric and wild appearance.

Dunn beckoned to the first mate on the second morning out, and began a gentle conversation. His voice was silky smooth when he wished it to be, and, for all his ferocious appearance, he seemed as pleasant a gentleman as one could hope to meet at a garden party where dainty teacups might meet rosy lips of sweet girls.

'Mr Ellis, who is the lad gazing at the binnacle?' (A question asked, though Dunn knew well the name of every member of his crew.)

'Mills, Sir.'

'Send him aloft, Mr Ellis. Let's give him something better to do shall we?'

'Aye-aye, sir.'

'Let's see if he has a head for heights.'

'Aye-aye, sir.'

And JP on that sunny day was sent on a vertical voyage up the foremast where he addressed himself to the topgallant sail and watched the riggers at work. Soon he was happy to be clambering over the rigging helping unfurl or furl the sails as the occasion demanded. His school training had, of course, included practice at these skills, but not on the open sea in the middle of a squall.

Supper-times were his second best moments, for afterwards, if the weather allowed, he would be able to rest awhile with full stomach while the night watch were about, and the food on board the *Thames* was more than satisfactory in both quality and quantity. But best of all were the nights he worked in the warm seas near Jamaica when the air was balmy and the sky was clear enough to count the stars.

*

JP did not converse easily with the other members of the crew, but he got on with his work silently, almost grimly one might say, never arguing with anyone over the tasks he was given. And so, time passed and he grew strong in body, though weak in spirit, for the temptations open to a lad when ashore on leave while his ship was in port were too attractive to be ignored. Indeed, he delighted in giving in to the cravings of the flesh, both outwardly in brothels, and inwardly in taverns. Gambling, though, held no interest for him. He had decided to save what little he was paid in order to improve his lot. Among his shipmates he acquired a reputation for miserliness, rarely standing his round of drinks, but they also developed a grudging admiration for his mind, for he was quick to spot sure opportunities. In London, he had invested a portion of his wages in stocks, while the others had spent everything. Little by little his holdings had grown, until, when on land, he could afford fair lodgings, and not have to put up with the same mean holes as his shipmates.

Was it love of work for its own sake that made John Powell Mills diligent in carrying out his tasks in the five years he spent as apprentice aboard the *Thames*, or did he have an ulterior motive? If you have been reading with attention, then you will know that the latter must have something more than a whiff of truth. But for some who work hard for the wrong reason, a kind of love of its own accord develops, and this can blossom into an interest in the task at hand for its own sake: so it was with JP. He almost believed in himself. Sometimes, he reached down into his soul while lying awake at night in his hammock, surrounded as he was by snores and other nocturnal sounds, and thought of the greatness that he was certain lay there preparing itself to shine forth from his brow so that it might dazzle the beholder.

And five years and a little more passed.

In May of 1837, the *Thames* returned to London from a successful voyage. JP, flush with money and self-belief was out of his indentures, and bid farewell to Captain Dunn and the *Thames*.

⋆

'I'm home, Ma,' calls JP as soon as he walks through the door.

These are the first words Frances Mills has heard her son speak for many months. She had known that he would appear before her sooner or later. The young man she sees before her is almost a stranger to her. He has grown: still of medium height, but already with powerful chest and arms, though he is only twenty-one. His suntanned skin darker than it had been before, he stands almost silhouetted in the low frame of the door, bending slightly so as not to bang his head on the lintel.

'Well, John, you're home again.' She moves towards him, and he to her, but they are awkward in each other's presence. Never close, they are almost as strangers now. 'Sit down, and I'll bring you something to eat.' She still speaks with a soft Irish accent.

And JP sits and disposes of some bread and cheese and a mug of warm ale without uttering a word while his mother looks on, trying to fathom her son, trying to find some association in her mind with the child she remembers. Oh, yes, she had seen him once or twice in the last five years. He had even written to her—once.

⋆

You may, reader, wonder what had become of his siblings, his brother Joseph and his sister whose name I never have managed to discover, but I have been able to find not a trace of either. Perhaps they had died in childhood, or perhaps they both merely disappeared into the mass of people that form that metaphorical sea called London. Frances did not mention them to JP, nor he to her. I have often found myself following a thread of inquiry like a clew until, all at once, it vanishes from under my finger leaving only puzzlement and frustration.

★

Now he was an Able Seaman, and signed to another vessel, the *Flora*, her master, Captain Leveque. The *Flora* was a sprightly barque plying the West India trade. Canadian-born Henry Leveque was in his prime, thirty-seven years old, upright as a redwood and with a powerful voice which could be heard above the crashing of a ship as it hurled itself against boisterous waves in a moderate gale. Well-liked by his crew, though overconfident in his abilities, his generosity of spirit saved many a wretch from himself and booze; for Captain Leveque was that rare fish, a tee-total sailor, but one who expects his men to restrain from drunkenness when aboard. The ladies loved him, and he loved them in return.

JP rejoiced in his good fortune, for as an able seaman under the command of so popular a captain, he felt certain that his own status would be in the ascendant, and so it proved, at least for the seven months that he worked on the *Flora*. In December, though, he found himself in a bad way with influenza, and had to leave the ship, which sailed away without him. At least he was in London. Ill and weak, he went to stay with his mother, who seemed pleased to be able to nurse him. He fretted on shore and in bed, but it was two months before he felt well enough to seek work.

His luck changed, and, using his experience as a passport to success, he signed on as an able seaman on the *Elbe*, voyaging round the Mediterranean and trading with Holland.

Oh, joy! The chief mate of the *Elbe* fell ill the day it was due to depart. The captain, casting his eye about for a replacement at short notice, selected JP as the smartest option available, and, aged twenty-one, John Powell Mills took his place as second in command.

In the succeeding years he worked as chief mate on a number of vessels. His time on the *Elbe* lasted twelve months, then came the *Clarinda*—ten months in the West-Indies, and the *Margaret*—voyaging to the Colonies (transporting convicts to New South Wales) and the East Indies.

JP found his time on the *Thames* a somewhat sobering experience. It was the first time he had worked on a convict ship, and certain matters disturbed him. The convicts were all women, and all under the jurisdiction, while on board, of the Surgeon Superintendent Dr Colin Arrott Browning, a Scot with very particular views. The Admiralty had ruled that all Surgeons Superintendent of Convict Ships were required to give to them, after each voyage, 'a regular Sick-Book, with Journal and Nosological Synopsis…in a complete and Scientific state' and Browning was a stickler for regulations and always did so, making all entries with fine exactitude in a neat, sloping hand. He had been a ship's doctor for nearly twenty-seven years by 1840 when JP became Chief Mate of the *Margaret*; outwardly kindly, he was not happy if he was ever contradicted, and that kindly aspect was a mask to his true character. 'Convicts,' he complained, 'are presented to me, by the matrons and governors of prisons, dressed cleanly, and with the appearance of rude health, whereas they may be suffering from heaven-knows-what illness, and are not fit to travel on so arduous a journey.' His complaints on this matter were, to his fury, ignored by the authorities, and he recorded with bitterness the death from advanced syphilis of one of the prisoners on the *Margaret*. Browning had deeply held Christian beliefs, which he tried to inculcate into the minds of the prisoners, though with little success, however well-meant his efforts were.

'Arbitrary forgiveness has no place in my administration of discipline,' he remarked to JP, as one of the more contrary prisoners was brought before him to be punished for stealing.

'That was well said,' he continued, 'I must make a note of that.'

The prisoner asked forgiveness.

'Forgive you! *How* can I forgive you? You deliberately, with the knowledge of your duty, transgressed. You must now take your punishment. A personal offence, I shall always be enabled to forgive in the spirit of the Gospel, but the forgiveness of your present offence is a very different matter, for it was an offence against *law*.'

The prisoner was put in irons for a number of days. Browning drew the line at flogging: 'I do not flog the prisoners, though it is authorised by Act of Parliament, for it is a mode of punishment to which I strongly object.'

At the start of the voyage there were on board 131 female convicts, 21 convicts' children, and 17 non-convict settlers. During the passage, one convict died, and two children were born.

Dr Browning caught a bad cold towards the end of the voyage and was confined to his bed for some days, undergoing the operation of cupping. JP, who had formed a dislike for the Doctor, but who had been asked to visit, kept away from his sickbed, sending the Third Mate, Mr Long to enquire after his health.

And so, JP looked upon his work on the *Margaret* not as high adventure, but as a chore to be borne. Nevertheless, he stayed with that ship for two years.

*

Then came the *Beaulah*—one month of work only, falling out with the captain as he was offered other work before the ship sailed to India. Then a year on the *Lord Lowther*, carrying Government stores to China—1,000 tons of bread for the army and navy as well as several flat-bottomed boats for service in Chinese rivers; then three months on the Cambridge (to India), returning home to London in September of 1843. Thus, time passed, and he grew stronger still, though he found himself on occasion slightly short of breath. On shore, he consulted a doctor, for he had little trust in ships' doctors. He was prodded and poked, and eventually given the diagnosis: mild asthma. JP was relieved but irritated, regarding his condition as a weakness; this made him think less of himself, but he found he could forget his troubles with generous internal applications of rum or brandy.

5
Rachel

JP suddenly discovered that he was prosperous. He was saving money and his friends looked at him with a kind of respect that he had never known before. He looked forward to the time when he could stand on the deck of a ship as a captain, like a knight astride his steed. Meanwhile, when ashore, he would swagger into taverns and public houses, order whatever he desired, slap the money on the counter, and glory in his success as the heady waters in his glass made their way down his throat and into his belly where they burned like a coal fire on a wintry evening.

His glance one day, during that fleeting stay in London, September 1843, fell upon a young woman whose appearance pleased him. Yorkshire born Rachel Masterman lived with her brother William and their younger sister Mary in premises above their aunt's public house in Deptford, Greenwich. Unlike other girls, she did not buckle at the knees at the sight of JP, whose curiosity was thus aroused: and so a-courting he went. He smartened his appearance and trimmed his beard close, disdaining to shave as some did when on shore. His beard was important to him, lending an air of authority, and, after all, shaving is a serious thing to contemplate when at sea, for even when the waters are comparatively calm a sudden motion of the ship might cause a razor-clutching hand to do unwanted injury. Rachel told JP that she was twenty-seven, the same age as he; he brought her flowers and sweets, and she was flattered. Her aunt Sarah was more cautious.

'Watch him, lass, there's more to him and less to him.' Which curiously unenlightening statement was one of her stock expressions. But Rachel was not inexperienced in the ways of men. She made herself pretty for JP, and flattered him. She had, of course, lied about her age, for she was at the time thirty-one, and had considered herself to be long on the shelf as far as marriage was concerned. However, she determined, to the surprise of her friends, to try once more for lasting security.

'After all,' she told them, 'he will be away at sea much of the time, and then I can do as I will.'

She had been let down before, and was determined not to be so again. Her brother William, younger but protective of her, had been kept largely in ignorance of her previous beaus, and also of the pregnancy which had lasted only three months, at which time she had arranged for a termination—with her aunt Sarah's advice (a dangerous and illegal proceeding), as she had not been quite certain of the father's identity.

*

JP was soon off again, Chief Mate of the *Thomas Coutts*, bound for East India, returning in May of 1844. His luck was in. He had been recommended for a captaincy, and with it came a pay packet to match his new status.

And so, in June of that year, he married Rachel Masterman. The new Mr and Mrs Mills took the rooms above the public house, while William Masterman and his sister Mary found other lodgings.

Shortly after his marriage to Rachel, JP was back at sea, Master of the *King William*, and on his way to the West Indies. He was not back with his wife for nearly seven months, then home for two, and off again this time for a fifteen months voyage, Master of another vessel, the *Tory*. When asked his destination by friends he told them that the *Tory* would be heading to Calcutta and the Indian Colonies. Rachel, got on with her own life while he was gone, dutifully unfaithful as she had always intended to be: living at times with her aunt, and sometimes with her brother.

6
Mills, the *Tory*, the *Eleanor*, and Family Life

Captain Mills put aside any superstitious twinges of doubt he had felt about the forthcoming voyage on the *Tory*: earlier that year Captain George Johnstone, master of another ship of the same name, had been charged with murdering his Chief Mate, the Second Mate and another seaman, and injuring a number of other sailors during the course of the return voyage from Hong Kong, having conceived the notion that the crew were about to mutiny. Johnstone was later found not guilty by virtue of insanity and spent the rest of his days in a lunatic asylum, but at the time of his trial, JP was mid-ocean.

'While I am Master, I am Monarch of all I Survey.' With that thought, Captain Mills stood on the quarterdeck of the *Tory* with legs firmly planted as if they gained sustenance from the wood. The ship was two days out, a pretty (though unfavourable) breeze was blowing on that fine March day in 1845. The *Tory* was busily tacking so as to beat a course forward, and Mills felt that he could command the world. His Chief Mate was James Hill, a handsome, but surly fellow who had a way of becoming suddenly charming when he liked, particularly when there was female company. The two men understood each other well, and had mutual respect. Hill had been chosen as Mate not by Mills, whose prerogative it should have been to make the choice, but by the *Tory's* owner. Any resentment this might have induced was instantly put aside at their first meeting, and they became drinking companions. Never forgetting who was the superior in rank, Hill gave deferential treatment to his captain; Mills was flattered, for though he was three years older than the Chief Mate, Hill had a naturalness about him that might have made him seem to be the more senior of the two.

And John Powell Mills ceased thinking of himself as the callow JP of yore, but instead regarded himself as Captain Mills, Ship's Master.

He had been, though, somewhat embarrassed by the truth of the matter, for the ship was not heading for trade in fine goods with the Indian Colonies, but to Van Diemen's land with one hundred and seventy convicts, all women, convicted of petty crimes to sentences of between seven and twelve years. Some of the women brought their children with them, twenty-four all together, and he knew that he would be in for a noisy time.

There were compensations: not only did he get on well with the Chief Mate, James Hill, but also with the ship's Surgeon Superintendent, Dr John Sloan, an experienced ship's doctor with a wealth of amusing stories to keep them occupied when time seemed to lag. At mealtimes, they were joined by two sisters who travelled in the steerage, and whose business it was to supervise the convicts in their daily duties and keep them and their children under control. The matrons, Rebecca and Elizabeth Stewart, however, were not, in the Captain's opinion, of a sort to grace his table, and he always felt a sense of relief when they withdrew afterwards. The *Tory* left Woolwich, London on March 23rd, and arrived in Hobart, Van Diemen's Land on July 4th after a fairly uneventful passage.

Dr Sloan was a methodical man who took his responsibilities very seriously. It was he, not Captain Mills who had charge of the convicts, a captain's duty being, merely (!), to navigate the ship safely to its destination. Sloan looked after the women as well as he was able, keeping a detailed log in the same kind of neat sloping hand as Dr Browning of the *Margaret*, recording lesser illnesses alongside more worrying sickness carefully in the ship's Medical Journal. All but one of his patients lived, and that one, a boy of twenty months who died of scrofula. He recorded cases of sea-sickness, pneumonia, rheumatism, bronchitis, colds, dysentery, upset stomachs and colic as well as one case of gonorrhoea and two of syphilis (both contracted before boarding). Sea-sickness was the commonest complaint, particularly among the older women. Mills admired Sloan for this meticulousness, and watched as the women went about the chores they were given with an occasional raised eyebrow when he saw how those who had been deemed termagants behaved almost docilely.

After nineteen days, the *Tory* arrived at Tenerife. The weather had been intensely cold to begin with, but became less unpleasant as the ship continued her path. It was Dr Sloan who had desired the *Tory* to put in at Tenerife. 'After all, Captain,' he told Mills, 'Tenerife affords every facility to a ship's needs, particularly after a tedious voyage, and the women will be pleased not to feel continually sick.' Mills harrumphed, but agreed, for the port was easy to approach, and he was not disinclined to stretch his legs on land.

Once in the town, Dr Sloan was able to procure supplies of beef, vegetables, bread, and fresh water. Some of the prisoners had saved a little money and asked him to buy them fruit. He recorded this in his journal, carefully noting that the recipients had found the fruit, 'highly refreshing after the enervation produced by seasickness.' The rest of the voyage continued smoothly as before.

Sloan was a stickler for cleanliness and insisted on following the rules laid down for this to the letter. The women cleaned their berths regularly and kept themselves clean as well. He was surprised, and noted this in his journal also: 'I must do the prisoners the justice to state that they were almost all disposed to carry out my views on this point, which I have no doubt conduced most materially to their health, and comfort,' he wrote, following this with information that he allowed some of the prisoners access to part of the poop deck where they could work at making or mending their clothes. And, despite the fact that he made absolutely certain that there was no interaction between the women and the sailors, and that he was inclined, if any of the prisoners misbehaved, to shut the miscreants in a specially constructed cabin within the prison hold, for the ship was a prison, remember—despite this, he was generally liked by his charges, and he honestly believed he was doing his best for them. Those he had placed in solitary confinement were always contrite afterwards; but he deplored the 'silent system' then used in Millbank Prison to control prisoners who were awaiting transportation to the colonies.

As noted at the start of this narrative, it has been my own work to inspect some of Her Majesty's prisons. I must remark that the humanity shown by Dr Sloan seems to me highly commendable. And now that I myself work at Millbank Prison as Surgeon in full charge of medical matters, I see to it that things are managed differently, for we have a duty to humanity, the criminal as well as the good; my studies of the former indicate to me that though the monotony and labour of the treadmills is currently thought to be the best way to punish, the future must surely lead to other, more humane, methods of rehabilitating the criminal.

*

Dr Sloan's notes regarding the voyage of the *Tory* include the following interesting information:

*

The chocolate supplied for breakfast was loathed to such an extent, that the greater portion was thrown overboard. After having made several futile attempts to reconcile the women to its use, I resolved to substitute tea in lieu…

I found the preserved potatoes after a short period, highly relished, and feel assured they were very beneficial as an anti-scorbutic…

Several of the elderly females suffered from the depressing passions of the mind, and were peculiarly liable to diseases of debility, particularly while under the influence of conscious guilt, and self reproach. I found it necessary under such circumstances to issue a more generous diet.

*

I have shown you matters relating to life on board the convict ships *Margaret* and *Tory* that you might contrast them with later voyages to be detailed hereafter.

*

The next voyage in the *Tory* did, finally, find JP en route to India to trade with the merchants of Calcutta, and he felt a sense of relief, though his trust in the ship's owners to employ him as he felt they should had been badly damaged. He resolved to move on and find himself another berth.

Rachel seemed cold towards him whenever he was home. The kind of welcome he always hoped for was never forthcoming. In August of 1846, he became Master of the *Eleanor*, another barque, this time voyaging to Mauritius. He was not happy inside himself, though he enjoyed his time at sea. A suspicion that all was not well at home nagged at him and kept him awake at nights. He drank more than before; it helped him sleep.

October 1847 saw him again between ships, and home in London. Rachel greeted him sulkily when he arrived, and he, not willing to put up with her moods, and expecting his conjugal rights, became argumentative and brutal towards her.

But time and tide wait for no man, as the saying goes, and the sea called him again. A new appointment had come his way, and he felt the need to leave a situation which had become unbearable to him. Strangely, Rachel seemed unwilling to let him go, and shouted at him, accusing him of deserting her and unfaithfulness.

7
The *Subraon*

Now, at last, comes a description of the passage of the *Subraon* to Australia. How might one adequately describe the poor conditions that existed on board a ship making such a voyage; what of the unhappy events that occurred on this vessel? They were a scandal, an iniquity, the result of an appallingly mis-thought idea—but none of these goes near the truth; and it ought to be stated at once that conditions on other ships, both before and after, have been far worse. I think not only of the appalling scheme devised by Earl Grey to transport poor, lost and starving souls to far away places, but also of all kinds of enforced transportation involving the packing together of too many people in one place as if they were so much cargo.

Captain Mills was appointed Master of the barque *Subraon* in late 1847 following the death of the previous incumbent, Captain Hodnett. His pride at being selected manifested itself in a new set of clothes and a visit to a barber. The *Subraon* was the largest ship he had captained, and also the newest—built only a year earlier, and he felt his selection to be a great personal compliment, for Captain Hodnett, who had died on board while the ship was returning from India, had been a well-respected sea-dog of the old school. The sea had been Hodnett's life; unmarried and with no children, he had bequeathed all his worldly goods to his dearly beloved mother, something that Mills, whose opinion of his own female parent was less than adoring, was unlikely to do. He chose James Hill to be the

Chief Mate, for he was a man he felt he could trust. There was an understanding between the two which had proved financially useful on the last voyage they had shared.

The *Subraon* was a sizeable barque weighing 510 tons. She was built in Sunderland, three-masted and as tight a vessel as could be desired. She was sheathed with felt and yellow metal, and on inspection had been deemed to be a Class A vessel. The ship's owners, Messrs Soames and Co. of London, had allowed Captain Mills a share in the profits from her voyages, and he looked forward to a time when a more financially interesting mission than delivering half-starved Irish emigrants to Australia would be possible. He comforted himself with the thought that not only was the *Subraon* a smart vessel, but also able to outrun most other ships of her class, which meant that he might soon be back in London. Not that the speediness of the ship meant that they could travel unprotected; when sailing in dangerous waters it was important to have means of defence, and there were four small cannons on board—for emergency use only as it was unlikely that the *Subraon* would be able to withstand serious attack by pirates for any length of time.

★

On a morning shortly before departure, JP lay late in bed with a sore head and a bloated stomach, and Rachel, returning to the bedroom from the kitchen where she had been preparing breakfast, was surprised and a little annoyed to see him there still.

'You lazy pig, get up!'

JP groaned and clutched his stomach. 'Bring me some ale,' he said thickly.

But Rachel, who wanted him up and out of the house, ran out to find a doctor. Shortly afterwards she arrived home with Dr Downing, who went straight up to see the patient. Downing was the type to stand no nonsense from anyone. Approaching middle age, he was stern, but with a breezy manner and a habit of saying exactly what he thought. His examination was brief.

'Mrs Mills, will you step inside?' he called. Once she was present, he began to speak with her, almost as if JP was not there. 'I've examined your husband,' he said. 'Really, there's no need to tell you the cause of his discomfort, I'm certain that you both know what the reason is, and how to deal with it. (Don't interrupt, sir, I'm talking with your wife. Consider yourself lucky that she fetched me.) Complete avoidance of all alcoholic drinks whatsoever, that's the cure for him. I would have recommended a sea voyage, but I understand that he's off to sea quite soon. He'll be out of your control then, madam, and there's no telling what he'll do. (You stay where you are, do you realise what you've done… what you're doing?) If he continues to carry on the way he has been, it will be an early grave from a diseased liver. I'd say I've never seen anything like it before, but it's an old story. I'll prescribe a tonic for him and send it round later with my bill. Good day to you both.'

And with that, the good doctor left. JP pulled a face with gritted teeth at the doctor's back, and then sank back upon the bed with a groan. The room spun about him, and the foul taste in his mouth made him retch.

The day of departure was soon upon them. JP left once more, and Rachel, unable to know her own mind, went back to her old ways and found a new, though short-lived, love. So it was that when she gave birth to her first child, a son, a few months later, she named him after her husband. JP never really knew the truth of the matter, or, at least, if he suspected, he kept his own counsel. But his drinking of spirits increased in both frequency and volume.

*

On a cold Friday, the 10th of December, at the turn of the tide, the Blue Peter flag was hoisted. Captain Mills ordered the

Boatswain to weigh anchor, the capstan on the quarterdeck was duly turned under the Boatswain's supervision, the anchor was raised, and a steam-tug pulled the *Subraon* into the dirty waters of the *Thames*. She eased her way out of London, the Union Jack flying from the jack staff at the end of the bow sprit, and in stately fashion made her way down the *Thames* and into the North Sea. Taking a route through the choppy English Channel, she put in at Plymouth where her passengers and supplies were to be taken on board.

*

Crew:

Master—Captain John Powell Mills
Chief Mate—Mr James George Hill
Second Mate—Mr Thomas Day
Third Mate—Mr Charles Carwardine
Ship's Surgeon Superintendent—Dr Frederick
               Acret
Able Seaman—Augustus Reynolds
Able Seaman—Peter Murphy
Able Seaman—Thomas Sheppard
Able Seaman—James Edward

Various other members of the crew including the Boatswain (or Bosun), the Carpenter, a sailmaker, the Cook, the Steward, the ship's apprentices, and a number of able and ordinary seamen.

*

Plymouth: December 1847. Preparations for taking on board one hundred and ninety-eight government-assisted emigrants continued: a frenzy of activity in the biting cold. The *Subraon* was anchored a little way out: everything and everyone had to be ferried over—a time-consuming business. But who is the large gentleman who, unconcerned at the disruption he causes, ploughs his way through the sea of dockyard hands and sailors? He makes his way over to where Captain Mills stands apart from all others on the quay, a solitary figure; none should dare to interrupt the Captain while he is deep in thought.

'Good day to you, Captain Mills.'

'Good day, sir.'

'I represent the Board of Governors of the Dublin Orphan Institution. Now, with regard to your passengers, I have been informed that you have room for a further number, having recently been let down.'

'Sir, my vessel is better for the fewer.'

'But I have with me…'

'Say no more, sir! Do you think it a pleasure to me, who should be trading with eastern potentates, to be employed ferrying government-assisted paupers to the other side of the world, that you would encumber me with more of 'em?'

'You will be recompensed for the increase in numbers. There are but eleven: young ladies from Dublin, orphans all.' And he indicated a group of girls standing a little way off with an older lady and a clergyman.

'Young ladies will be more trouble than they are worth,' responded Captain Mills.

'But we will increase your fee—a private arrangement, you understand.'

'I would expect double.'

'Twice the usual amount? It is extreme, but—well let us make it so. Understand, Captain, this is something of an experiment, for if these orphans are successfully transplanted, there are hundreds more who will follow.'

'And who is to have charge of these eleven girls during their time on board?'

43

'Why, Captain, they will be responsible for themselves and for each other. They are responsible young ladies and have been well-taught. You will find that they give no trouble.'

'It is not trouble from them I fear. If they are unaccompanied, who will…'

'…keep an eye on their well-being, Captain Mills? Why who but yourself. I know you will say you don't have time, but they have been trained to domestic service. They could make you comfortable. Use one or two to keep your cabin clean, serve coffee in the mornings et cetera. Double fee for you, don't forget. See, I have their names here so that you may add them to your manifest.'

Mills took the list and glanced at it. The large gentleman took out a pocket watch and pursed his lips. 'I have another appointment,' he said, 'so I must hurry away. Look after these girls, Captain Mills, I entrust them to your care. Once we, the Board of Governors of the Orphan Institution, have been informed that they have safely reached their destination, we may ask you to effect more work of this sort. Good day, sir, I trust you will have a good voyage.'

The large gentleman offered his hand, which Mills shook without thinking, and then hurried away, pausing a moment to speak to the clergyman. Mills looked after him, and shrugged. He looked briefly at the girls, turned on his heel, and walked away without making any salutation.

Let us be clear at once. There were indeed eleven orphan girls from the Dublin Orphan Institution, but a statement that they were able to look after themselves should be seen either as an example of gross naivety, or simply as a bold-faced untruth.

*

Orphan girls:

Alicia Ashbridge, 19 years, cook.

Ann Brennan, 17 years, house servant.
Ellen Busby, 17 years, house servant.
Augusta Cooper, 17 years, house servant.
Martha Magee, 18 years, nursemaid.
Patience Newcomen, 17 years, nursemaid.
Dorcas Newman, 19 years, nursemaid.
Mary Preston, 18 years, housemaid.
Emma Smith, 16 years, house servant.
Mary Sneyd, 18 years, house servant.
Ellen Stephens, 17 years, nursemaid.

*

All were listed as members of the Church of England. Emma Smith was the most literate, Alicia Ashbridge was the oldest and most sensible, and therefore regarded by the others as the leader, while Martha Magee had the most dominant personality, and felt that the other girls would be best led by herself. Dorcas Newman was the quietest and the most popular among the eleven.

On the quay, the eleven girls stood shivering. Wrapped in shawls which were too thin, they huddled together for warmth. They were, though, very excited, and their talk was all of the future. Meanwhile, the matron of the Orphan Institution and the clergyman, who were there to see them safely on board, stood to one side and looked severely at them.

'I'm told it's much warmer there.'

'I can't wait till we're there.'

'Have patience, Patience.'

'Oh, ha ha, that's an old joke! Keep it to yourself next time you think of something so funny as that, will you!'

'Behave yourselves, girls. Don't forget to thank the Almighty for his benefits to you,' said the clergyman.

'Yes, Mr Smart.'

The matron looked stern and drew herself up. 'Mary, have you got your bag?'

'Yes, Ma'am.'

It began to rain, and they huddled together tighter still. The other passengers and Captain Mills had already boarded. Most of them were below deck where it was comparatively dry. From the quarterdeck, Mills watched all. Standing with him were the Chief Mate and the Second Mate.

'Nearly ready, Mr Hill.'

'Off with the tide, Captain?'

'As soon as, Mr Day. Once everyone is stowed below, we set off with no further ado. See to it, Mr Day.'

'Aye, aye, sir.'

And the Second Mate went to speak to the Boatswain.

On the quay, the Third Mate was now shepherding the girls towards the boat that would ferry them to the *Subraon*. Emma Smith trembled. 'I'm scared,' she said.

Dorcas put her arm round her. 'Don't worry, we won't be at sea for too long, and I'll look after you.'

Once on the ship, they were shown down the stairs to the women's quarters.

'Those are the girls you mentioned?' asked James Hill.

'Indeed,' answered the Captain.

'Some are better looking than others.'

''You mind your duties, Mr Hill, and don't think too much about girls. They'll be more trouble than they're worth, I've no doubt.' And the Captain's mind wandered to the extra fee he was being paid. 'More trouble than they're worth,' he said, but this time to himself.

*

Life for the emigrants would be hard during the passage to Australia. The more fortunate ones had poky cabins, one to a family, each with narrow wooden benches which were to be used as beds. For others, it was a different story: men and women were placed in different holds; husbands were separated from wives at night—there were no married quarters for those travelling steerage. Children stayed with their mothers; adolescent boys with their fathers. Mattresses filled with straw were laid on the floors; hammocks were strung up above these in some places. The girls from the Dublin Orphan Institution were given an area slightly apart from the other women, separated from them by a large oilcloth which had been strung up on a rope and weighted at the bottom. (The crew, of course, had their own sleeping quarters away from the passengers.)

The women argued over their space while the men fought over theirs. The air down there was close, despite the cold, and often unpleasant. Those who had family cabins were, in truth, little better off than the others, for the cabins were so small as to make the air inside almost unbreathable after they were occupied only a short time, especially in warmer climes: two or three or more people sleeping in a room 6 feet by 6 feet by seven feet high is not a pleasant thought. Some cabins were slightly larger, but more people slept within.

Records of the passengers show that 163 were Roman Catholic, 31 were Church of England, and 15 were Presbyterian. 117 were female, 92 were male. There were 34 married couples. 72 of the passengers were minors, 6 less than a year old—3 of whom were born on board during the voyage. Two of the babies born during the voyage were given the ship's name '*Subraon*' as a middle name.

Of the passengers who stated a profession or calling there were 53 farm labourers, 24 farm servants, 12 house servants, 9 housemaids, 8 nursemaids, 4 kitchen maids, 2 cooks, 2 grooms, 1 groom and coachman, 1 carman, 1 carpenter, 1 coachman, 1 dairymaid, 1 dressmaker, 1 laundress and 1 ploughman.

*

Finally, on Christmas Day, the ship began the voyage to Australia. Most of the passengers had come up onto the deck. The Captain gave the order to weigh anchor, and, as it was Christmas, the sailors began singing 'I saw three ships' instead of a shanty. All joined in, whatever their religion, passengers as well as sailors. There was little wind that day, and the *Subraon* was hauled out of the harbour by a steam-tug. While it was towed, the emigrants crowded the ship's bulwarks on the main and quarter decks gazing towards the land. It was England they were saying their farewells to, they had already wished Ireland and the friends they were leaving a tearful goodbye. But there were few people on the land now who were there to see them leave or to wish them well on their voyage. They had been told to expect the voyage to last at least three months, and so it proved. There was a fine drizzle in the air which seemed to freeze itself to everything it touched. Some of the smaller children soon began to get restless in the cold. They were scolded by their mothers for their rudeness on a holy day, and fell silent. Eventually, the emigrants began to make their way below deck to their berths. Life on board the *Subraon* began to find its own normality, though different, perhaps, to anything you or I would describe as normal.

Those passengers still on deck were ushered out of the way by the sailors. All at once, a command was given, awestruck, those emigrants still on deck watched as the sails were unfurled, and the masts, which had been as bare as empty coat-racks or hat-stands, became full of life. A wind sprung up, the sails were filled with majestic dimension, and the ship sailed out into the North Atlantic Ocean.

8
The Voyage of the *Subraon*

From The Private Journal of Frederick Acret, Surgeon
Christmas Day 1847

This job is no sinecure. By some miracle I managed to persuade the ship's owners that I was the man for the job. Perhaps my history of army service in the Canadian provinces gave them a certain sense of security as to my hardiness under adverse conditions. I hope I am up to it—but finding this position was not easy, these people usually prefer experienced men, and I have not long been qualified as a doctor of medicine. I joined the ship at Plymouth as previously arranged. When I arrived on board some of the crew were lounging about the deck eying up the girls. The Captain was noticeable by his absence. One of the men lifted my sea-chest onto the deck, mopped at his face with his neck cloth, and then, instead of following my instructions, just stood there with his eyes almost bursting from his head. Despite my impatience, for it was very cold, I had to admit that the scene presented to me was truly remarkable. For though many took passage to Australia at that time, the emigrants were so unfamiliar with ships, that they created confusion and turmoil by constantly standing in the most inconvenient places. Moreover, the clothing that some of the girls wore was inappropriate with regard both to the time of year and to their modesty; although they were expected by their sponsors to be modestly presentable at all times, a lack either of self-awareness or judgment meant that they were not properly prepared to be amongst sailors who had, for the most part, been on board ship for months on end without even sight of any feminine company. Coldness was all that prevented them from exposing themselves in a totally unacceptable manner.

I have laid in some brandy, for medicinal purposes, to be kept under lock and key in my cabin. I expect to have plenty of call for spirits during the voyage by the passengers, and although there are a goodly number of casks of the stuff in the hold for such a purpose (under my control for dispensing to those in need), I deemed it important to have my own private supply, though I hope to have little recourse to it. We leave today.

I brought with me a book published only eight years ago which I hope may be of use to those passengers who can read and who wish to consult it, under my supervision, of course.

Tegg's Handbook for Emigrants, given to me by my friend William Tegg, son of the book's publisher states on the title page that it contains 'Useful Information and Practical Directions on Domestic, Mechanical, Surgical, Medical, and other subjects, calculated to increase the comforts, and add to the conveniences of the colonist.' William's father, Thomas, was a delightful man, and it is my hope that this volume will be of great benefit. For my part, naturally, it is the Surgical and Medical matters which are of the greatest interest, though, naturally, I expect there to be little information held there with which I am unfamiliar. However, the book does contain a useful and comprehensive reference list of medicines which a layperson may find gives guidance. There are several pages of information about emetics, purgatives, anodynes or narcotics, and tonics.

On reading through this list, I was surprised to find that the cost for an efficient medicine chest exceeds ten pounds sterling. It is needless to say that I have not been permitted to carry on this voyage all the items recommended in Tegg. I am, though, surprised to see listed some substances which I believe to be positively injurious under any circumstances. Croton oil, for example, is such a powerful purgative, that I would never recommend its use, nor would I have thought it wise to gargle with Sulphuric Acid, however diluted it is. I do agree, though, that Laudanum and, indeed, powdered Opium are useful and necessary items.

The instructions in the book on Bleeding and Cupping, and Dentistry, I think are unwise. They are meant for the layman, but really these matters require an experienced and well-taught practitioner.

All together one hundred and twenty-two pages are given over to medical and related matters, including a pharmacopoeia and information on minor operations, and how to deal with wounds, burns and scalds, corns and bunions, bites of rabid animals, insect stings, epilepsy, colic, rheumatism, various infectious diseases, women's complaints, midwifery, and poisoning.

The early chapters deal with more practical matters concerning life in the colonies, including building, decorating, baking, cooking, and brewing.

Perhaps, though, the most significant advice for the emigrant comes in two paragraphs early in the book, where one can read how to prepare for a long voyage by taking care to live abstemiously and making certain to take four grains of calomel every night for a fortnight in order to limit future suffering from sea-sickness. Of course, by the time any emigrant reads that it will be too late as they will already have embarked. The other useful advice in the two paragraphs mentioned is to avoid drinking warm liquids during a voyage, as that increases the tendency to sea-sickness, but any who are seasick are advised to take a dose of carbonate of soda solution to neutralise stomach acid.

I mean to start as I would continue. This is a new beginning for me, and I will strictly limit and regulate my intake of all spirituous liquids from now on.'

★

26 December 1847—5 a.m. James Hill was keeping watch. It had been a hard night. Not many had slept, what with the excitement of the departure from Plymouth, but the sea was calm at that moment, giving temporary peace to passengers and crew. It was not long, however, before the swell of the Atlantic waves took hold upon the barque and began tossing her in its arms. The deck was wet from the sea foam that swept over it. The *Subraon* held firm to her course; this weather was not troubling to the sailors. Dorcas Newman went walking towards the ship's head—the WCs below deck were already in a dreadful state. The crew (those that were on the deck) were working hard. Of the other passengers there were none to be seen. Dorcas, returning from the head, slipped and fell, crying out as she did so.

Although it may seem a fast way of making acquaintance, please remember that time on board ship is finite. A man meets a woman, or a boy a girl, and they talk. An opportunity once missed may not be found again. James Hill was not far away from Dorcas when she fell. Their conversation went like this:

★

Hill: Let me help you.

Dorcas: I can manage… *[Hill raises her up and then steadies her.]* Thank you.

Hill: What is your name?

Dorcas: And why would you want to know? I'm sure you already do anyway.

Hill: You are Dorcas. I've never met anyone with that name before.

Dorcas: It was my mother's name. My father called her Dolly, though.

Hill: I shall call you Dolly.
Dorcas: I must get back to my friends.

*

And she left him. But this bald conversation does not indicate the looks that passed between the two of them, nor the subtle weight of words that can carry an extra meaning. Dorcas had never felt the arms of a young man lift her before. Her heart felt strangely raised, and she realised that this journey might do more than just offer a chance of another life in another world, but also give her a kind of freedom which she had never known before.

James Hill watched her as she left, and smiled while tilting his head slightly in a thoughtful manner. He took from an inside pocket a hip-flask, unscrewed the lid and took a nip of the contents (not his first that morning) merely to keep out the cold, though spirits, or any alcoholic drink, were strictly forbidden while on duty. The flask had been a present, not a particularly expensive one, but it was inscribed 'J from J'.

*

Early the following morning, Captain Mills assembled his three officers in the cabin for an important talk. The sea was choppy, but unproblematic, and the operation of the ship was temporarily in the hands of the boatswain. The Captain was in a fine mood; though wishing that he was carrying a more rewarding cargo, he enjoyed giving commands—particularly if they were of great moment, but delivered in a subtle manner.

'Mr Hill, drinks for all,' he uttered in the easiest of voices with a grin which was intended to be pleasant, but gave the appearance of one who would not put up with being crossed.

James Hill poured four glasses of brandy from the decanter on the Captain's table.

'Gentlemen,' began Mills, 'let us begin with an understanding. We are here not to profit ourselves by taking advantage of others less fortunate than ourselves, but to assist those who are in need. Mind you, we must not be wasteful. Suggestions, Gentlemen!' He sat down; the others remained standing.

It must not be supposed that the Captain was actually in need of suggestions. He had his methods, and all had been worked out in advance with his trusted Chief Mate. It only remained to see that the others would accept what he deemed to be necessary.

*

Hill: The supplies on board have been carefully logged, but there are means of protecting them in order to minimise waste, if you take my meaning.

Mills: Well put Mr Hill. How could one go about ensuring this, Mr Carwardine?

Carwardine: If I take your meaning, and I think I do, might I suggest that if we apply a small charge to those luxuries with which some would like to refresh themselves, and which they may expect to be supplied to them gratis, savings in usage might be made...

Hill: ...and a profit might accrue also—shared to each of us in proportion as befits our rank, naturally. *[Hill bows almost imperceptibly towards the Captain, who sits with no expression on his face.]*

Day: I counsel caution.

Hill: How so, Mr Day?

Day: If word of this gets out...

Hill: But it won't, will it? I have made a list of prices for all items, particularly drinks. All passengers will be expected to...

contribute if they are in need. Mr Carwardine will see that they are made aware of this requirement. *[Carwardine takes the list from Hill as if it is no surprise to him.]*

Mills: Another drink, Gentlemen? Please help yourselves. *[An unusual liberality on his part.]*

Day: With regard to the Doctor…

Mills: Let's fetch him in. BOY! *[This to the ship's apprentice who waits outside.]* Fetch Dr Acret. Gentlemen, while we await the arrival of the good doctor, let us discuss the other matter.

＊

All knew the significance of that remark, for Dr Acret had suggested that the best way of protecting the eleven orphan girls from the unwanted attention of unmarried emigrant men, might best be served by employing them in keeping the officers' cabins tidy. Carwardine smiled; Mr Day protested that he had no interest in the girls except that they should be protected. The Captain protested that all would be done to ensure the safety of the girls.

Hill: I have drawn up a list of duties for them.

Day: How will that benefit them?

Hill: They will be paid for their work—those that do work, that is.

Carwardine: *[Examining the list]* I see you have chosen the best-looking girl to look after you!

Mills: Enough, Mr Carwardine! I will have no disagreements on my ship. Mr Hill…?

Hill: I mentioned the possibility of such an arrangement to one or two of the girls; they seemed most amenable. None of us will be disadvantaged by this arrangement.

Mills: It all seems highly satisfactory to me. Now, leave me, gentlemen. I would interview the Doctor alone, I have other matters to discuss with him.

*

From The Private Journal of Frederick Acret, Surgeon
Monday 27 December 1847

No sooner were we out of the English Channel than we met the force of the Atlantic. I supposed that the Captain would furl the sails; this he refused absolutely to do. When I remonstrated with him, he replied that he was not one to "shorten the sail at the first sign of bad weather," adding with a scornful look, "Anyone who goes to sea needs courage. That goes for the Master of a vessel and also for the crew, and also for the ship's Surgeon." He ignored me when I mentioned the wretchedness of the poor emigrants, most of whom spend their time spewing up whatever they manage to put in their stomachs. The sea washes over everything, and there is nowhere dry on board. I have been obliged to keep to my quarters with a bucket by my bed. I was never a good sailor even when the sea was calm. A little drop of something to keep out the cold is welcome.

*

One morning after breakfast, (which that day had consisted of porridge made from groats and tea for most of the emigrants and the crew, and coffee and bread rolls for the officers and those few of the emigrants who paid extra), five emigrants, three men and two women, assembled nervously near the door to the Captain's cabin, where he had been eating with Mr Day and Mr Carwardine, Mr Hill being on duty. The emigrants looked at each other as if none was willing to make the first move. Just as they had made up their minds not to carry out their mission and thereby disturb Captain Mills, but to return below deck, the door suddenly opened, and the Captain himself stood there surprised to see them.

'Yes?' he said haughtily.

'Captain Mills, sir, good morning.'

'Good morning,' came the curt answer, and the Captain made as if to walk on.

'Before you go, Captain, we wondered if we might have a word.'

The Captain looked sternly at the emigrants.

'I have little time this morning, but I will give you one minute,' he said impatiently.

'We wondered, Captain, about the water ration. Some of us are rather thirsty, and we wondered if, perhaps, a mistake had been made. For, surely, the ration is a little small.'

'There was no mistake,' responded the Captain. 'You are receiving what you are due, and, indeed, all that can be spared. Good day!'

The Captain left abruptly and went up onto the poop deck where the others were not permitted to follow. The emigrants stood, flummoxed and thwarted, for there was nothing left to do but return whence they had come, and to report back on the result of their plea.

Below, many were suffering through lack of water. Their hopes were shattered by the news of the brief interview with the Captain; some cursed, others wept. The next ration of water was not due to be dispensed for some hours.

*

From the Diary of Emma Smith
Monday 3rd January 1848

I curse the day that we ever agreed to come on this dreadful journey. We have been on this hell-hole for over a week, and I have no doubt that Captain Mills is the only one on board happy to be here. New the ship may be, clean it is not; it is freezing cold, and there is hardly a dry place on board. I am certain the Captain intends to make the voyage last as long as he possibly can. Good God, are we girls to suffer the insults of all. The other passengers, especially the women, look down on us as if we were the filth of the earth, while the crew never cease ogling with their great leery eyes. They are all too bold. Some of the girls seem to think it flattering and make sheep's eyes at the men when they think no one is looking. Just because I'm the youngest of our party, they think I'm to be kept in the dark, but I keep my eyes open. The day before yesterday was New Year's Day. Some of the crew decorated the rigging with coloured cloth triangles. The passengers were almost polite to us, and Captain Mills deigned to come over to us and hope we were fine. Freezing cold it was, and we girls all huddled together while the Captain read the service. In the middle of it all he suddenly stops. 'Who put those rags there?' he says quietly. There was no answer, and he continued with the service. After he had finished, he stalked over to one of the officers, not the chief mate, but another one whose name I don't know. 'Have the d— goodness to see that those things are removed. I'll not have my ship spoiled even on a day like today.' The other goes off and starts shouting at a group of men who were doing something with ropes.

Martha tells me that that officer is the Second Mate, Mr Day. 'Keep clear of him,' she says 'he's a regular b—.' Her language is appalling. I wish I was back home.

On Sunday, there was another service, but it was given us by the Third Mate, Mr Car… something-or-other. The Captain was nowhere to be seen. Most of the passengers are Roman Catholic, but a few of us are Church of England. Nearly everyone was there though—it passes the time. What a dull time we are having. The sea is rough, but I heard one of the men say it was calm which surprised me. I must close now as someone is coming.

★

Scene: The Captain's cabin. Present: Captain Mills, Chief Mate James Hill, Alicia Ashbridge, Augusta Cooper, Martha Magee, Dorcas Newman and Emma Smith; (the Second and Third Mates having left the room before the arrival of the girls).

The Captain begins. (No one would dare speak before he spoke to them.) 'Young ladies, welcome. You are here as Government Assisted Migrants, and there is nothing wrong in that, nothing at all. We who run this vessel have only your very best interests at heart, and that is why you are here.'

No one dared ask why only five had been thus invited, but the reason can easily be deduced. It was simply that five of the eleven (those present) were deemed by the Captain and his officers to be—not unattractive, whereas the others were less interesting to them.

'Ladies, you are young and unprotected. We would give you the security of knowing that, as long as you are aboard the *Subraon*, nothing untoward could possibly happen to disturb your sensibilities.'

This was a long speech for Captain Mills. He turned to the Mate who stood by. 'Continue, if you would, Mr Hill,' and the Captain gave a smile which he supposed to be friendly, but which only succeeded in making the girls present feel uncomfortable, though, if you had asked them, they would have been unable to say why.

Hill took up where his commander had left off. 'We wondered if you would be willing to help us with a few domestic chores which sailors such as we have little time for. Oh, you will be rewarded. I myself have worked out a schedule of light duties and wages. If you are kind enough to accept, I will happily show you how it all works.'

Hill was a charmer, there can be no doubt of that. 'Believable,' 'trustworthy', 'a gentleman' are the expressions that might come to the mind of any who had the pleasure of his acquaintance. Dorcas smiled. She had no doubts that it would be to their advantage to take such a kind offer. Emma was unsure, but Alicia, whose lead the others would follow had made her mind up, and Emma overcame her doubts, though she kept a secret dislike for the Captain.

During the weeks that followed the five chosen orphans were often, apparently, at their duties. Their reward, mild flirtation with the officers, and a sip or two of spirits —'merely to keep out the cold,' the men said to the orphans. All accepted the offer, after all the officers were gentlemen, were they not? All were seen, more than once, slightly the worse for drink. Alicia, Augusta and Martha in particular seemed happy to be plied with spirits, though each put up a show of resistance to begin with, all having been warned during their time in the Institution against the evil of the demon drink.

*

From the Diary of Emma Smith
Thursday 6th January 1848

There is no privacy to be had anywhere here for a girl. That was Martha Magee who nearly caught me writing the other day, and I haven't had a chance to put pencil to paper till now. There is plenty of gossip amongst the others. It seems that Augusta and Alicia have already been given some money by Captain Mills for tidying his cabin. Martha says that she knows just what sort of tidying they were doing, but she's just jealous. I've been talking to Dorcas who's almost pretty when she smiles, but she's so quiet that I really have to work hard to worm anything out of her. The others seem to like her a lot. Dorcas says not to take any notice of Martha and not to confide anything to her either. 'That Martha's a gossip,' she says.

*

From the Diary of Emma Smith
Friday 7th January 1848

I wish I was back home, even if there was nothing much to eat. Why did I agree to leave? Ann Brennan's a saucy wanton. Flaunting herself at the Chief Mate. I heard her. 'Oh Jim,' she says to him, sweet as pie, 'just look at this will you?' He takes no notice of her. Frankly I'm not surprised, he could choose any girl, he's so smart. This morning, Augusta and Alicia had a huge argument. Dorcas hurried me away so I would not hear what it was about. But I already knew. Each one wanted pride of place as servant to Captain Mills. I don't know why, he's a brute! I overheard that from a conversation between two of the passengers, Mrs Black, who was holding her baby to keep her warm, and Mary Ann Dixon. They seem to be quite friendly, as I often see them together. It might be because they are both Presbyterians, and there are not many of them on board, poor things. Mrs Black had been knitting a baby shawl for her daughter. She said that when her husband had wished the Captain the time of day, the Captain had turned roughly from him, and shouted at one of the men to keep the d— passengers out of his sight. I'm keeping well away from him. This evening there's to be an entertainment. One of the men has brought a fiddle with him, and he's going to play for us if the weather stays fine. I should think there will be some dancing on deck, so that will warm us up a bit. It seems that the Captain has allowed it to go ahead on the condition that none of the crew join in.

*

Life on board could be dull. The emigrants told each other stories and sang songs. The men were expected to work at chores assigned to them, some did so willingly, others were lazy and shirked their tasks at every opportunity, hiding in discreet corners and playing cards: gambling away future earnings. The latter were the ones who became depressed and felt ill, for there is a satisfaction in completing tasks well which they never gave themselves the opportunity of finding.

The sailors were used to the motion of a ship; unlike the emigrants, they managed to keep steady even though the ground beneath their feet constantly shifted from side to side. Sometimes they would sing as they worked. The passengers joined with the choruses once they knew them, and when the sails were being set, the air would be filled with hauling songs such as *Reuben Renzo*, *Haul on the Bowline* and *Haul Away Joe*.

But the singing of the sailors belied the dissatisfaction some were already feeling, for though they were given good rations of food and drink, they found the behaviour of the officers to be demanding but sloppy. They needed leadership, good or bad as the case may be, but Captain Mills was not often seen on deck. A captain's presence gives confidence to his crew, but this crew had to sing to lift their spirits, rather than singing because they were already feeling so inspired that sing they must.

*

From the Diary of Emma Smith
Wednesday 12th January 1848

I hardly know where to begin telling of the dreadful thing that happened while John Kelehan was playing his fiddle, and we were all up and dancing. For once, the other passengers did not seem to mind us girls mixing with them, though why they should be so uppity I could not say; they have been assisted in their passage to Australia just as we have. Mr Hill the First Mate took it upon himself to join in the dancing despite the Captain's orders, and ended up dancing with Dorcas of all people. There were a few noses out of joint when that happened, but Mr Hill soon had to leave to attend to his duties. We were all enjoying ourselves, and there was lots of laughter. But in one corner there was one man who was not laughing. Amongst the passengers are two brothers, Patrick and Thomas, both huge fellows and not too young. One was dancing with Alicia; the other one was glaring on with furled brows and a scowl that could sink a million ships. No one likes the Shea brothers, and they don't like each other it would seem. Up jumps Patrick, the younger one, from the corner, leaps over two of the dancers with a knife in his hand, and flings himself at his brother. Everyone scattered in all directions. Alicia fell down in a faint. Thomas was sprawled on the deck with his face bleeding. Patrick Shea had drawn back his knife hand and would probably have struck out at his brother, but his arm was caught by a burly sailor who had sprung down from the quarterdeck. Patrick, big though he is, was no match for the sailor, and others soon appeared having heard the shouting of the men and the screaming of the women. Patrick has been put in irons in the hold; Thomas is with Dr Acret who will no doubt be applying a styptic to his face. The party was at once at an end; Captain Mills is pacing the deck with a face like the blackest thunder, and all passengers have been sent below deck.

*

John Kelehan, while he had been accompanying the dancing, had been, as he himself would have put it, 'eyeing up the talent,'—that is, looking at the girls and working out which of the prettiest were married or already spoken for. Dorcas stood next to him after she had danced with Mr Hill, and John Kelehan found her pleasing to his eye. She saw him looking at her and turned her head away shyly.

'After all,' thought John Kelehan to himself, 'she's not bad looking, and no one seems to have staked a claim to her.' The Chief Mate had danced with her, this he had seen, but since James Hill was known to be a married man, where was the harm in that?

*

The days came and went, days filled with hunger and thirst, cold and sea-sickness, mealtimes signalled by the ringing of the bell; the emigrants learned the signals quickly, it's important to recognise that a meal should be ready when you are hungry. Four bells, 6 a.m.—everyone up! Six bells, 7 a.m.—everyone out. Eight bells meant breakfast at 8 a.m. Two bells, lunch at 1 p.m. Four bells was the signal for the evening meal at 6 p.m. Some of the passengers were given a rota so that they might assist in preparation and serving of the meals, others were expected to work at different tasks.

Rules for the emigrants, set down by the Passenger Act of 1847, were posted below deck, so that all might be aware of them. Since many were illiterate, the rules had to read to them. Since some were not too bright, and not well-behaved, it was necessary to remind them of the restrictions placed upon them and of their duties.

*

Extract from *The Colonisation Circular*
Issued by Her Majesty's Colonial Land and Emigration Commissioners—March 1847

The following are the Regulations to be observed on board Emigrant Ships proceeding to Australia under the superintendence of the Commissioners:—

To be hung up in at least one conspicuous place between decks.

1. The emigrants are to be out of bed at seven, the children to be washed and dressed and the decks swept, including the space under the bottom boards of the berths, which are to be lifted for the purpose every morning.

2. The beds are to be rolled up, and, weather permitting, carried on deck.

3. Breakfast at eight.

4. The decks to be cleaned at nine, by dry holy-stoning or scraping, each mess being answerable that their sleeping-berths are well brushed out, and the space in front kept clean.

5. A party of six or more is to be formed from all the males above 15, taken in rotation, to clean such parts of the deck as do not belong to any particular mess, and also the ladders, the hospitals, and the water-closets, and to be sweepers for the day. The decks to be swept after every meal.

6. The single women are to keep their part of the deck and their berths clean and if they need assistance their male relatives must give it them.

7. One or more women, as may be necessary, will be taken in rotation to attend any sick in the female hospital.

8. Immediately after breakfast, all the children, weather permitting, are to be sent on deck to be inspected by the sur-

geon, or the teacher, and seen to be clean, and then sent to school.

9. The bottom boards of the berths should be removed and dry-scrubbed and taken on deck, weather permitting, once or twice a-week, as the surgeon superintendent may direct. The bedding should also be well shaken and aired on deck at least twice a-week, if the weather permit.

10. Every mess is to have a head man to be responsible for the order and regularity of it, and whose duty it will be to report to the surgeon any misconduct or neglect requiring correction.

11. For the general enforcement of the present regulations, and of cleanliness and good order, constables are to be appointed from amongst the emigrants, in such manner as the surgeon superintendent may think proper.

12. The constables will attend daily at the serving out of the provisions, to see that each mess receives its proper allowance, and that justice is done; and a scale of the victualling will be affixed in some conspicuous part of the ship, for the information of all concerned, or delivered to each passenger with his embarkation order.

13. The coppers are to be cleaned daily, and the constables will inspect them every morning, and report to the surgeon superintendent whether or not they are clean.

14. No gambling is allowed.

15. No smoking is permitted between decks.

16. Spirits and gunpowder are not allowed to be brought on board. If discovered, they will be taken from the party.

17. Dinner at one.

18. Tea at six.

19. All to be in bed by ten o'clock.

20. A lamp is to be kept burning all night at each of the three hatchways, and it is not to be removed; and a lamp in each hospital, when occupied. No other lights are to be allowed after eight, p.m.

21. The married men in rotation will keep a watch in their part of the 'tween decks during the night. There should be two or three in each watch, and the night should be divided into three watches; the first from eight, p.m. to midnight, the second from midnight till four o'clock, and the morning watch from four to seven, a.m. The business of the watch will be, to prevent irregularities—to assist any persons taken ill—to attend to the hatchways, deck-ventilators, and scuttles, seeing that they are open or shut, according to the weather and the surgeon's directions—and to make any complaint that may be necessary to the surgeon superintendent.

22. Washing-days, every Monday and Friday, or on such other days as the surgeon superintendent may appoint, having regard to weather and other circumstances; but no washing or drying of wet clothes is, on any pretence whatever, to be suffered between decks.

23. On every Sunday, at half-past ten, the emigrants are to be mustered in the order of their berths, the surgeon superintendent passing along and inspecting them, to see that they are personally clean, and have on clean linen, and clean and decent apparel. Afterwards Divine Service is to be performed, and the Lord's Day to be as religiously observed as circumstances will admit.

24. On Thursday also a muster in clean linen and apparel.

25. The heavy luggage is to be put in the hold. The emigrants will have access to their boxes at intervals of three or four weeks, as the surgeon superintendent may direct.

26. One man may be taken, in rotation, if necessary, to act as the cook's assistant.

27. The surgeon superintendent is to appoint one man, if he think proper, to be his assistant in the hospital, or generally in attendance on the sick.

28. The surgeon superintendent will select one person to act as teacher to the children, and will appoint fit hours for school.

29. The teacher and the constables are to be exempt from the duty of cleaning decks amongst the messes, or from taking their turn in the party of general cleaners and sweepers. The man acting as cook's assistant for the day, if there be one, and the hospital man, will also be exempt from those duties.

30. All questions that may arise on the preceding Regulations are to be decided conclusively by the authority of the surgeon superintendent, who is entirely responsible for the care and good management of the emigrants, and whose authority is to be respected in all cases accordingly.

31. The surgeon superintendent is enjoined to refuse any extra comforts when in course of issue, and to deny any other indulgence he may think proper, to any persons who wilfully neglect or obstruct the established rules; and in case of gross misconduct or insubordination, he will report it to the Governor on arrival, with the name of the offender.

32. Finally, there are two remarks which it is desirable the emigrants should bear in mind,

First, —That it must very much depend on the attention they pay to the Rules provided for cleanliness and airiness, whether they reach their destination in high health and spirits, as many do, or, on the contrary, suffering under some of the infectious disorders which proceed from dirt and negligence at sea.

Secondly, —That on landing in the colony, their conduct during the voyage is sure to become known, and that while persons who arrive in a happy and orderly ship may expect the best offers of employment, those who bear the character of having been quarrelsome and refractory will naturally be avoided.

*

How well these regulations worked may become apparent in the following pages.

*

The emigrants had brought with them tools to practise their trades where needed, and each was given a small amount of storage space in the deepest hold in which the tools and spare clothes might be stored. Once every few weeks they were permitted to collect a change of clothing from the hold. Most soon became accustomed to the smell of unwashed clothes between decks; it was hard to keep clean.

The food was not good, but it filled the stomach and lay there like lead for a short while. But there is too little nutrition in adulterated flour and other produce, and everyone felt hungry again soon after meals were over. The crew, who ate better food in their own mess hall, watched the passengers sometimes as they ate their poor stuff in a frenzy. They referred to breakfast, lunch and supper as 'feeding time,' and this soon became the term amongst some of the emigrants also. The ship's cook, a Scot with an unintelligible accent and a way of either over- or under-cooking everything, was also expected to be in charge of slaughtering any livestock which was selected to be prepared for the table. He supposed that there might be amongst those of the emigrants who were farm labourers some who might happily assist in this task. He was soon disabused of this supposition, as those who were willing to help in this messy chore were totally incompetent.

But mealtimes were looked upon as highlights of the day, in spite of their meagreness—it could be argued that for some the little they received was a feast, for it was certainly more than they had been able to eat back at home. The cook, moreover, knew how to create something that had a smell which gave promise of something memorable and savoury, though perhaps that smell reminded one mostly of over-boiled cabbage. He created stocks to add to his stews, which gave off an aroma which caressed the nose and insides of the mouth, so that all who were able might be found standing near his galley drinking in the smell with open mouths. It was just that there was never enough, and that the promise of something good always led to disappointment upon actual tasting.

When eight bells sounded, the cook would be found presiding over a large cauldron, holding in his right hand a ladle with a long handle so that it might reach to the bottom. It was observed by all, however, that this long-handle was balanced by a small bowl at the end, which did not allow for large portions to be scooped up and placed on the plates which were given to the passengers.

The Captain and crew had other eating arrangements: larger portions of better cooked ingredients.

Many of the male emigrants had brought tobacco with them, and this allowed them to comfort their post-prandial hunger pangs with pipe smoke. Many of the women, too, smoked when given the chance, closing their eyes to narrow slits as they inhaled the rough fragrant smoke, and speaking to each other with smoky breath. The men were quieter when they smoked, preferring to contemplate their own thoughts, building castles in the sky, while the smoke was carried away by the wind, for it was forbidden to smoke below deck or in the cabins.

Despite the cold wind of those early days, some of the passengers spent time above deck, gazing into the distance, though no land was in sight, or looking down into the cold, green sea, which seemed to gaze jealously back up at them as if to say, 'Come down to me and I will rock you in my arms till you sleep an eternal sleep.' Some were fascinated by the angles and shapes made by the ship's wake, others kept well away from the sides for fear of falling in. Mothers were continually heard telling their children to come away from the sides of the ship; one small child was discovered to have improvised, from two pieces of wood and a tray, a platform for himself to stand on so that he could see over the side more easily.

*

From the Diary of Emma Smith
Saturday 15th January 1848

Freezing cold it is here, and we are all more than a bit thirsty. The Captain rationed our drinking water severely almost as soon as we left Plymouth, but we were never given a reason. I heard two of the menfolk talking about another connected matter. They were both furious, but were speaking very low. It seems that the crew's water has not been rationed. After the fight earlier this week, Alicia has been very quiet. Indeed, she hardly says a word, she was very badly shaken. Dorcas spent some time comforting her, she always has had a calming influence on any of us who are troubled or unhappy. Mrs Black's baby, who I think is called Margaret Jane was crying all night last night, and no one could do anything about it. Eventually, Dorcas got out of her bed, and asked if she could hold the child. No sooner was she in Dorcas's arms than she went to sleep. We were all amazed. Dorcas truly has such a way with her. I'm sure that once we are all in Australia and have found good husbands, she will make a wonderful mother. Mrs Black has said she will knit Dorcas a muffler if she helps with the baby sometimes, and if she can find any more wool. Martha is now assigned to keep the Captain's cabin tidy in place of Alicia and Augusta.

*

From The Private Journal of Frederick Acret, Surgeon
Saturday 15th January 1848

My God! Are there no depths to which this captain will not sink? He has given orders to limit or strictly ration the water for the emigrants. I remonstrated with him, but he shouted me down. Thomas Shea, one of the passengers, was injured by his brother in a brawl over a girl. Nothing has been seen of her on deck for some time. She has been keeping a very low profile, and I'm not surprised.

The Captain seems rather too interested in the orphan girls. Two of them were given the task of keeping his cabin clean, but one of the others seems now to have replaced them. Indeed, young Martha is constantly going in and out of there, while he hardly shows his face. I overheard Captain Mills bragging to the Chief Mate that he could have any girl or woman on board if he liked. The two men laughed a bit at that, so I don't know how serious that remark was.

*

Below deck there were a number of water closets for the use of the passengers. Since there were too few WCs, though, and those were often overflowing, some of the emigrants took to various strategies in order to avoid using them. Some did not open their bowels for days at a time, going around with that leaden feeling that comes from near permanent constipation. Others would make trips to the ship's head, where the latrines were supposedly only for the sailors' use.

The five orphan girls working for the officers had at least the advantage of being able to use the WCs meant for their employers.

Sickness and diarrhoea soon became a problem among the emigrants, and when a fever (somewhat unsurprisingly) broke out among them, it was up to Dr Acret to treat the unfortunate ones. His constant inebriation did not help him in his task. He would have dosed them all with spirits, but since the Captain had ordered that the rum on board should only be given to those who paid for it, and many couldn't (or wouldn't), only a few were thus dosed.

And here let me state that in my opinion the use of spirituous liquors for medicinal purposes of any sort is probably unwise. Tegg's Handbook, which he carried with him, and which I have seen, is, I feel, particularly at fault for recommending that so many remedies are dissolved in proof spirit or brandy. Though paregoric or camphorated opium tincture may be beneficial despite its alcoholic content, pure spirits, as Dr Acret apparently wished to use, and in quantity, can lead only to drunkenness.

One morning, Dorcas visited the Doctor complaining of an aching feeling in her stomach and a slight cough. She appeared pale if anything, rather than feverish, and Dr Acret, giving her a cursory glance went to his medicine chest. From a bottle he measured out a tablespoon of ipecacuanha wine, mixed it into a glass of water, and gave it to her to drink. She thanked him and left.

'These people who come to me with nothing wrong,' he thought to himself, 'they really make me ill.'

*

From the Diary of Emma Smith
Undated entry

I cannot bear to write. The injustice of it all. One of the passengers accused Dorcas of stealing drinking water. We all knew that she could not be guilty, but the Captain was in a rage this morning after a ferocious argument with Dr Acret which many heard. He ordered Dorcas to be punished—without waiting to hear her side of the story. James Hill, the First Mate started to protest, but he was at once overruled by the Captain. After a wait that seemed an hour, but may only have been a few minutes, Dorcas was led out of the Captain's cabin, where she had been given her sentence, and before us all was bound hand and foot, and with a rope tied round her waist was roughly hoisted to the top of the mainmast. We girls were all crying and screaming. Her distress was… You can imagine how she was affected by this. When she was brought down, barely conscious, we rushed forward to give assistance, and as soon as she was untied, carried her to our little corner where we have been comforting her. Mr Hill seemed to be quite anguished by the matter, but was unable to express himself fully before the Captain for obvious reasons. He came by later to ask how she did, but Martha saw him off with some very sharp and well-chosen words. Dorcas seems all but dead. How this will end, I cannot say.

*

From the Diary of Emma Smith
Undated entry

How I hate Captain Mills for what he has done to poor Dorcas.

*

Among the emigrants on the *Subraon* was a farm labourer from Clonlara, Clare called Donald McNamara. Twenty-five years old, he was a scrawny fellow with a wretched and unwashed appearance. This was due in no small measure to the fact that he had a great aversion to the use of soap and water. At the best of times he was dirty, but now, when clean water was not given for washing, and since all were forced to the necessity of using cold seawater for that purpose, and since soap was hard to come by, McNamara positively revelled in the filth which accumulated on his body. To put it mildly, he stank. It was hard to keep clean on the *Subraon*, but most made an effort to do so. Dreadful was the thought that McNamara might approach, and those who slept not far from him, all unmarried fellows, as he was, shunned him and were horrified and disgusted. Eventually, four of them went to lay their problem before the Chief Mate.

James Hill was sympathetic, but was not certain that he would be able to assist. However, he agreed to speak to the man to encourage him to clean himself and his clothes. McNamara, when faced with his fellow emigrants, whose previous entreaties he had ignored, and the Chief Mate, stuck his chin out, and insolently declared, 'I will not! Who the hell do you think you are? I know all about your little games, you jumped up, little fucker!'

Hill signalled to the four who stood with him. The emigrants bodily lifted the struggling McNamara, stripped him bare, and thrust him head first into a large tun filled with seawater. James Hill took a large scrubbing brush, usually used for swabbing the deck, and furiously scrubbed at McNamara's skin while the other was prevented by his fellow countrymen from escaping the barrel. His yells and curses were soon silenced by several duckings under the water. From not far away, others gathered to view the entertainment.

Eventually, the barrel was tilted over, and McNamara rolled out. Too exhausted now to express his fury, he lay panting like a dog. Someone thrust a blanket at him. Gradually the crowd dispersed, helped on the way by the scowls of Captain Mills who had come out onto the deck to see what all the fuss was about.

McNamara took care not to let himself get into that filthy state again during the voyage, but he held a grudge against James Hill for a very long time. Dr Acret, who had observed the proceedings from a little way off, nodded at Hill as they passed each other later. 'That was a good trick,' he said. 'I hope he doesn't try to get his own back.'

'Not a chance of it,' said Hill.

*

From the Diary of Emma Smith
Undated Entry

I have discovered that Martha, for all her criticising the behaviour of others, has a shameful secret of her own. She thought to fool us all by playing the part of Miss Innocence—but I saw her going off with Third Mate Mr Carwadine. I am ashamed to admit that I followed to spy, and heard them canoodling in one of the cargo holds. I hid behind a crate and heard it all. Certain I am that had it not been for a voice calling for him, he would have gone all the way with her then and there, and that she would not have objected, so disappointed she seemed at his departure.

I don't know if I will tell anyone of this, or if I should tell. I think I will not do so, but I will remember. I don't think that was their first meeting of this sort. Martha is shameless. Her talk is always of men and their bodies (though always as though she was shocked by it all). "Look at the muscles on him," she said of Mr Carwardine when she first saw him. I remember that clearly. I think she was 'rescued' from the streets of Dublin, so I'm sure she was never the pure little miss she pretends to be. The other day one of the sailors ripped the front of his trousers open on a marlinspike while up in the rigging fiddling with a rope. Those of us who were there looked away, except for Martha who insisted on telling us what she saw. Really, a man's naked body is no pleasure to see, though he may be useful as a protector in times of need and also as a husband.

*

One blustery morning, Captain Mills, like one obsessed, strode around the deck, examining the sailors and their work. A few of the male emigrants had been looking out over the bulwarks at the sea, where many Portuguese men-of-war could be seen like tiny yachts navigating stormy seas in large convoy. The emigrants made themselves scarce at the sight of the Captain, while Able Seaman Augustus Reynolds, who had been standing with them, immediately made himself busy.

'The old man's on the warpath,' murmured Reynolds partly to himself and partly to the disappearing backs of the emigrants. 'I haven't seen him so active for days.'

Reynolds wiped his sweaty face with his sleeve, and decided not to get himself a drink of water until the Captain had gone back into his cabin. He had little respect for British authority. A Canadian born and bred, he had taken part eleven years earlier in the rebellions against the government, and had then made himself scarce. Though he felt bereft at not being able to return to Montreal and his parents, and angry that Canada had not been granted independence, he felt that perhaps in Australia there lay the promise of a safe life out of immediate British jurisdiction. But, even though the sailors were permitted water to drink (within moderation) if they needed it, it seemed wiser not to let Captain Mills actually watch him go to the water butt. It had not rained for some days, so supplies of water were not increasing. Life on board the *Subraon* had been an experience not worth the repeating, and he was already considering not making the return journey to England.

Meanwhile, the passengers took what water they could when they were allowed to do so. Gradually, they became dirtier and dirtier as there was not enough water on board to permit washing of their bodies or their clothes. The smells below deck were now unbearable.

JP was depressed, and he wore a scowl on his face that might have sunk a ship with a glance, so it was no wonder that no one wanted to be under his eye. In point of fact, he was thinking of Rachel and of finding a solution to his home-woes, and took no notice of Reynolds or the emigrants. A touch of indigestion had not helped his mood, and he found it hard to concentrate. 'A stiff tot of rum will sort me out,' he thought to himself. 'Perhaps two!' and he returned to his cabin.

*

From The Private Journal of Frederick Acret, Surgeon
Tuesday 22nd February 1848

Mrs Ferry was delivered safely of a son this evening. Naturally, she was attended by the other ladies, but I was called to look the new baby over after he had been born, and then to register the birth in the ship's records. They have named him Charles

Subraon after the ship. The mother is doing well. All the young ladies on the ship were crooning over the baby as soon as they were allowed to see him. I've just time for a quick nip of something to keep the cold out, and then it's bed for me.

*

The days pass; it is evening: cold and dark. Two seamen speak with each other as they work.

'I've not seen the Captain for days,' says Able Seaman Murphy to Able Seaman Reynolds.

'I've seen him, but not sober,' responds the other.

'Who's minding the wheel?' says Murphy.

Reynolds looks round. 'Hill,' he says.

'Oh, Hell! Does he know where we're going? The man's a nightmare. Half-seas-over half the time, and asleep the other half.'

'But when he's in his cabin, it's not just sleeping he'll be doing, you can be sure of that,' says Reynolds, 'he'll be a-comfortin' a poor injured party. The two men laugh grimly. 'But it's no laughing matter,' says Reynolds. 'I don't give a toss if wants to play with girls, but he needs to be campusments when he's at the wheel. And the same goes for the others!'

James Hill, meanwhile, stands by the ship's wheel, wrapped in an oilcloth coat. Before him is the small cuddy, little bigger than a cupboard, in which stands the binnacle upon which the ship's compass is mounted. The entrance to the cuddy faces the wheel, and above the compass is an oil lamp which is kept lit at nighttime so that the direction of travel can easily be ascertained by its light. Hill, however, is in a world of his own. He has allowed his imagination to take flight, and he pictures himself captain of his own ship, with wife and family at home. His wife's face, though, is indistinct; a vision of Dorcas hovers before his eyes, and he thinks lustful thoughts of thighs and smooth skin.

*

Ann Brennan, Ellen Busby, Patience Newcomen, Mary Preston, Mary Sneyd and Ellen Stephens sat together in the screened-off area reserved for them. These were the girls deemed by the Captain and the mates to be less interesting to them. They had been talking about Dorcas's punishment. All were shocked by the brutality shown by the Captain, and some feared for themselves.

Patience frowned as she examined her dirty fingernails. 'Dorcas and the others are still working for them,' she said. As there was no answer she continued, 'I tell you, it will come to no good end.'

The others still said nothing. 'Who do they think they are?' she added eventually, leaving the others to deduce whether she was speaking of the other orphans or the sailors who were employing them.

Ellen Busby, who the others considered to be slower than they were, gave her opinion, surprising the others who were not used to her saying much at all.

'They are not bad girls, most of them.'

'It's not the girls we have to worry about,' said Ann Brennan, 'it's those sailor chaps. I wish we had never come. And that Captain is always sneaking around trying to kiss all the girls. I tell you, there's no safety to be had on this ship.'

At that moment, a head appeared from behind the oil-cloth. It was Mary Ann Dixon. 'Anyone seen Dorcas?' she asked. 'Mrs Black was looking for her. Says she has something to give her.'

The girls were not happy about their situation, nor with each other, but a kind of loyalty made them all deny knowledge of Dorcas's whereabouts and Mary Ann continued her search.

'I'm cold,' said Ellen Stephens to no one in particular, 'especially my feet, they're like two chunks of ice. '

'Sit by me,' Mary Sneyd said to her, 'I'll warm them for you.' And she held Ellen, who was the smallest of them, close to her, and began to rub her feet.

Mary Preston began to cry.

'Not homesick for that dreadful place we've just come from, are you?' said Patience.

'I feel sick,' was the reply.

'Don't you puke on me!'

But they all wished they were back home and had never left.

*

Mrs Black found Dorcas standing by the side of the ship gazing out over the ocean.

'It's so vast,' said Dorcas.

'Here you are,' said Mrs Black, and she held out a pair of mittens. 'It's not much I know, but there wasn't much wool left.'

Dorcas thanked her. 'Where's the baby?' she asked.

'My husband is holding her a while.'

And the two looked out over the water.

'Is he nice, your husband?' said Dorcas eventually.

'Oh, yes, he's a good man,' said the other. 'We're really looking forward to a new life together, him and me and the baby.'

Dorcas felt a longing spring up in her mind: a new life and someone to share it with.

*

From the Diary of Emma Smith
Undated entry

Dorcas has told me, in confidence that she is in love— with James Hill the Chief Mate. Poor, sweet thing, she confided in me her secret. He, meanwhile, doesn't seem to look at any of us, including her. Those others of us who are helping keep house for the Mates have tried to get him to notice her, but he studiously avoids all eye contact. I do hope it all turns out well, she deserves happiness after all her earlier troubles. I will never tell a soul; I write this here for no other eyes but my own.

Meanwhile, Martha has been seeing to the Captain's cabin, and is always there, and this despite her bold looks towards the Third Mate. What a contrast there is between Martha's unbridled show of lust for Mr Carwardine, and sweet Dorcas's pure love for Mr Hill.

*

From the Diary of Emma Smith
Undated entry

It seems that Mr Hill had noticed Dorcas after all. I saw them talking together. She told me that he kissed her. 'I love him, Emma,' she whispered to me last night. 'When he holds me in his arms I think I will melt.'

I hope he is not a deceiver—I cannot think he is, he has such an honest face, and, I will say this, his voice is very mellow, though he is from Liverpool. I wonder if they will be married. She says he hasn't asked her yet, but is sure he will.

Martha and Ellen Busby had words. Ellen accused Martha of fornication; Martha denied it. I thought that Ellen was talking about Mr Carwardine, but it turns out that it was the Captain she meant. Apparently, Martha is always in his cabin.

Another thing: that Mr Carwardine keeps looking at me in a most disconcerting manner. Whenever I turn round, he always seems to be there, and I wish he wasn't.

*

Ships bound for Australia often stop at Cape Town for a few days. The *Subraon* did not; two days after passing the southernmost tip of Africa, and the ship was making good headway.

The journey round the Cape itself had been a terrible time for all. The ferocious winds blew in the opposite direction to that desired. The Captain navigated the *Subraon* so that she sailed some distance south of Cape Town in order to take advantage of the Agulhas current as it curved back on itself eastward after it had swept south-west down the eastern coast of Africa. The screams from below deck at every pitch and toss of the ship as the terrified passengers clung onto each other were largely inaudible above as the sailors struggled bravely to keep the *Subraon* under control. Below deck, many of the passengers had tied themselves down in order to avoid being flung about. Above, the Captain had already ordered that the sails be furled, and, with a face like stone, looked out from under his sou'wester as his men went about their work.

In his cabin, Dr Acret wrapped himself in a blanket and lay in his bed. He had looked out as the storm had started, but had then thought better of it.

The passengers missed the sights seen by the sailors as they worked on deck as the ship passed south of Cape Town. From the starboard side of the ship they had seen distant icebergs, seemingly small from where the men stood, but immense in reality and a danger to any ship unfortunate enough to sail too close.

But as the days passed, the weather changed for the better, and the *Subraon* sailed inexorably on through sub-tropical climes, keeping to the 39th parallel, well north of the colder Antarctic current, eastward until the Agulhas current met the South Indian Ocean current, onwards to Australia. Captain Mills planned to steer the ship so that she would curve northward slightly, passing a little north of the Île Amsterdam which lay approximately halfway between Cape Town and Sydney.

★

An early March morning: weather fine. Upon the deck, near the forecastle, Eliza Bews stood, rod in hand, pointing at a large slate balanced on a barrel. She, her husband John and their children had left their home in Cornwall and were the only emigrants on board not from Ireland.

John Bews had been appointed to the position of schoolmaster by Dr Acret, his wife had been made his assistant, but it was she who did most of the schooling. Most of the passengers who had children had agreed to let their children be schooled, and John Bews had agreed to teach them—for a small fee. Those children whose parents had paid sat hard by, gazing at the large slate. Eliza Bews pointed at the letters, naming each one in turn, while the children made efforts to copy them down on their own small slates using scraps of chalk. Bews remained nearby all the while, to see that none of their charges misbehaved or absconded. They had agreed with the children's parents not to touch upon any matters concerning religion since they were both Church of England and their pupils were mostly Catholic.

And so, the children gathered around on that hot day and listened to the lesson, though all were disinclined to learn.

A little way off Mary Bradley, housemaid from Derry, eighteen years old and illiterate was watching, wishing that she too could join the young students. She could neither read nor write and yearned to improve herself, but felt unable due to shyness to present herself to the teachers. The children told over their letters, not absorbing much.

Overhead a large bird could be seen wheeling between the clouds. 'Albatross,' called a voice from above, and despite threats from Mr and Mrs Bews the children all stood and watched the bird pass over the ship and into the distance: the only entertainment they had had for days, and nothing and nobody could stop them enjoying it.

Mrs Bews noticed Mary Bradley looking on and beckoned her over.

'If you are happy to help, you can join the class to learn,' said Mrs Bews who seemed to understand the difficulty the other showed.

'What could I offer, I can't read?'

'Start by helping keep the children in order.' Eliza dropped her voice almost to a whisper, 'Frankly my husband is not very good at that.'

And so, Mary Bradley joined the class as an unpaid assistant.

*

From The Private Journal of Frederick Acret, Surgeon
March 1848

This interminable voyage is almost as insufferable as the Captain's behaviour. I feel unable to do anything to ameliorate the situation of the passengers who must endure such privations. I am in an invidious position. I think this will be the last voyage I make; certainly, travelling with this captain is something I will not consider, not after the way he spoke to me today. Not for the first time we disagreed on a matter of importance. In matters medical, surely it is the ship's doctor who must have the final say. But I was overruled and roundly insulted before the crew into the bargain. I will not serve under this captain again.

*

March 1848
A fever has broken out among the emigrants. Despite the Captain's orders, I have seen to it that any affected are given adequate liquid comforts, though they may be charged for it (which is against regulations).

Fourteen passengers have now been affected by the fever. One of them, Hugh O'Neill is very seriously ill. His wife is nursing him, but I fear he will not live.

*

24 March 1848
Hugh O' Neill died this morning of the fever. He was the fourth person to die of the same cause, the other three being members of the crew who also came down with it. All help was given to them, but there was nothing to be done, The Captain has ordered that they all be buried at sea.

*

Those who had died were sewn up in their hammocks, and after a brief burial service read by the Captain, were consigned to the waters which surrounded the ship: a sombre moment watched solemnly by all, especially the children. Mrs O'Neill watched with dull eyes, and was then escorted away by her closest friends.

9
Night

Nighttime. Calm sea. On deck, the sailors on watch stood looking out over the inky blackness. The sky was cloudy, and no stars could be seen. Mr Day was on duty and slowly paced the ship, looking, though in desultory fashion, to see that all was in order. A.B. Peter Murphy, standing on the starboard side, stifled a yawn.

'Not tired already, are you?' asked the Second Mate.

'No, it's cold. I always yawn when I'm cold.'

Mr Day turned away. Murphy shuffled over to the port side, where he was joined by A.B. Thomas Sheppard. The two men spoke in whispers, intentionally lisping as they did, so that no sibilant sounds might carry to the ears of the Second Mate.

'Thpoke to Guth' [Augustus Reynolds] said Sheppard. 'He thaid we're not the only oneth fed up. If enough of uth agree, the Thubraon won't get any further than Thydney.'

'I'm blowed if I thail with her and thith lot after we get there,' said Murphy.

'We'll have to bide our time, we don't want to be accuthed of mutiny.'

The two seamen shook hands, and Sheppard left to get back to his hammock.

*

Nighttime. In the emigrant's mess hall, supper, such as it was, had finished. Most of those who had dined at the last sitting had dispersed to their berths or to the deck. In one corner of the mess hall, a small number of emigrants remained. One of them had spread out a large, but very tatty, map onto a refectory table. The small party sat, or knelt on the benches, or stood close by and leaned over it. By the subtle light of the oil lamp which hung on the wall, giving out a strong fishy aroma as the whale oil inside burned away, they attempted to plot the course of the *Subraon* so far.

*

Nighttime. Time to change the watch. Mr Hill and Mr Day met on deck. They spoke stiffly with each other: both studiously polite, but brief.

'Mr Hill.'

'Mr Day.'

'An uncomfortable sort of voyage, this.'

'What voyage is not?'

'True, true.'

And other courteous nothings passed between them.

'I'll be glad to get back home to my wife,' said Mr Day.

'As will I to mine,' responded the other.

But their conversation, which continued after this a while, had been overheard by more than one other person. The Captain had been on deck at the time (a rare appearance). He was not so sure of the pleasure he would have at being back with his own wife. It was unfortunate that Dorcas had also been on deck at that moment, invisible to the men as she breathed the night air, so stuffy it was below where the women slumbered and snored.

*

In the emigrant's mess hall the conversation of those present continued.

'By my reckoning, this is where we were at about noon, and this is our current position.'

'That can't be right, We've been heading South-West for the last few hours.'

'South-West, how do you make that out?'

'I don't. I asked Carwardine. He said we have to head towards the Argentine in order to pick up the current to the Cape of Good Hope.'

'Man, where have you been? That was days ago, and it was towards Rio de Janeiro we were heading. He was having you on! Don't believe a word these sailor chaps tell you.'

'I suppose you studied navigation, then! Another talent to add to your list!'

'As a matter of fact…'

'Listen to him, he knows what he's about.'

'Quiet, woman! This is men's talk,' said the second man.

'Oh, is it, now? I'll tell you, Mr Know-it-all, he knows more than you ever will.'

'Shut your mouth, or…'

'Or what?'

'Or I'll shut it for you!'

'Don't you talk to a lady like that!' said the first man.

'What lady?' said the other.

'Why you… Take that!'

'Where's me stick. I'll give you what for!'

'Come on, then!'

And a space was suddenly cleared for a fight. No one tried to stop it—everyone had been so bored that any entertainment was welcome. Other men returned to the mess hall to watch. Women, too, began to arrive.

The two who had been arguing squared up to each other, and with bare fists began to circle around the space like prize-fighters, each aiming jabs, or dodging them as was needful. The noise rose to a deafening roar; two or three of the sailors also began to watch the proceedings.

The fight was not really ill-natured. The challenge had been made half in jest, and the two men, once each had bloodied the nose of his opponent, began to laugh. Then, each clasping the other in his arms, they began to roll on the wooden floor. One of the women began to sing and stamp her feet, and suddenly the fight had turned into a dance.

★

Nighttime. Much later. By the light of a stump of candle John Kelehan, groom from Tullanore, and Martin Sheahan, carman from Doonass, sit in the men's dormitory, steerage, playing chess, and this despite the fact that the emigrants are, strictly speaking, all supposed to be in bed after the evening four bells for 10 p.m. has been sounded. The chessboard is battered, and several of the pieces have been improvised out of scraps of wood and old nails. The calm sea allows them to do this now; it is a way of passing the time quietly.

A week ago this would have been impossible, for the swell of the Atlantic and the gales which rolled northward tossed the ship so violently and unpredictably that no chess piece would have remained upright for long.

During those rough times, the emigrants had been battened down below decks and lay miserably in their berths, while empty bottles rolled and slid over the floor as the ship tilted this way and that. No one attempted to tidy them away because everyone felt so ill. The sailors, for whom the rough ocean was nothing but a way of life to be relished, laughed at the emigrant men, calling them lazy, lily-livered land-lubbers (and worse). The younger male emigrants had been assigned chores both above deck and below, but none had been in a fit state to do much at all.

But now, all is comparatively calm, and the two chess-players play on, ignoring the deep snores which reverberate around them.

'What'll you do in Australia, John?' asks Martin quietly.

'I suppose I'll find someone who needs their horses taken care of. That's all I know really. I left a real beauty behind, you know.'

'A girl, you mean?'

'No,' says John, 'a horse.'

'I think I'll find me a girl,' says Martin.'You're in check, by the way.'

'What about them that's on this boat?'

'Too lazy, most of 'em. You've seen what they're all like!' He chuckles.

'Some might be not too bad,' says John.

'Man, you're a fool if you think of startin' with any on this barge.'

But John is not sure he agrees with his friend. There are distinct possibilities in his mind.

And so they continue a while until even they become too weary to carry on, and roll themselves into their mattresses and sleep.

*

Nighttime. The passengers are all cocooned in their blankets. The *Subraon* ploughs her way through the southern Indian Ocean. The creaks of the hull and the snores of the sleepers together with the movement of the ship might give the impression of a weird barcarolle.

In his cabin, Captain Mills lies awake in his own bed. Unable to sleep, he stares up at the ceiling and wonders if he is wasting his life away. Sleeping is hard for him at the best of times; he is a martyr to insomnia. At this moment, sleeping is even more difficult than usual as he is not alone. He looks down to his left, where a feminine arm lies draped on the cover, and sighs. The girl next to him stirs slightly and carries on sleeping. He releases himself from the bed, pulls on his trousers and his boots, and leaves the cabin, walking onto the deck where he can see the stars and the moon and try to imagine he is a ship's apprentice again.

Back in the Captain's cabin, Martha sleeps on.

*

Early morning in the women's area: many are up and awake and speaking in loud voices. Another day, the same as every other was dawning. The monotony of the voyage was unbearable, and there was little rest from the bickering that, like a continuous stream of invective, went on throughout the waking hours.

'I have something I need to say,' said Dorcas to Emma. She trembled as she said it. It had been some hours since she had overheard Hill and Day, and she had been trying to find an opportunity to speak to her friend alone ever since. She needed courage as well, for what she needed to say was hard. They sat together in a corner where the lower deck met the stairs to the quarterdeck.

'What do you want to tell me?' Emma asked happily—supposing a new delightful game that might take their minds from the awfulness of the voyage. The other seemed unhappy, though, and Emma, seeing the troubled look on Dorcas's face, became solemn all at once.

'Tell me,' she said.

'Emma, it's serious.'

'What is?'

'I don't know how to say this.'

'Try,' said Emma.

'I'm going to have a baby.'

'But that's impossible… How can that be…? When…?'

'I don't know. How can you ask questions now? I'm overdue.'

'I had no idea…'

'Emma, what am I going to do, what am I going to do?' whispered Dorcas desperately. 'I thought he loved me—but he has a wife, he has a wife already. I think I shall die!'

'Who is he?' asked Emma, though she already knew what the answer would be.

'James… James Hill. He promised to marry me. What shall I do?'

'Dorcas, please—don't do anything stupid. Let me think a moment. Just let me think.'

'Emma, you can't tell anyone, you mustn't.'

'What about—*him*?'

'Especially not him.'

There was a pause as the two girls sat holding each other. Eventually, Emma spoke. 'Are you absolutely certain?' Dorcas nodded miserably. 'Don't worry,' said Emma, 'I'll look after you.'

Dorcas, tired from her troubles took her solace in sleep. Emma covered her friend with her shawl, and stayed close by to watch her.

*

Night came again. In the mess hall, all was quiet. Captain Mills, still unable to sleep despite the alcohol circulating in his veins, had been walking silently round the ship, inspecting all: a kind of pretence, for any who might see, that he was alert. He gazed round the room where the emigrants had lately been eating, and was surprised to find, stretched out on one of the tables, one of the emigrants fast asleep. He gestured to the ship's boy who was busily wiping the tables down, and asked in a low voice who the person was.

'I don't know her name,' came the reply, 'but she's here most nights, at least for the last two or three.'

'Wake her!'

And the boy went over and shook her gently. The girl stretched and then stood up abruptly when she realised what was happening. 'A plain little thing,' thought the Captain to himself. 'Let's have some fun.'

'Name, miss?' he barked hoarsely.

'Margaret Tuohy, sir,' came the answer.

'And what the devil are you doing here?'

'Sleeping, sir.'

'I can see that you were sleeping, why were you sleeping here?'

'Well, you see…'

'No, I do not see!'

'There are rats on this ship, sir. They bother me at night when I'm in my bed. So I thought I would come here to sleep instead, though it is cold…'

'If I see you here again, it won't be the rats that bother you; if you're cold, you could try wrapping yourself up in my bed of a night. I'll show you something that'll worry you more that a rat!'

But Margaret Tuohy, pushed past the Captain, and hurried back to her own berth in the female quarters. As for the Captain, he sat on one of the benches, doubled up in silent laughter, while the boy looked on.

10
James Hill

James Hill was dressing in his cabin. He caught sight of his reflection in the small mirror that he had fixed to the inside of the door, and smiled at what he saw, nodding as if to a familiar acquaintance. In a hidden compartment within his sea-chest he kept a small cask of something to warm him or to help him pass away the hours. And, since he had a key to the ship's stores and access to the medicinal spirits on board, he had found no difficulty in keeping his private supply topped up. He had made certain that Captain Mills also had a regular supply, and the two kept this as a secret between them. Dr Acret, meanwhile, had been denied a key, and had to ask every time he needed spirits with which to dose a sick passenger; and though the good doctor cared somewhat about his fellow man, and resented this, he had no intention of sharing his own private supply in case of need. He had his own private sorrows to drown.

Hill pulled on his coat, and, ready to step out onto the deck, reached for his hip-flask for that customary little nip of brandy to prepare him for his duties. But it was not in its usual place. He searched his pockets one by one, dug into the chest, and then began a more systematic search. But it was not to be found. The ship's bell rang for the change of the watch, and cursing he strode out onto the deck without his flask and without his usual nip.

The Captain stood not far away. 'Anything the matter, Mr Hill?'

95

'No, sir.'

'Proceed, Mr Hill.'

And Hill went about his work casting a suspicious look back at his commander as he went. 'Though surely,' he muttered to himself, 'he has enough of his own and more than I have into the bargain.'

That James Hill thought a great deal of himself goes without saying. He began once more to think of a time when he might be Master of his own ship. In his mind he could see it already. How different he would be from Captain Mills, how benevolent, how wise he would be, and how loved. He was so lost in his thoughts that when Emma Smith went up to him, he didn't notice that she was there for a moment, not even when she began to speak. It was only after she tugged at his sleeve that he came out of his reverie. She began telling him something which he could not at first understand. But when he realised what it was she was telling him, he left her abruptly.

'What kind of trouble have I got myself into now?' he asked himself. 'You fool! Idiot! Thank God Dorcas will be staying in Australia and Jenny won't find out about her.'

Dorcas, who had instructed Emma that on no account must she tell James about her condition, had almost counted on James finding out. She saw her friend go to the Chief Mate and deduced the subject of their conversation; but then, embarrassed and horrified at the thought of a confrontation with the man who had ruined her, she went and hid her face from him by standing by the port side of the ship and firmly gazing out to sea.

James Hill approached her, and she turned to face him. The wind blew her hair over her head so that it covered her face. The tears in her eyes were, in reality, from the wind, but she knew instinctively how to make them play to her advantage. Hill gazed at her.

'Don't you think you should go below?'

'And why should I?' she answered almost defiantly.

'You best know the reason for that, I think.'

'James, what are we going to do?'

'I'll speak to Dr Acret,' came the answer. 'He will know the best thing you can do.'

Dorcas did not notice the subtle shift, from the first-person-plural which she had used in her question, to the second-person-singular he had used in his answer. James, though he liked, even loved, Dorcas, already thought of the problem they had created between them as *her* problem.

*

Captain Mills soon tired of Martha as he had done with the girls who had preceded her. Martha now kept Mr Carwardine's cabin clean. Nor did she object too strongly, for Carwardine was a handsome fellow who knew how to keep a girl happy, and she had already spent a considerable amount of time in his company.

*

From the Diary of Emma Smith
Undated entry

I am to keep the Captain's cabin tidy. He has said that he will pay me well, and that I won't have to work too hard. I was a little surprised by his behaviour, though, for he seemed to want other favours. I think the others would be very jealous if they found out what I've been up to.

*

One morning there was considerable excitement among the passengers as a school of killer whales was seen to be following the *Subraon* only two ship's lengths distant, and almost in its wake. The older children and their teachers were given permission to go up onto the poop deck, where they stood holding on to the taffrail watching. The children's loud chattering made it evident to the seamen standing nearby, keeping an eye out for their safety, that they considered the whales to be making great sport.

'And so they are,' muttered Able Seaman Peter Murphy to his companion, 'but a whale's idea of sport differs from a child's. It's hunting sharks or the young of big whales that they are about.'

The children were all too soon called back down to their lessons. Eliza Bews had preceded them finding that the swell of the waves made her giddy up on the poop deck.

*

From The Private Journal of Frederick Acret, Surgeon
April 1848

Mr Hill has come to me with a problem. He has made an unfortunate alliance with one of the orphan girls, Miss Newman, quite a pretty girl. She told him but a short while ago that she is now pregnant with his child. Apparently, they commenced intimate relations the day after we left Plymouth. Who would have guessed it? No wonder he was so affected by her punishment: I was too. He asked for my help, but, whatever my faults, and however much I sympathise with their plight, I am no abortionist—and were I so, it would be a very dangerous undertaking here where there are no proper facilities. As it is I have had babies to deliver on board, and with no little trouble. I hope she does not go to one of the ladies here for help. I have heard of girls mutilated in the past by such practices.

The worst of it all is that Hill has confessed to me that he is already married. His wife lives in London. I hope the poor girl

he has got into trouble doesn't find out. She's a fragile thing—
God knows what might happen if she did.

I must restrict my drinking somewhat, as I seem to have mis-
laid a pair of forceps and a probe.

*

Dorcas sat in the cabin which Mrs Black shared with her husband and baby daughter. Little Margaret Jane was in her arms,
and Dorcas rocked her while singing a soft lullaby. Husband
and wife had gone for a walk on the deck. As she sang, tears
rolled down her face. Mrs Black, then, returning without her
husband, stood in the doorway amazed.

'Why, whatever is the matter?'

And Dorcas, unable to keep her own secret, blurted out the
cause of her unhappiness and her shame. The other, taking the
baby and placing her in a crude wooden crib, comforted the
crying girl as best she could.

'Who else knows of this?'

'Only Emma, I haven't told anyone else.'

Unable to bear it any longer, she tore herself away, and flung
out of the cabin.

*

'Dorcas, I brought you some water,' says Emma as she passes
through the curtain which separated the sleeping area of the
orphan girls from the other women. But Dorcas is not there.

Emma, surprised, but not yet too afraid, begins searching the
ship. Faster and faster she walks, until she is running here and
there calling her friend's name. The other girls, not knowing
that there is anything wrong, join the search as if it were a
game of hide-and-seek. But soon they realise that all is not as
they had supposed. How can someone disappear on a ship?

Now all the girls are running around below and above the deck, calling Dorcas's name; asking all they meet, but no one can answer, none has seen her. Surely there is nowhere to go—except —

'Dorcas!' Emma shrieks, 'Has anyone seen her? Has anyone seen Dorcas?'

James Hill appears. 'Emma, what's happening?'

'It's Dorcas, I can't find her, she's gone. I think she may have fallen overboard!'

11
Dorcas

Emma says 'fallen,' but her mind says, 'jumped!' Deeply distressed, she stands rooted to the spot and trembling as if she had the fever to end all fevers.

Suddenly, the ship is a hive of activity.

'Lower a boat!' shouts the Mate, and the men jump to it.

'Oh, Dorcas!' wails Emma; the crew and the other passengers are now very alarmed too.

Some of the male passengers hang over the sides of the ship trying to spot the missing girl in the water, though the ship must by now be well past the place where she went over the side. Sailors climb the rigging to get a better view—but there is nothing. Nothing!

Then a cry from below: 'She is in the cargo hold. She's been found.'

'Thank God!' Emma and the other girls weep. Emma runs down the stairs to the hold. 'Thank God!'

And then she reaches the bay where Dorcas is lying on a pile of empty sacks and old ropes. Her dress is stained red, red, red.

'Oh, my God! Oh, my GOD!' screams Emma in shock. 'Dorcas, what has happened, what did you do?'

But it is all too obvious. Near Dorcas, on the floor, lie two bloody knitting needles and bloody rags as well. Emma turns, horrified. The sailor who found Dorcas is nowhere to be seen. James Hill arrives and gazes on the scene before him, aghast.

'Stay with her,' he says, 'I'll get the doctor. Only let him be sober!'

As Hill turns to leave, his foot kicks accidentally at something in the shadow of a crate. He bends to pick it up. It is his missing hip-flask—empty, of course. He pushes past the crowd of people who are beginning to assemble outside. Two of the crew hold back the passengers and the orphan girls and usher them away. Mrs Black, who arrived distraught, does not try to approach too near, but hangs back with a hand over her mouth; she is led away by her husband. Dorcas is left with Emma.

*

From The Private Journal of Frederick Acret, Surgeon
April 1848

The very worst has happened to that orphan girl. She attempted to terminate her own pregnancy, and is now terribly injured and in no little pain. Who told her how to go about such a dreadful task, and, more importantly, who gave her the tools to do it? I despair of humankind! I write this in a brief interval that has been granted me that I may recover some fortitude with a small glass or two of brandy. I had not left her side for hours, but finally managed to stop her bleeding, though I fear only temporarily. She is very weak, and I must return to her side immediately. God grant me the ability to save her life, but I fear the case is already hopeless.

*

'Dorcas, my dear, Dorcas, my love. Do wake, they've spotted land. We shall arrive in Australia soon, and I shall look after you till you are well.' Emma put her head by her friend and caressed her hair. But there was no response. Dorcas lay in a room hardly bigger than a closet, but she was silent. 'I'll get Dr Acret,' said Emma.

The Doctor, once fetched, motioned everyone out including Emma and closed the door. His bloodshot eyes told tales of long hours awake, and too much brandy. By the light of the dim lamp in the room he looked at the girl lying there, and bit his lower lip. Emma remained outside the door, crying bitterly. Others came and went.

*

April 12, 1848: The *Subraon* arrived at Port Jackson, Sydney, New South Wales, Australia. The passage itself had been comparatively easy, though navigation through Bass Straits, the sea between Van Diemen's Land and Victoria, had been particularly difficult. All on board were suffering from great stress, some more than others. On board the end of a tragedy was playing itself out. A curtain came down on a young life, once so merry and full of promise.

*

From the Diary of Emma Smith
Thursday 13th April 1848

Dorcas! Not Dorcas! Everyone's lovely girl, dead! We stood there, horrified by the news. Utterly bereft. The tears, then, cascading down our cheeks, we girls huddled together for comfort. To give credit where it's due, even the other passengers seemed shocked at the disaster which had befallen us, even those who had been the first to condemn her. Dr Acret seemed exhausted; he had sat with her continuously for forty-eight hours without sleep. The Captain was not to be seen. James Hill, appearing as from nowhere, rushed into the small room where Dorcas lay lifeless. Then it was that the Captain appeared by our sides. He gave us a glance betokening sympathy, and then followed the First Mate, closing the door after him so that we could not see what was happening inside. We could hear, though, a sound of abject wailing from within.

For the rest of my life, I will not forget Dorcas, who was so kind to me and was our joy and comfort in times of woe. Her quiet and gentle ways, her laughter, her sadnesses will stand for her as a memorial in my mind. Already, I seem to have difficulty recalling her face as it was before her trouble. All I see is the pain etched upon her cheeks. She was treated with great cruelty and injustice, and I cannot forgive those who were guilty of such vile acts.

We are to stay aboard the ship until called for. We must get our things, such as they are, ready for departure: ten girls bereft! Martha put her arms round me when she saw how distressed I was. She and Dorcas never got on, but even she was affected by her death. She will help me collect my things, for I cannot bear to leave. I can hardly see, my eyes are so swollen. Dorcas's body is to be looked after once we have left.

12
The Desertion of Augustus Reynolds

Before the emigrants were allowed to disembark, the Health Officer, Arthur Savage, arrived on board to make his inspection together with the Tide Surveyor (a glorified term for a customs inspector) Edmund Minto Gibbes. Dr Acret told Savage of the fever and the four deaths that had resulted, and Savage, though he was not happy with the state of the *Subraon*, could find no reason to put the ship in quarantine, since the fever had ended so many days earlier. Gibbs inspected the cargo, such as it was, and found nothing to worry him, allowing the goods to be unloaded so that they could be prepared for auction.

*

The authorities did not waste time. The day after the ship's arrival, the Office of the Colonial Secretary advertised in a supplement to the New South Wales Government Gazette as follows:

On Saturday the Fifteenth instant, persons desiring to obtain female servants from this Ship will be admitted on board between the hours of 10, a.m., and 4, p.m., but it is to be understood that the hiring will be restricted to the unmarried females. On Monday, the Seventeenth instant, and following days, between the hours of 10, a.m., and 4, p.m., the hiring of the remainder of the Immigrants will be proceeded with.

*

Like so much cattle, therefore, were the passengers treated. Dr Acret, as Surgeon Superintendent, would be in charge of making certain of the respectability of the hiring parties, in particular with reference to unmarried females who were 'recommended not to accept situations in Inns or other Houses of public entertainment, as it is considered that such places are better suited to servants who have been for some time in the Colony, than to Immigrant girls on their first arrival'.

The emigrants were sent to their various places of employment by land or by sea. A number were taken by the ship Columbine to Brisbane, nearly all these became ill; the most seriously so, John Brown and Maurice Collins, spent some time in hospital under the care of Dr Keith Ballow of Brisbane. Collins recovered, but the doctor feared the worst for Brown.

*

Captain Mills sat in his cabin. He did not feel well; there was a dull ache in the pit of his stomach, and his throat was tight. On the table before him an empty decanter and an empty, but used, glass told their own tale. He was worried: not feeling guilty, or sorry (except for himself). That he had drunk too much speaks for itself, but his burden had not been eased. There was to be an inquiry. The ship was to be held in Port Jackson until that inquiry was over. Even then there was no guarantee that he would be permitted to sail away as if nothing had happened. So he sat there, head in his hands, indecisive and nauseous.

There was a knock at the door. Thomas Day entered. He was now Chief Mate, James Hill having been escorted from the *Subraon* by the authorities along with Carwardine.

'Sorry to disturb you, Captain, something has arisen which may need your attention.'

Mills raised his head and his eyebrows.

'Six of the men are refusing to return to work,' Day continued.

'Are they aware that the articles they signed are binding on them till our return to England?'

'They are, Captain.'

'Who speaks for them?'

'Reynolds, sir. He seems to be the leader.'

'Fetch them in.'

'I'm sorry, Captain, they have gone ashore and are refusing to return.'

Captain Mills heaved himself out of his chair. His face drawn, lips pursed, white with fury he banged his fists on the table. 'I'll see to this now,' he grunted through clenched teeth.

He staggered out onto the deck like a wild man. The sunlight dazzled him, but he gathered himself together, and left the ship to make a formal complaint against the six absentees and have them arrested for breaking the terms of their articles.

*

In his own cabin, Dr Acret paced the short distance between bed and door. He wanted to make a clean breast of everything, but found himself unequal to the task. 'One more glass, just one more, and I will be ready. I will be a ship's surgeon no more! Oh, what a mess!'

One glass more turned into two and then three. He sat at his table.

'Why did I take work on this wretched tub? Why wasn't I stronger?'

And as he half spoke and half thought these words, his head slumped onto his chest, and with a hand over his eyes he began to weep—not for the loss of life of a young girl, but for himself and the end of a career for which he once had such high hopes.

*

Of the six who had broken their contracts, three absolutely refused to return to the *Subraon* under any conditions. Augustus Reynolds, Peter Murphy and Thomas Sheppard were duly arrested by the port authority and held until the case against them could be heard. The other three sheepishly returned to the ship, though they did not avoid the charge.

On Saturday 27th May, They were brought before the magistrate, Captain Browne, to answer the charge of refusing to work on the *Subraon* or to proceed with her to sea. Reynolds was the first to be brought in; each case had to be heard individually. George Robert Nichols prosecuted. A stern man with a high forehead, Nichols was a reformer, but he would brook no nonsense from wrong-doers. Thirty-nine years old, he had a reputation for liking a stiff drink or two (or more) and suffered chronically with gout which made him exceedingly bad-tempered.

Captain Mills was sworn, and stated that his complaint was true, and that the six he complained of had absented themselves from the ship. Thomas Day, now Chief Mate, confirmed the same under oath.

Reynolds was called to take the stand.

Nichols gazed at him for a moment, and then asked if there was good reason for his refusal to return to work and go to sea in the *Subraon*.

'I will not return to the *Subraon*, nor will I proceed to sea in her. It would not be safe to do so.'

'Indeed,' interposed Nichols, 'may I ask the reason for this.'

'My reason is simply this. The officers of the *Subraon* were constantly drunk during the voyage out, especially at night. I have no intention of endangering my life by placing it in the hands of those who are not capable of seeing to my safety,'

'Did you, as has been written in the charges against you, demand your discharge?'

'I did, sir.'

'And have you any proof of what you say?'

'I would ask that Peter Murphy be asked to give evidence to support my statements.'

'I have no doubt,' responded Nichols, 'that he will support your statement, since he has also been charged with the same offence.'

'Let us hear what the other has to say, Mr Nicholls,' said Captain Browne wearily.

Peter Murphy, when asked about the behaviour of the mates, made the following declaration: 'All the officers of the ship were drunk every night.'

'What did you consider to be the effect of this wanton drunkenness?' asked Nichols.

'That the safety of the ship and the lives of the crew and the passengers were endangered by their conduct. Why, I have seen James Hill, the previous Chief Mate, Mr Day, the present Chief Mate, and the Third Mate repeatedly drunk.'

Captain Browne, though tired, was nevertheless able to perceive a vagueness in this last statement worthy of further inquiry. 'I want you to be very careful how you answer this question,' he remarked.'Just how often have you seen the officers of the *Subraon* drunk?'

'Sir,' came the response, 'I cannot say how often Mr Hill and Mr Day were drunk, but I'll take my oath that I have seen them so full fifty times during the voyage.'

'And how often would you say the ship was placed in danger as a result of this?' asked Mr Nichols.

'I have never actually seen it in danger from the drunkenness of the officers because we had very fine weather. There was an occasion, though, when I was left for three hours at the wheel while Mr Day the Second Mate was sleeping in the hencoop.

On that occasion it was impossible to get an officer to order a light to the binnacle. I was steering in the dark, gentlemen, with no idea of the direction to take as a result.'

'And what was the reaction of the Captain to this behaviour?'

'The Captain never came on deck at night, so I cannot say if he knew his officers were drunk.'

'Did you tell him of this?'

'No.'

'Did you tell the other members of the crew that you and the others were intending to knock off-duty and leave the ship?'

'No.'

'Where do you suppose they got their drink?'

'I cannot say, but Mr Hill was always drunk for the first two and a half months of the voyage; Mr Day was drunk three or four times a night.'

At this point the witness Murphy was dismissed, and Reynolds took the stand once more. He, on being asked if he had anything more to say, proposed calling the others who were in custody, as they would all say the same as Murphy. Captain Browne, thoroughly bored by now, was not amenable to this idea, and so, instead, two other seamen from the *Subraon* were sent for.

'I was in the Chief Mate's watch… Yes, I regularly saw him in liquor, though I couldn't say if he was drunk or not… I don't know how many times, but quite often, I should say… I cannot say that his being drunk put the ship in danger, though when he was drunk, he used to order unnecessary work to be done.' Thus, the first seaman.

The second seaman called was James Edward. 'I was in the Second Mate's watch… He was repeatedly in liquor while on duty… I would not say he was drunk, but, certainly, he was in liquor…

'This was very often the case, and when in that state he would often go to sleep on his watch… He would sleep in the hencoop, sometimes elsewhere. It was very difficult to rouse him. Once, while I was at the wheel, I put the binnacle lamp out to give me an excuse to awaken him, but I don't know that the ship was ever in danger because of the conduct of the officers.'

On being asked whether he would continue to sail on the *Subraon*, Edward replied, 'I would willingly sail round the world with this ship, but I do not think it would be safe to sail with the same officers, but I am no tell-tale. As for the Captain, he was hardly on deck at all.'

Mr Nichols then remarked that the safety of the ship was evidently not endangered by the conduct of the officers and that the men had never complained to the Captain of it, and that Captain Mills had never observed it.

Captain Browne then made his decision, albeit in a rather roundabout way: 'I feel myself placed in a position of great embarrassment with regard to this case because I am a party to the enquiry currently pending with regard to this vessel, the *Subraon*, as to many irregularities which may have taken place, which are also connected with the conduct of the officers. I do not think, however, that sufficient reason has been shown for refusing to do duty, although if the conduct of the officers were as described, I would consider the seamen perfectly justified in refusing to proceed with the ship; they have no right to be called upon to expose their lives to unnecessary risk. Under all these circumstances, I cannot make up my mind to send the prisoners to gaol for thirty days for the offence, which is the punishment prescribed, but since I am not unbiased, and regretting that I have heard this case at all, I will postpone a decision until the coming Tuesday so that the case might be heard by another magistrate.'

The following Tuesday, the case was briefly heard again by another magistrate. The three who had returned to their duties were released under caution. The others, Reynolds, Murphy and Sheppard, were each sentenced to 30 days imprisonment in Darlinghurst Gaol, and were released on the 29th of June, after which they, too, returned to their duties.

13
Captain Mills

As for the Captain, his woes were far from over. Embarrassed as he was by the accusations made concerning his running of the *Subraon*, they were nothing when compared to the awful inquiry which was about to be made concerning his conduct directly. The conclusions reached appalled him.

A selection from his private journal shows the frame of mind he was in during the voyage. His shaky handwriting clearly betrays one affected by over-indulgence in alcohol.

*

From the Private Journal of Captain Mills

— I have never been one for great speaking. When I first went to sea it was a relief to me that I could be silent for much of the time, so I will be brief.

— A few thoughts
— Why can't everyone leave me alone
— Just get on with it for God's sake
— I am tired
— I could almost wish myself back on land
— Martha, Martha, Martha.

— The women passengers are all so stupid: chattering away so that it is impossible to think whenever they are around. The men are so ignorant.

— The girl who cleans my cabin doesn't know what she is about, but I watched as she cleaned yesterday, and she was a welcome distraction.

— Saucy wanton, the way she moves around when cleaning the floor. ' Is that what they taught you back home?' I asked. 'You never mind, it's got nothing to do with you,' she answered.

— Little minx—I think she's flirting with me.

— Wrote a letter to my wife, though God knows when I'll get a chance to send it to her. I hope she is behaving herself.

— Emma, Emma, Emma, Emma.

— Weather is kind to us. We make good progress. Mr Hill tells me that some of the passengers are seasick. On a mill-pond! I ask you!

— Supplies holding out well.

— Plan: ration supplies now, be generous later when we know there is enough to see us through.

— Nothing but complaints from the passengers. Who found this doctor? He is absolutely useless.

— Hill and Carwardine joined me for a libation yesterday evening. Mr Day on duty. Day thinks too much of himself. Carwardine is not to be trusted with the women. Hill does well for me, but I have to keep an eye on him.

— A passenger died. Recorded in the log, what a day. His wife is being consoled by her friends.

*

The inquiry of the Immigration Board into the events which had taken place on the *Subraon* began. Evidence was so overwhelming that it came to a speedy conclusion. The panel's low opinion of all involved in the events included the orphan girls, but they were truly shocked by the behaviour of the officers and the Captain.

*

Acret at the Inquiry:

Question to Dr Acret: How is it, Doctor, that you did not discover the pregnancy of Miss Newman when you treated her for the fever from which she and others were suffering.

Answer from Dr Acret: The girl in question was herself unaware of the significance of symptoms related to such an event. I myself, gentlemen, was busy treating the sick. I cannot answer for what might have happened as a consequence of matters which were not brought to my attention. Moreover, there was not a whisper of such a matter among the single women who were her friends. How could they possibly know of such matters. They could not, gentlemen, being unmarried, and therefore inexperienced.

Question to Dr Acret: Captain Mills noted in the ship's log that you were habitually drunk, and that he was forced to confine you to your cabin for over three weeks while you showed all signs of delirium tremens. How do you respond to that charge?

Answer from Dr Acret: This is utterly false. I was never so confined, I have never suffered from delirium tremens, and I was never seen to be drunk.

*

Hill at the Inquiry:

Question to Mr Hill: A serious complaint of assault has been laid against you by Mr Donald McNamara, that you viciously, and in the company of four other men, brutally injured him by rubbing him harshly with a scrubbing brush, causing him numerous abrasions. How do you answer this charge?

Answer from Mr Hill: There was no injury done to the man by any of my actions. It was, however, deemed necessary to secure him in order to clean him. This was done for the sake of preserving the good hygiene of the ship.

Inquiry: We will hear from Dr Acret as to the hygiene on the *Subraon*, and the necessity of your actions.

Dr Acret was recalled.

Question to Dr Acret: What is your opinion of the treatment of Mr Donald McNamara by Mr Hill, and the scrubbing he was given?

Answer from Dr Acret: I should say that the scrubbing McNamara received did him more good than harm. He was certainly much cleaner afterwards.

*

A report was made to the Colonial Secretary, Sir Charles Fitz Roy, who communicated its findings back to Earl Grey in London. The matter was discussed in the House of Lords. To summarise the report, the following charges were proved or unproved:

*

1. PROVED— That there was insufficient water issued to the Emigrants during much of the voyage, according to the fixed scale. This was particularly so during the first half of the voyage. Later on, the Captain had increased the allowance, though not by enough. He had tried to show that this increase was to his credit. The inquiry disagreed.

2. UNPROVED—A portion of the *draught* porter put on board as a medicinal comforter was withheld from use. Mills told Acret that it had all been drunk three weeks be-

fore arrival, but there was, in fact, an unopened cask. Acret accused Mills of having intentionally done this, stating that the Chief Mate had told him of the remaining cask. The Chief Mate, however, did not support Acret's assertion to the Inquiry.

3. PROVED—A portion of the *bottled* porter put on board for the use of the Emigrants was not issued to them, and they were issued with an inferior drink.

4. PROVED— Inferior rum was served to the Emigrants instead of that put on board for their use and furthermore that rum was mixed with water. Inquiry found that other rum was substituted, though its inferiority could not be proved.

5. PROVED—The emigrants were said not to have been given the spirits put on board for them to be given free for medicinal purposes, unless they paid (not all could). Furthermore, Mills sold marine soap to the emigrants instead of giving it to them gratis, in order to benefit himself.

6. PROVED— Spirits and fermented liquors were sold to the passengers at unreasonably high and extravagant prices from Mills' own stores, and from the ship's stores with Mills' express sanction and authority. He should have forbidden this practice. Immigrants paid 4 shillings for a bottle of sherry, which he should have supplied at 2 shillings.

7. PROVED—That the Master did not "strictly prohibit and prevent on the part of the crew or officers any intercourse whatever with the female passengers on board," as required…, but, on the contrary, he failed to prevent communication between the sailors and the females and between the officers and certain of the single females, who waited on them as servants with his express sanction. He

allowed an unrestrained freedom of intercourse, which was encouraged by his own example, he also having had a female constantly in his cabin, and his offence in this particular being aggravated by the circumstance of these females being young, unprotected and friendless girls from a Foundling Institution in Dublin. This charge is proved beyond all doubt to its full extent, and the ruinous consequence to the females, who in violation of the terms of the Charter Party were allowed to frequent the Cuddy and the Officers' cabins, appear to us to demand the infliction of a very heavy penalty... Dorcas Newman, who waited upon the Chief Officer and who has been represented to us as a very interesting young girl and a great favourite in the Institution from which she was sent, fell a victim, as will be seen from the evidence to the consequence of a miscarriage and died before she could be landed from the vessel. Martha Magee, whose intimacy with the third Officer is exposed in the evidence, is now, we have very recently learned, the inmate of a notorious brothel in Sydney, having returned hither from a distant part of the Country to which she had been removed by the Government in order to place her beyond the Third Mate's reach and where she had been in a respectable service. Emma Smith, who waited upon the Captain, has been frequently seen under circumstances which leave no doubt that she is receiving the wages of prostitution, though she has not yet become a Public Woman; of several of the other orphans by this vessel, we have reason to fear that we shall ere long hear of their having exchanged their homes and employments for the easier mode of earning money, which Emma Smith has recommended to at least one of them. The incompetence of the Surgeon Superintendent, Dr Acret, is indisputable. However, we find the charges laid against him by the Master of the *Subraon*, Captain Mills, that he was habitually drunk and was confined to his cabin to be entirely false, despite their entry in the ship's log.

*

It was also found that the Captain had used improper and corrupting language to Emma Smith, and the girls were repeatedly seen intoxicated with liquor given them by the Captain and Officers.

The Inquiry recommended that the usual gratuities should be withheld from Captain Mills, James Hill and Mr Carwardine for their mismanagement of the *Subraon* during her voyage to Sydney.

Dr Acret decided to remain in Australia, and though the Inquiry found that he, too, was undeserving of any gratuity, it did find that he had been put in an untenable position by the unscrupulous behaviour of the officers of the *Subraon*. However, he had studied to conceal many irregularities during the ship's passage, he had denied any knowledge of the improper intimacy between the Chief Mate and Dorcas Newman, and had made false entries of treatments given in his medical journal while he had been unwell. On the other hand, his behaviour to the Immigrants was kind and attentive, and that spoke well of him. His errors chiefly arose from inexperience, and the Inquiry felt that with different Master and Officers he would have discharged his duties satisfactorily. The Inquiry therefore recommended that he should receive a payment of £100 as a donation so that he should not be left without resources since he was now so far from his friends.

But in his mind, Dr Acret nursed great doubts. 'Suppose,' he thought, 'just suppose it was all for nothing: that the girl was not pregnant after all…'

.

14
Sydney to Wellington and the death of Job Hudson

The Inquiry having made its report to the Colonial Secretary, the *Subraon* proceeded on its way to Wellington, New Zealand, leaving its anchorage in Newcastle, New South Wales; Captain Mills was still in command. Though the barque was considered a fast vessel, the journey took two weeks as the weather was very bad. On board in the hold, replacing the emigrants, was a new cargo, livestock to be sold at public auction in Wellington by James Smith and Co. There were 100 head of cattle, 38 horses, and 450 sheep. They were well treated because they were valuable, but the inclement weather made them ill; many did not eat well on the voyage, and were not in good condition on arrival. Also on board were 40 boxes of candles, 24 casks of oranges, 20 casks of ale, 1 case of cheese, 4 packages of tweeds, 2 carts and harnesses, and other items.

There were some passengers also, Mr Swann and Mr Brodsiak and their families and a builder called Job Hudson, originally from Sydney, who had obtained a contract for the creation of the barracks at Newcastle, NSW.

Mr Hudson was not a pleasant man. He was known to have a violent temper, and had been sued for common assault at least once. Some years before, his second wife had left him under circumstances which had made him angry and embittered. The following advertisement gives a clear indication of the depths of his feelings:

*

Sydney Herald—2 September 1841

  Whereas my wife Mary Anne Hudson, (formerly Hewson), did abandon my house and protection, and her home, on the 25th day of August, instant, and is no longer resident with me, this is to caution the Public against giving any trust or credit to the said Mary Anne Hudson: she having no authority to contract any debts while from under the protection of her Husband, and should shopkeepers or others, give trust or credit to the said Mary Anne Hudson, I will not defray any such debts nor any of them. The Public are also cautioned against purchasing any lands, Tenements, Horses, Cattle, Chattels of any description from my wife, Mary Anne Hudson or (Hewson), as I will not sanction such sales, and will seek recovery of such of my goods, in Courts of Justice.

  Signed JOB HUDSON

*

The voyage of the *Subraon* continued to be difficult. In the first place, Job Hudson was a hard drinker, and drank to great excess during that passage. He became so wild in his behaviour that he jumped overboard and was drowned. He left a widow (having married a third time) and several children by his first and second wives. There were suspicious mutterings among some that Mills had acquired an interest in Hudson's business, but they came to nothing, and he affected not to notice them.

15
Earthquake

On Thursday 28th September, a severe gale blew up. This caused some loss of the stock of hard goods as well as delay. On the night of Thursday the 5th of October, the *Subraon* finally arrived at Wellington. The passage had taken thirteen days.

Captain Mills carried with him copies of the latest newspapers from Sydney which contained news from England. Though some months out of date, this was gratefully received by the New Zealanders.

*

The day soon came to leave New Zealand and return home. Mills was glad. 'I'll not be sorry to see the back of this place,' he thought.

The *Subraon* would head first to Sydney, before making the voyage back to England—at least, that was the plan. Some days before, an advertisement in the *New Zealand Spectator and Cook's Strait Guardian* had appeared, offering passage on the ship in glowing terms:

*

FOR SYDNEY DIRECT

The splendid new British built barque *Subraon*
510 tons register, J.P. Mills Commander, will sail on Saturday,
next, 14th instant: (wind and weather permitting) has superior
accommodations.

For Freight or Passage, early application to be made to Captain Mills, or to JAMES SMITH & CO.

Wellington, October 10, 1848.

*

Unfortunately, the weather did not permit such an early sailing, and the voyage was delayed by some days, which meant that the *Subraon* was still anchored in Wellington Harbour when the following calamitous event occurred. At about half past one in the morning of Monday the 16th of October 1848 the inhabitants of Wellington were woken by a hollow roaring sound. Within a few seconds, the whole town was in the embrace of the severest earthquake known within living memory. Houses tumbled down in an instant, bricks were sent flying through the air. Men, women, and children ran shrieking in all directions in great confusion. The shockwaves continued for six hours, and when daylight came, the town was in a very sad way. Most buildings had been very badly damaged, and many of the inhabitants had narrowly missed being seriously hurt. That day a number of smaller tremors occurred; and these continued through the night. On Tuesday afternoon, there was another severe earthquake.

Houses rocked and quivered like a ship in a gale of wind at sea. Several buildings fell in on themselves; others were so shaken as to endanger the inmates or those who passed beneath. A father and his two young children were buried beneath a falling wall. His daughter was instantly killed, and his son died soon after being dug out. The grieving father had been very badly injured.

The crew of the *Subraon*, still anchored in the harbour, along with other ships, watched the collapse of the town. The inhabitants no longer trusted the safety of their own houses, and stayed outside all night long. Captain Mills, as soon as was possible, offered to take as many as would like on board to take refuge from the earthquakes which still continued. Many gratefully took him up on his offer.

Also at anchor in the harbour was H.M.S. *Fly*. When the first great earthquake had begun, Captain Oliver had thought for a moment that his ship had been grounded, so powerfully was the shock felt on board. All his men had run up onto the deck to find out what was happening.

On Thursday 19th, there were still further shocks, and numerous brick buildings completely collapsed. No wooden buildings were destroyed during this calamity, and many took refuge in them.

*

Friday the 20th of October was set apart by proclamation by His Excellency the Lieutenant Governor, to be observed as a general day of public fast, prayer and humiliation. The audiences were unusually large, attentive and devout. The following Sunday, a service of thanks for the delivery of the survivors was held on the *Subraon*, where those on board of all faiths were given a sermon by the Reverend Samuel Ironside, a Wesleyan Methodist missionary from Yorkshire, who had worked tirelessly to convert the Maoris to Christianity. Although his pious speaking was not to everyone's taste, all listened in silence.

For Captain Mills, this sermonising was a reminder of a childhood from which he had tried so hard to escape. On being introduced to Reverend Ironside, he had, after shaking that gentleman's hand and inquiring after his health, turned and walked into his cabin where he sat gazing at charts with a small measure of brandy nearby. Ironside, always so full of himself, had not noticed the Captain's departure. He went onto the quarter deck, gazed down at the assembled company and began to speak in his usual rotund Yorkshire tones, sounding far older than his thirty-four years. He had a habit of lifting his chin as if he was stretching his neck, before gazing back down with wide eyes and a fixed glare whenever he wished to make an important point. One of the young boys present began to giggle, but was instantly silenced by his mother with a dig in the ribs which he instantly transferred to his small sister who began to cry silently.

After the sermon, the audience spoke to each other, mingling among themselves. Those who were returning to the town waited for the boats to carry them back. One of the congregation, an officious schoolmaster named Charles Hinchcliffe, approached a young lady, who he had discovered was of the Hebrew faith. There were only twenty-eight Jewish inhabitants of Wellington at that time, and Hinchcliffe had made it his business to know about every one. His face was stern, and he stared at her accusingly, which made her most uncomfortable. Finally, and without introduction, he spoke. 'Unless you abjure your faith, and acknowledge the divinity of Jesus, there is no hope of salvation for you.'

Taken rather aback, the lady stood dumbfounded. Her male companion, who was standing nearby, turned to face Hinchcliffe. 'I don't know who you think you are,' he said, 'or if you are ordained or not, but this I do know, that you have shown yourself to be an insolent and ignorant pretender to the faith you profess.' With that, he took the lady by her arm, and the two turned their back on Hinchcliffe and climbed into one of the boats.

Hinchcliffe was left with a red face, burning with fury. He went over to Reverend Ironside. 'Did you see that? That's what you get for trying to help people.' But Ironside had nothing but contempt for Hinchcliffe who he regarded as a deeply flawed individual because he was known to drink too much, whereas he, Ironside, was a teetotaller.

*

After the earthquake and its aftershocks, many settlers, fearful of another such visitation, determined to leave the Colony for Australia, and took passage in the *Subraon* with their families, bound for Sydney. Some who would have left, though, were prevented from doing so, for they owed money in Wellington, and their creditors took legal action to prevent their departure.

16
Shipwreck

Finally, the weather was deemed favourable enough for departure. Unfamiliar with the seas around Wellington, JP hired the local official pilot to navigate the ship out into open water. Captain James Calder, the pilot had much experience, but was something of a daredevil and a showoff to boot.

So it was that in the late afternoon of Thursday the 26th of October, the *Subraon* left for Sydney with passengers on board. James Hill had been restored to his position as Chief Mate. In the cabins were Mr and Mrs Fitzherbert and their son, the two Miss Parks sisters, Dr and Mrs Hansard and their three children, Captain Young of the 65th Regiment, Mrs Murch, her 3 children and her servant, Mr and Mrs Maxton, and their two children, Captain Nagle, Mr. Beamish, Mr. Robinson, Mr and Mrs Spinks and their two daughters, Mr and Mrs Dean and their five children. In the steerage were Mrs. Mathews, Mrs. Gill and her four children, Mr W. Smith, Mr Hill, Mr Thomas Wilson, Mrs Waldren and her four children, Mr Jackson, Mr and Mrs J. Brown and their three children, Mrs Hartley and her daughter, Mr Watson, Mr and Mrs Wilson, and Mr and Mrs Bishop and their baby.

A strong wind blew from the south; the entrance or exit to Wellington harbour has an inner and an outer passage: the inner, Chaffers Passage being the narrower, divided from the outer, Cook's Strait, by Barrett Reef, a group of rocks highly dangerous to ships. Captain Mills may not have been familiar with

Wellington harbour, but he knew the *Subraon*, and the way she behaved under these conditions. The wind was fresh, and the waves exhibited all the signs of a swell that would increase in size. Moreover, the currents in both passages were known to be strong and very unpredictable.

'Mr Calder,' shouted Mills above the sound of the wind which was whipping up, 'take the outer passage, the ship will not manage the inner.'

Calder, who had been unable to make his mind up which passage to take, though knowing the outer was far broader, was, nonetheless, disinclined to take orders from any man who knew the waters less well than he. Having navigated through Chaffers Passage successfully on other occasions, he now determined that this was the way he must take, and no other.

Wellington harbour faces south; Calder, at the wheel, had to tack the ship from side to side in order to make headway against the wind.

'To hell with that,' he muttered to himself. 'I know what I'm doing.' A few moments later: 'there we go,' as he turned the wheel clockwise so that the *Subraon* headed into the narrower strait. He continued tacking forward. The wind grew stronger. Captain Mills swallowed down his fury at the blind disobedience of the Pilot.

'You'll miss stays, Mr Calder,' shouted the Captain, (by which he meant that the ship might not turn in time).

'I never have yet!' shouted Calder back.

Calder turned the *Subraon* away from Barrett Reef; the ship was now heading towards the mainland, where other rocky places were known to lurk beneath the waves. Captain Mills gritted his teeth, furious with himself for having let the stupid fellow anywhere near the *Subraon*. The Pilot though was struggling with the wheel, which did not want to turn as he would like.

'He'll sink us all, Captain!' shouted Mr Day.

Day grabbed at the wheel to lend extra strength to the turning. It was the last turn necessary before clearing Chaffers Passage, and entering into open waters. The rest of the crew looked on anxiously. The wheel turned, but it was too late. The shore was too close, and with a mighty crack and judder, the *Subraon* hit the rocks at speed. Great cries and yells arose from the passengers, who had previously been exhorted to silence.

It was eight o'clock in the evening. The ship, pierced by the rocks under the larboard counter, where she met the water, lurched to her starboard side, but remained stuck on the rocks about one hundred yards away from the shore. Captain Mills, became calm, and, looking at Calder, said through tight lips, 'What did I tell you?' Calder was cowed into silence. (He was later dismissed from his position as Harbour Pilot.)

Captain Mills did not lose his head; in a crisis, he was the man to be with; the passengers, though, were in a state of utter confusion. He immediately assumed command, and together with his officers and men began organising the passengers, women and children first, so as to take them off the ship and get them to safety. They worked with great self-possession and coolness, and soon two of the *Subraon's* boats and the boat which had been brought by Calder the Pilot to carry him back to the harbour were filled with passengers. The swell of the water was great, and the wind had not abated, so that the journey to the shore was very difficult. Eventually, all were safely landed in a small bay about three quarters of a mile from Calder's station. Many of the women had lost their shoes, but they wrapped their feet with blankets, and all made their way there to take shelter. Once inside, they were given hot drinks and blankets to keep them warm. Many stayed the rest of the night there, while others obtained shelter under temporary tents formed from sails erected on the beach. Meanwhile, someone was sent back to the town to raise the alarm.

At 3 o'clock in the morning, news reached the harbour authorities that the *Subraon* had struck a reef. The news was taken to Captain Oliver of H.M.S. *Fly*, still at anchor in the harbour. He immediately despatched five well-manned boats to give assistance. Several boats were also sent by Messrs J. Smith & Co, the *Subraon* agents, with about thirty men.

Captain Oliver of the *Fly* was in personal attendance, and, for most of the day, he and his men *Subraon* to rescue the property and cargo from the stricken **Subraon**. Great hopes were entertained that the ship might be floated off the rocks when the tide rose so that she could be brought into the harbour, but those hopes proved to be vain. The *Subraon* was stuck fast and filling with water.

Now that the earthquakes seemed to have abated, most of the passengers elected to stay in Wellington after all instead of making their way to Sydney. Captain Mills, though, was determined to return to London. He left what remained of the *Subraon* beneath the waves at the southern end of Breaker Bay, Wellington Harbour.

*

Meanwhile, back in London, Rachel had a new baby to look after. Not even her brother knew her secret, for the dates were not so far out that she could not get away with claiming that her husband was the father. 1848 had been a difficult year for her, for a cholera epidemic had broken out, and it was particularly virulent in Rotherhithe. Her friends and neighbours all had family members who had been carried off, but she herself and her baby were, remarkably, unaffected.

When Captain John Powell Mills arrived back in England in early 1849 he was tired and disillusioned, and ready to resume all the advantages of married life. Rachel showed him the newborn boy, and he, not wishing to admit of being cuckolded, went along with her explanation. He watched her suspiciously over the next few days, but there was no sign of any other man with any interest in her. This was hardly surprising, as the affair with her lover had been short-lived. Mills, though, hit out at her, and she, with tears in her eyes promised never to stray again. He accepted her back into his household, for they had become estranged, and she had been staying with her brother William.

'I will never go to sea again,' he told Rachel over a breakfast of bread, cheese and ale. There was a long silence; Rachel received this news with mixed feelings; they continued eating.

After a few minutes, Rachel spoke: 'What will you do, John?'

He thought he would do nothing at all, at least for a while, but he knew that inactivity did not suit him. 'I don't know,' he said. 'I have some money, maybe we should invest in something new.'

Now that he was back in Rotherhithe, he discovered self-pride. He had been embarrassed by the affair of the *Subraon*, and would soon be surprised by the stories told in the press of those events, resenting the exaggerations of the letter-writers who seemed to insist on sharing their opinions. He refused to admit to any responsibility for the fate of the ship or of Dorcas Newman.

Rachel, trying her best to be practical, went about her daily chores in a matter-of-fact manner which irritated him.

One May morning, just after he had returned home from a coffee shop where he had been discussing past times with some of his old cronies over steaming mugs of bitter coffee, Rachel stopped her ironing, and said in a business-like tone, 'Well, I've found a job for you.'

This only added to his irritation with his wife, for he felt that it implied criticism of his own efforts to occupy himself; but, though he took no pleasure in her statement, feeling that it undermined his natural masculine superiority, he felt hope rise up within. He was, he owned, thoroughly fed up with doing nothing, and needed something to regain his self-respect. But his aforementioned pride would not allow him to consider taking on any work he felt to be beneath his dignity. Perhaps, though, there might be something in her discovery, whatever it might be; maybe she had found something worthwhile.

'Yes,' she continued, 'my brother William has an opening in his business. You would be an ideal person to work for him.'

This was not what he wanted to hear, but she carried on regardless. 'If you can let him have, say, one thousand pounds, I'm certain he would be happy to take you into his business. I know he has great plans and would use it wisely.'

'If I give him that kind of money, it'll be William who works for me, I think you'll find.'

'I'm not sure that's what he has in mind.'

'You've seen him, then?'

'Yes.'

'And talked with him about my affairs?'

'Yes,' came the answer—a little warily this time.

But he did not hit out at her as she thought he might, but stood mid-thought, considering.

'I'll go and see him,' he said eventually.

Rachel had nothing but admiration for her younger brother, and she hoped that this bringing together of brother and husband might help her feel secure.

Mills turned on his heels, and instead of sitting down to rest, as had been his intention, he left their home and set out for William Masterman's zinc works. He saw to it that his way led past the China Hall Public House, outside which two old sailors were sitting at a wooden table weeping in each other's arms. He barely glanced at them before entering the bar in order to obtain something liquid with which to fortify himself, and so it was not until the following day that he finally found himself meeting his brother-in-law.

They had never really got on well with each other. Masterman thought Mills coarse, Mills thought Masterman a fool. William Masterman was a bullish, red-faced man, now thirty-four. Rachel loved her brother for he had been a rock to her in times of need. Mills could not deny that the zinc works might be a good way to invest his money, for it had been doing well. The two men met at the office of Masterman's lawyer. Mills had brought his own legal advisor. The four had a not unpleasant meeting, and Mills agreed to go into partnership with his brother-in-law.

After the partnership agreement had been drawn up and signed, Masterman looked at his sister's husband, and coolly said, 'Mind, now, this is a grand business, and we can make a tidy sum, but we must be prudent'

Mills, though, also had ideas for the business, and prudence was not one of them. A new idea had occurred to him. Was not the zinc works employed in producing sheathing for ships' hulls? What if they were to sheath the hull of their own ship? And he became thoughtful. 'A ship of our own, perhaps a small fleet,' he thought. 'I could be captain…'

Thus, with thoughts of this sort, lies the path to success or troubles, and only a soothsayer may predict what the outcome may be. One might confidently predict the latter to be more likely, and that confidence would not be ill-conceived; but, for now, we will let that partnership be launched upon its way, and will return to it in due course.

*

A year later, Rachel gave birth to a second child, a daughter they named Rachel Masterman Powell Mills, and in 1851 their second son John Masterman Powell Walker Thackeray Mills was born. Unlike their older brother John Powell Mills Jnr. they would live respectable lives. John Powell Mills Jnr., he who we met at the start of this tale, did not consider himself, as he grew older, to be so much a part of the family as were his younger siblings. His father often lost his temper with him, and for a while, the lad went to live with his uncle until it became time to find work on his own account. Once he had left the family behind, they did not hear of him much again, until they all but forgot his existence (except for his mother, of course).

*

To return awhile to the case of the *Subraon*: I read through piles of newspaper and parliamentary reports. My horror at what I read there increased as I realised that the case of the *Subraon* was but one example, and perhaps not the very worst, of the appalling treatment meted out to poor emigrants travelling to new lives in far-off corners of the Empire. I feel greatly saddened by what I have discovered, but most of all my heart goes out to poor Dorcas Newman, for she had been a light to her friends in times of trouble, uncaring of her own woes, and yet it was she who had come to the end of her life—something which happens to all, but it is to be hoped at not so young an age, and, in any case, without the load of suffering she had to bear.

And allow me to state my surprise that no charges were ever brought against any of the officers of the *Subraon*. Captain Mills continued his pursuit of a maritime life as ship's master. Acret, who had qualified as a surgeon at the age of thirty-two—shortly before he joined the *Subraon*, remained in Australia, where he married, had children, and in 1867 died of drink. James Hill made his way back to England and continued as a sailor.

*

26 February 1850, House of Lords: The Earl of Mountcashell stood to speak.

*

'My Lords, I apologise for the lateness of the hour, but I feel that this matter is of great importance, and I feel bound to bring it to your attention now, as otherwise there will be no opportunity to do so till after the Easter recess.

'My Lords, some of you will be aware of the despatches from Governor Fitz Roy of New South Wales to Earl Grey last year, regarding the conduct of the Surgeon Superintendent, Master and Officers of the emigrant ship *Subraon*. Charges of the gravest and most serious character had been preferred against the Captain and other Officers of the vessel, though the Captain complained that he was not allowed to bring forward witnesses on his own behalf, and no witnesses were examined on oath.

'The charges made were as follows: that the Captain violated the Passengers Act in not allowing a sufficient supply of food, and that he had not afforded sufficient protection to the female emigrants on board. That the Doctor, instead of protecting the female emigrants, according to his instructions, proposed to have them engaged as servants to wait upon the Captain and himself in their cabins. One of those unfortunate girls became in the family way, and it was reported that means were used to procure an abortion. The fact, however, was that she died on the passage.

'I would like to read an extract of a pamphlet published by Mr. Sidney, in which the following summary was given of cases reported in the blue book on Emigration, ordered by the House of Commons, July 1849. The Immigrant Board of Sydney observes—"It is impossible to convey a just idea of the gross abuses and infamous misconduct which occurred (on board the *Subraon*) owing to the 'imbecility' of the surgeon-superintendent. Unrestrained intercourse took place between the sailors and the women, and between certain officers and certain single women. Among these were girls from a foundling institution in Dublin for whom every promise of care and attention was given. One of them, a very interesting girl too, was seduced by the chief officer, and died in consequence of miscarriage before she could be landed from the vessel."

'Now, emigration orders strictly prohibit any of the crew from having any intercourse whatever with the female passengers. It appears, however, that, in consequence of the intimacies that sprang up in opposition to the terms of the charter party, several of the females were ruined and are now inmates of a notorious brothel in Sydney, and there is apparently reason to fear that others will follow their example.

'I believe that, up to this hour, the Poor Law Guardians of the Dublin Union who selected the girls are unaware of the fate of the unfortunate person who lost her life.

'I hope that matters will be laid before Parliament in order that other unprotected females might not be exposed to similar perils without at least having some warning.

'I emphasise that some of the crimes were so heinous they led to the death of one individual who had been seduced by one of the persons on board. Moreover, spirituous liquors were fully vended and given freely to the female emigrants. Nor is the *Subraon* the only example of a ship in which abuses of this kind have been known to take place. We have discussed other vessels on other occasions. I propose, therefore, that measures should be taken to ensure the summary punishment of seduction and violence on board emigrant ships.'

*

Earl Grey replied, and implied that although the charges were grave, they were exaggerated, and opposed the noble lord's motion on the ground of the public expense it would involve.

*

Mountcashell's address was reported in *The Times*, and shortly after he himself received a letter from Captain Mills. Mountcashell sent this letter to that newspaper, where it appeared a few days later.

*

The Earl of Mountcashell's covering letter to *The Times*—published March 7th 1850

EMIGRANT SHIPS
TO THE EDITOR OF THE TIMES
Conservative Club, St. James's, March 2

Sir,—I think the enclosed letter, from the Captain of the *Subraon* to me, worthy of public notice. Whilst it explains the position in which he was placed (upon his own showing) it confirms facts which I felt it to be my duty to bring under the notice of the House of Lords. It is high time that sound and stringent measures should be adopted by the Secretary of the Colonies for the safety of emigrants, especially females; and if ample proof was wanting, Captain Mills would supply it.

I am, Sir, your obedient servant,
MOUNTCASHELL.

I have read strong testimonials as to the humanity and courage displayed by Captain Mills when his ill-fated ship was lost on the coast of New Zealand.

*

Mills letter of March 1st 1850 to the Earl of Mountcashell—published in *The Times* 7 March 1850

My Lord,—It would be futile for me, after what has been done by partial judges, to exonerate myself from the many false persecutions laid to my charge when commanding the *Subraon*, conveying emigrants. I write this under the oppression of deep sorrow, having been sixteen months out of employment, and not the least hopes of ever again getting employment, solely through the mismanagement of the surgeon-superintendent appointed by Government over the emigrants.

My Lord, you say it is impossible to form a just idea of the infamous conduct and gross abuses that took place upon the *Subraon*, and owing to the imbecility of the surgeon. My Lord, don't for one moment think the surgeon was such a meek creature. His talk was disgusting about his debauchery when a student; he was one of those sort of people who are under the abject dominion of every vice, and only for show did he cloak his acts on board my ship; so much so, that no fault could be found of him until the last six weeks of the passage, when he developed his character by shutting himself up 26 days beastly intoxicated, and his old complaint of *delirium tremens* unfolded itself. During his drunkenness I had the whole of the emigrants cast on my hands; at this time there were 29 cases of typhus fever, and every day an increase of the malady. Had I not taken the whole responsibility, the whole of the emigrants would have suffered, and no doubt two-thirds of them would have died. I had every corner, bed places, and all parts of the ship, four days successively fumigated. Night and day was my whole attention paid to them, and I do believe, so tranquil was my vessel with the people on board, that no person but the officers of the ship knew of the surgeon's drunkenness. I assure you, my Lord, that my aims were pure for the poor people on board; without making myself conspicuous to gain any affection from them, my study was to do all the kindness consistent with my duty for them.

Women in their travail I was obliged to attend, and the whole of the emigrants have frequently acknowledged my kindness to them with the exception of a few vile creatures.

My Lord, don't think me a character that would screen myself by laying blame on others. May the hand and arm that writes you this drop from my body if I had one feeling but of purity towards the poor people under my command. Had I to accuse myself of committing one crime, I should consider myself worthy of all the torture that could be put upon me. Unfortunately, all my kindness has been construed into crime; it is only time that will exonerate me, and when some of the emigrants have time to reconsider the palpable lies that were told. Whatever may have been done unknowing to me, I feel thankful I cannot accuse myself of doing anything wrong towards the emigrants,

My Lord, you say unrestrained intercourse took place between sailors and women. I have only to say, if such were the case, it was unknown to me. I was so strict with the men that I did not allow them even to speak to a woman, and the whole of the females were authorised to remain on the poop of the ship, where no communication could be had.

My Lord, you say a girl was seduced by the Chief Mate of the vessel. Far from my contradicting such a statement as true; but, my Lord, you must be told that the statement was from a boy only, and I assure you that the mate was no friend to any of my boys, I am sorry to say. Let it be true, then, my Lord, what was the method I then pursued? I ordered my mate to his cabin, and kept him in close confinement, and instantly on my arrival I sent him out of the ship, and this only on the statement of a little boy, subjecting myself to a law controversy for three weeks before my arrival at Sydney. What with the surgeon being beastly drunk, my mate in confinement, the ravages of typhus fever, and difficult navigation in Bass's Straits, I assure you, my Lord, I had no time but to be vigilant.

In concluding, my Lord, I have to remark to you that twice before I have gone out with a cargo of all females. I have been highly complimented on my arrival at Hobart Town on the manner and humanity of treatment towards the people. This vessel was the *Tory*; the surgeon-superintendent Mr. Sloane, R.N., a person of good repute; it is from him that any information respecting my treatment of females could be got—a man acquainted with ships and sea, not a raw student just coming from school with his head full of nothing but the debauchery and wantonness of all his mad frolics, to which I always turned a deaf ear when my surgeon commenced them.

My Lord, my surgeon had nothing to lose, as his object was to get to Sydney, where he had influential friends, and, as he termed it, the 'lousy' sum he would get from his trouble with the emigrants was not worth troubling about. On the other hand, my Lord, I had my owners to study, and my reputation. The surgeon being invested with so much power, I judged it prudent not to thwart him, and many times, I have remonstrated with him about his neglect, all to no purpose. I have begged him to come down and see a poor man dying, when he replied, 'Let them go to Hell.'

My Lord, we have no fair trial; as a master of a ship we are a doomed class of men; whatever is said of us must necessarily be authentic. At the investigation in Sydney there was nothing of prudence. I was not allowed to bring any witness on my behalf; no person was put on his oath; all was taken as evidence against me, whilst I affirm on oath that not one wrong action was committed by me that I can accuse myself of; my study was to do the poor creatures all the good that was in my power, in consistence with my duty to those that employed me. Twice have the vile persecutions against me driven me deranged. My bread for my wife and family depended on my acting with justice. I will not trespass, my Lord, on your patience if you deem me worth your notice to accept this letter of facts. I could say a great deal of truth, but all will not mend my wound. I am wrongfully cast and must bear the stigma.

The brother of the Governor of South Australia, Sir H. Young was present on board my vessel when lost; to him I am indebted for a statement of my character by a letter from him on the occasion of shipwreck, and also to the inhabitants of New Zealand. I can assure you, my Lord, my character and feelings were the same to the emigrants as they were to the inhabitants of Wellington, New Zealand, and at the time of my vessel being wrecked with 60 passengers on board. I send, accompanied with this, two New Zealand papers, with the letters presented to me inserted therein. My Lord, if you notice the papers, may I beg you will return them when done with, for it would be the happiest day of my life could I clear myself of the vile persecutions laid to my charge? From a boy without parents I have pushed on to gain the head of my profession, and in the midst of it, reputation and employment are all lost through the neglect of a Government officer—the surgeon-superintendent.

I have the honour to be, my Lord,
Your Lordship's most obedient and
Very humble servant,

JOHN POWELL MILLS
Late Master of Emigrant Ship *Subraon*.

*

It was with great amazement that on digging further into this shocking affair, that I found that Chief Mate James Hill had also written a letter to *The Times* refuting completely the allegations that had been made against him. Although he and Captain Mills had worked well together for some time, they had parted company with a good deal of ill-feeling between them, largely brought about by an inability to agree what story to present as truth regarding the passage of the *Subraon* to Sydney. Hill told a version of events which differed in so many details from the official version, that I feel bound to present it here.

17
James Hill's Letter

On the afternoon of Friday the 8th of March 1850 James Hill, sat in a coffee house, and read the previous day's *Times*. He went hot and cold as he read the letter from his former captain, becoming more and more agitated as he did so, forgetting completely about the cup of coffee which was on the table before him. His mouth grew tighter and tighter as he read, he clenched his fists, and trembled. He had had been certain that an understanding between the Captain and himself had been reached, and felt this betrayal of trust to be more than he could bear. He called for paper, pen and ink, and fumed while he waited for those items to be brought to him. Hardly able to marshal his thoughts into order, he began to write, in a hurried scrawl, his own letter to *The Times*.

Once finished, he arranged for it to be sent immediately to the offices of that newspaper whose very title he cursed outwardly.

He had no illusions that it would be published the following day, and he was not disappointed in his expectation, though he cursed when he scanned the paper, and found it was not there. Nor was it there on Saturday; his agitation knew no bounds. He spent two sleepless nights, since there was no Sunday issue. Finally, he saw, with some satisfaction, that it was printed on Monday the 11th, although he trembled when he read it, for he could not foretell what reaction his letter might have. He read it several times that day, and often referred to it in the coming days.

*

Hill's letter to *The Times*—published 11 March 1850
8 March 1850

EMIGRANT SHIPS
TO THE EDITOR OF THE TIMES

Sir,—My attention has been called to a letter which appeared in *The Times* of yesterday on the subject of the ship *Subraon*, and I shall be much obliged to you if you will give insertion of a few words from me in reference to those portions of them which relate to myself. I will not so far trespass on your limited space as to attempt to refute the various assertions contained in Mr Mills's letter, which he terms 'facts,' but will confine myself to those observations which relate to myself. I allude to that part of his letter in which he writes that, far from his contradicting the statement made by Lord Mountcashell that a girl was seduced by the chief mate of the vessel, his Lordship must be told that the statement was from a boy only, and assuming it to be true, he tells his Lordship the method he then pursued was to order his mate to his cabin, and keep him in close confinement, and that instantly on his arrival in Sydney he sent him out of his ship, and that only on the statement of a little boy. Now, Sir, in answer to this, I beg most distinctly to deny that the Captain ever ordered me to my cabin during the two years I was acting under him in the *Tory* and *Subraon*, or that he sent me on shore after the arrival of the *Subraon* in Sydney.

Before the *Subraon* left Plymouth (Christmas 1847), the surgeon of the ship came to me and said it was the intention of the Captain and himself to have each a female emigrant to attend to their cabins and wait upon them. I told the surgeon I thought it would be bad policy in them to do so, and stated my belief that it would breed a disturbance in the ship.

This, the surgeon admitted, and acknowledged that I had endeavoured to dissuade him from doing it. I am sorry to say that my remonstrances had no weight, for about three weeks after leaving Plymouth the Captain sent for me, and told me that he and the surgeon had taken servants from amongst the emigrants to attend to their cabins, and that it was his wish that I should do the same; and that I should signify to the second and third mates that he (the captain) wished them to have their cabin attended to by a servant also.

Upon this, acting as I conceived it to be my duty (although, perhaps, unwisely), I obeyed the Captain's orders, and each officer of the ship had accordingly a servant to attend to his cabin. Everyone must be well aware of the bad results which might be expected from such an injudicious and improper arrangement. But, Sir, the alleged consequences were not verified by the oath of a single witness, and they are, I swear, many of them, entirely false, and others most grossly exaggerated and perverted. I can satisfactorily prove by numerous witnesses that, shortly after this arrangement as to the servants had been made, I signified to the Captain that I thought it an improper one, and I accordingly discharged the girl who had been attending to my cabin. At this, both Mr Mills and the surgeon were much annoyed (for reasons best known to the former), and frequently urged me to take her back again, saying that it was unfair to send her to live in the berth, which was inconveniently crowded with the other passengers. After some little time, I was persuaded by the Captain and surgeon, and, at the express wish of the girl herself, to allow her to attend to my cabin again, and to enjoy as before the use of it while I was on duty on deck.

The conduct of the Captain to this girl during the latter parts of the voyage, and the threats which she held out against him of exposing such on her arrival at Sydney, was, I believe, the sole inducement which led him a few days before our arrival there to prefer a charge against her of a serious nature, and to threaten her with irons. On my being made acquainted with this charge, I told the Captain that unless it was properly substantiated, or publicly retracted before my brother officers and the ship's crew, I could not discharge my duties as chief officer of the ship. This he refused to do, and I therefore went to my cabin and remained there till the arrival of the ship in Sydney. During the time I was in my cabin, the poor girl had been sent to her berth, where, as Captain Mills says, typhus fever was raging, and, as might have been expected, she soon caught it, and on the day after our arrival in Sydney died from it. Her illness was treated both by the surgeon of the ship and by Dr Savage of Sydney as typhus fever, and I have never heard that either of them attributed her death to any other cause.

I will not dwell on the accusation brought against me of having seduced this unfortunate girl, but must content myself here with simply denying the charge, which I do most solemnly.

In conclusion, allow me to add that I sincerely hope the matter will not rest where it is, but that a thorough investigation into it will be made, and the blame thrown upon those who ought to bear it. For my own part, I am most anxious that a strict inquiry should be made, and I shall be most happy to afford every information in my power to further such, and in doing so, will hold myself responsible for the truth of what I state. I will add that in the letter from Captain Young referred to in Mr Mills's letter, my name was coupled with the Captain's, and mentioned in terms of equal praise. I inclose you a certificate which I received from Captain Mills, and which I trust you will insert in your paper with this letter, and I beg to subscribe myself

Your most obedient servant
JAMES GEORGE HILL,
Late Chief-Officer of *Subraon*,
Thomsons's Cottages, Poplar, March 8, 1850.

*

Captain Mills' reference for James Hill
TO OWNERS AND MASTERS
Oct.20.

Gentlemen,— The bearer, James Hill, has sailed with me as Chief Mate, a period of two years to the colonies and India in two vessels, the *Tory* and *Subraon*, in the last vessel until the loss of her at New Zealand. During the whole time he has conducted himself entirely to my satisfaction, and specially at the loss of the vessel, always behaving in a steady and vigilant manner for the benefit of the ship. I recommend him as a good seaman, a sober and industrious man, an active and efficient officer, and quite competent to take command of any vessel.

JOHN POWELL MILLS
Late Master of the *Subraon*.

A true copy.
Trinity-house, London, Dec 6.1849 R. Irving Gray.

*

When the *Subraon* landed at Sydney, far from treating Dorcas's death as being from typhus fever, Dr Acret had told the Health Inspector that there had been no fever on board for some days, as a result, the vessel had not been put into quarantine. What, then, can one make of Hill's letter to *The Times*? Dorcas died one day after the ship's arrival. In his letter Hill stated that Dorcas died of typhus fever, and this, therefore cannot be true, unless Dr Acret lied merely to get himself ashore more quickly. Who was telling the truth? Was Dorcas pregnant, or had she been suffering from typhus? If she was pregnant, then who was the father, James Hill or another? As for Captain Mills, his part in this matter is hidden.

James Hill's letter was printed, but little noticed. Mountcashell mentioned it in passing during another debate in the Lords in the following words: 'As is natural, all parties endeavoured to exculpate themselves, but the crimes committed in that vessel were so gross, so enormous, that I can scarcely describe them to the house. Some of the crimes were so heinous that they led to the death of one individual, who, having been seduced by one of the persons on board, was induced to resort to means for the purpose of procuring an abortion'.

Hill qualified as a ship's master in 1851. Five years later, his ship, the *Anita*, sank off the coast of Sabanilla, New Granada with no lives lost.

*

Letter to Emma Smith from Robert Mundy Gover
London
December 1871

Dear Miss Smith
Please excuse me for writing to you in this fashion. I realise that we have never met and that you do not know me. I recently came across the enclosed document which I believe is your personal diary. I ask you also to excuse the breach of your privacy of which I have been guilty by virtue of reading it, although had I not done so, you would not be holding the book in your hands. Indeed, I only managed to infer that the book was yours and not that of another *Subraon* passenger by certain clues that you allowed yourself to place there, by accident I am certain, for your name does not appear on the cover, or on the fly leaf, or anywhere in the text. I would be most grateful if you would write and let me know what to your knowledge has become of the others who travelled with you, Ann Brennan, Ellen Busby,

Augusta Cooper, Martha Magee, Patience Newcomen, Mary Preston, Mary Sneyd and Ellen Stephens, as well as to your own fortunes. (I am aware of the fate of Dorcas Newman.) You may wonder at my impudence, or at the very least my curiosity. I ask you only to believe that my intentions are only for the best in my desire to right a great wrong that has been done.

Please accept my very best wishes,
Yours sincerely,
Robert Mundy Gover

*

Letter to Robert Mundy Gover from Emma Smith
Sydney
11th July 1872

Dear Mr Gover
Your letter of December 1871 received by me, I write with news of myself and some of the other girls who came with me on the *Subraon* in 1848. I must say I was surprised that you wrote never having got a letter before. There was eleven of us girls altogether. Dorcas you already know about. I can hardly bring myself to write about her. Always a favourite she was. What a tragic end to such a beautiful person. Even now I can hear her voice and see her sweet smile. But that's enough! Alicia did the best of us perhaps. She married some years ago. Had some children though they mostly died. Her youngest, Isabella, is eight. Joseph, Alicia's husband, works hard, but he's a gruff man and I have seen his mark on Alicia once or twice. He's a bit younger than her, but had no cause to be jealous. Ann has been in and out of Gaol a few times over the years. Darlinghurst Gaol is not the nicest place to be as you may imagine. The cause of her troubles: drink and something else which I can't bring myself to mention because it disgusted me

so. She's not the only one. Martha had her troubles too, but she put it all behind her and is quite respectable now. In point of fact she is too ready to condemn others for I have felt the force of her tongue unleashed against me. And for what? You may very well ask. For nothing at all. My only aim was to see that my friends lived tidy lives. Mary Sneyd, though, she had a child out of wedlock which shocked us all at the time, even Martha who wasn't then so respectable herself said she would never have credited Mary living in sin. I felt the same, though Joseph, her man, is pretty as a picture, even now that he's a bit older. I haven't seen or heard of Ellen Busby or Augusta for some years. They went into service upcountry, I believe. Mary Preston went to live in New Zealand. Ellen is too snooty now to take notice of anyone, though God knows why. I still see her from time to time but only from a distance. I almost can't bear to tell you what happened to Patience. She disappeared right after church one Sunday a month after we arrived and has never been seen or heard of since. We all knew why and who she had disappeared with, because a young man vanished on the same day. She was no picture, but she had a way with her that could charm your money out of your purse and into hers. We all supposed she had been killed. I thought we'd all be murdered in our beds, but it never happened. As for me, I live by myself and work hard. Please write again and let me know how you came by my journal which I thought was lost.

Yours
Emma Smith

*

November 1874. There were so many differing views of these events that it came as no surprise to discover yet another. My interest in the career of Captain Mills remained unabated. I spent many weekends walking around the docklands of London, taking in Deptford, Rotherhithe and Greenwich: taking my meals in taverns haunted by sailors and visiting coffee houses where merchants were known to hire captains for their sea ventures and where merchant ship masters were known to meet to discuss their trade. What was this obsession that occupied my thoughts when awake, and my dreams when asleep? I had never before felt such a need to follow a mystery from start to finish. I left visiting cards with landlords of public houses, and even considered advertising once more in *The Times* agony column.

On a bleak Saturday afternoon in November 1874, Mrs Latchford knocked at my door and told me that a gentleman wished to speak with me. He was shown into my room, and with one movement cast aside both hat and topcoat.

'Mr Gover, I believe. My name is Day.' A large man in his mid-fifties, perhaps: grizzled and weathered.

'Please sit, Mr Day.' He sat and remained silent for a while.

'How may I help you, sir,' I ventured.

'I believe you are making inquiries regarding the voyage of the *Subraon*. I was the Second Mate on that ill-fated journey. Probably you received the Captain's book some time ago.'

'Then it was you who sent it to me?'

'It was.'

'Sir, I am pleased to make your acquaintance…'

He interrupted me: 'I do not have much time, Mr Gover. I leave in a short while for India. Ask what you will.'

'Merely for an account, as you remember it, of that voyage. The Captain's book was decidedly short on information.'

He spoke for about an hour, refusing any refreshment, though smoking a curiously shaped pipe. During that time, I made notes: asking questions only rarely.

'I am now a First Mate, but on that voyage I was Second, while Mr Hill and Mr Carwardine were First and Third Mates. Captain Mills, the Master, was a difficult man. We were all rough seamen, but there was something about him which was different to most other captains I have served under. He had high expectations and a fearsome temper, but he was weak. The louder he shouted, the less he was respected by his men. I only saw him act bravely on one occasion. Most of the time he was holed up in his cabin from where he would issue orders.

'Dr Acret, the ship's surgeon was inebriated most of the time. He was known to fall down even when the sea was calm: he had no sense of balance being frequently half-seas-over. Completely incompetent and untrustworthy, but his heart was in the right place. Oh, yes, he really did care about the health of passengers and crew, he was just incapable or too unskilled to do them any good if they were ill.

'The Doctor and the Captain had a major falling out. No one was supposed to know what it was about, but we all did— even the passengers knew what had happened. Nobody spoke of it, though. Captain Mills would have made life a living hell for anyone who did, even more of a hell than it already was on the *Subraon*.

'The disagreement was over supplies, and particularly drink. The Doctor wanted to be free to give spirits to any he judged in need; the Captain refused to allow him a free hand. The Doctor accused him of profiteering; the Captain slapped him hard. Dr Acret was not sober at the time. He was visibly shaken after this meeting, one which had apparently started amicably. How did we know what had happened? No voices had been raised; their conversation had been whispered, but one of the emigrants had been standing not far from the Captain's cabin, where he had no business to be, and overheard it all. It was all over the ship in no time.

'The others were frequently drunk. Hill and Carwardine behaved abominably to the girls on board from the start: so did Captain Mills, though he was not seen about much. I kept to myself, kept my own counsel too. I'm not proud of myself. I did nothing to help, too aware of my own position. But I would never have actively hurt anyone on board, particularly the female passengers—I have sisters, Mr Gover, and I was brought up to respect the gentle sex.

'My goodness! Is that the time? I must be off! Good evening Mr Gover, thanks for your hospitality. I will be back in England in a few months and will be happy to give you more information then. I feel badly, very badly, about what happened, and that I did nothing to help… Good evening, sir.'

And with that, he left. I never did hear of him again, though I did try to find out what had become of him.

My interest in Captain Mills continued. Imagine my surprise at discovering that he had been involved in another scandal involving his later captaincy of another ship, this time carrying a party of emigrants to Canada. This must be left for another time, perhaps another investigation might uncover fully the tale of Captain Mills and the Mutiny on the *Colinda*.

Meanwhile, what more can be said than this?—Justice is in the hands of those who wield the sword. Blind though she may be, the sword-bearers are not. And perhaps, even Justice peeps through half-closed eyelids, looking askance around her, but powerless to act.

PART TWO

Captain Mills and the Mutiny on the *Colinda*

'And here I find a marvellous great company, newly flocked in, mothers and men, a people gathered for exile, a pitiable crowd. From all quarters they are assembled, ready in heart and fortune, to whatsoever land I will conduct them overseas.'

—Virgil's *The Aeneid*, translation by J.W. Mackail.

1
Mills v. Masterman

The partnership of John Powell Mills and his brother-in-law William Masterman did not run a smooth course, but was tossed on high waves in stormy seas of disagreement. Mills was certain that the way forward lay in buying their own ship, taking command himself. Life at home had become unendurable, for Rachel made his life a living hell, and what he received from her fist and her tongue he returned with interest; a sea voyage would take him away from her nagging. He found the perfect ship, the *Rob Roy*; all that remained was to convince Masterman to agree. Both men were too stubborn to allow the other seniority of place with regard to decision-making. Masterman believed that as original owner of the business, seniority was his. Mills believed that since he had advanced the largest part of money into the business, and that he had business development ideas which went far beyond those of his partner, the right to make final decisions belonged to him.

To begin with, there was the initial discussion, and that between two men who had so little in common that it seemed for a while more like tactical manoeuvrings between two gentle statesmen. Masterman, too, had ideas concerning the future of the business.

'Leave things as they are, for that will be best,' he said. And after uttering that aphorism, as he did at the start of every meeting, there was a considerable silence.

'Well, John,' said Masterman, rising as if to leave to carry out more important matters.

'Well, William,' replied Mills, not moving anywhere, and effectively blocking the exit of the other.

'Is there anything else?'

'I have an idea,' said Mills (Masterman clenched his teeth), 'that should make us a tidy sum. The *Rob Roy* is for sale, and I think that a voyage to Rio should pay dividends.'

'How much?' asked Masterman.

'We should make a tidy sum,' said the other pretending to misconstrue the true meaning of the question.

'No, how much will the tub cost us?'

'One thousand pounds is all we need find and then she will be ours to do with as we please.'

'Brother,' said Masterman, 'I doubt we have the funds for this purpose.'

'I have money, but if you wish to be a part of this venture you must dip into your own pockets.'

'How much?' groaned Masterman.

'Three hundred or so from you should see it done. I will supply the rest, and then,' said Mills with relish, 'take command myself.'

'Yes…' Masterman said doubtfully, 'but surely you won't be able to go yourself—there's that Soames business you have to take care of.'

Masterman spoke an uncomfortable truth which Mills did not wish to hear. He was in dispute with the firm of Soames and Co., one-time owners of the now sunken *Subraon*. They wanted him to pay their losses and the penalties they had been charged by the Government for not fulfilling their contract; he refused to do so.

'Let their insurers pay,' he said to Masterman. But the latter knew that it was not quite as simple as that, for the insurers had decided that Mills himself was liable for the costs since they deemed him to be at fault.

Mills had set his heart on another sea voyage, and had already been in discussion with a firm of merchants who wished to commission a vessel to set sail for Rio de Janeiro.

'What if they will not?' said Masterman, hoping that he was playing a trump card.

'Nevertheless,' Mills stated firmly, 'the *Rob Roy* must be bought. If necessary we can select another captain for the first voyage.'

Masterman was annoyed, but at that moment he needed Mills, for it was his sister's money that was keeping the company afloat. He agreed, though reluctantly, and Mills went ahead and acquired the *Rob Roy*. The ship was chartered for the voyage to Rio, though with Mills's friend John Long Cant as captain. Perhaps that was just as well, for shortly after, Mills was absent from work, insisting, in a letter to Masterman that he had influenza. Masterman, uncharitably, assumed he was suffering from a bad case of delirium tremens—the truth was somewhat different to either of these as we shall see.

While Mills was absent, Masterman saw to the running of the zinc works. He, too, had ideas regarding improving profits. He decided, though without his partner's approval, to rebuild their warehouse. Until that time, they had been using a rather rundown cottage which occupied part of their premises for this purpose. He had it demolished, and brought in workers to build a more accommodating building.

'Wait till John sees what I have done!' he said to Rachel when she came to visit him at the works one day. 'He will see that others can have grand ideas.'

*

In 1850, John Powell Mills, late Master of the *Subraon*, sued his wife's brother, William Masterman. The case was heard on 20th July in the Court of Chancery before the Right Honourable Thomas Wilde, Baron Truro of Bowes, Lord High Chancellor of Great Britain.

Mills's solicitor was Lewis Jacobs, of 6 Crosby Square, Bishopsgate, London.

Masterman's solicitors were Bridger and Collins, of 37 King William Street, London Bridge.

The two firms did not see each other as rivals, but as associates whose joint interest was ensuring that their fees would more than justify their work. The Lord Chancellor watched over the proceedings with hawk-like attention.

*

Mills's Complaint

Mills stated that on 7 May 1849 he had entered into partnership with William Masterman as Zinc Workers. Premises in Peckham, Surrey had been bought at Mills's expense (so he said) and, for the benefit of the business, a trading ship—the Rob Roy—had also been purchased for £1,000. Mills had paid £710 and Masterman the balance of £290. The *Rob Roy* had been purchased at his suggestion, and he himself was to take command for the proposed trading voyages for the benefit of the partnership, though owing to a dispute at that time with his previous employer, shipowners Soames and Company, he was unable to leave England, and another had taken his place as captain. The *Rob Roy* had been chartered by the George Jones Ship Company on behalf of Messrs Nathan Brothers for a voyage to Rio de Janeiro in the Brazils.

Mills had prepared his case thoroughly, and had been well-coached in his part by Mr Jacobs: 'Mr Masterman caused a cottage on our premises to be pulled down so that a warehouse might be built, though he did not consult me in the matter. I had fallen sick just at that time, and was confined to bed. So I was also unaware that he caused the work to be stopped, leaving all in an unfinished state, because he had run out of money. He had been using our partnership funds without my knowledge to finance this building project to make profit for himself, not telling me so that he would not have to give me my due share.'

'Is there anything else you would add?' said the Lord Chancellor, knowing full well, having thoroughly read the long submissions supplied to him that there was.

Mills continued: 'Yes, my Lord. When the *Rob Roy* arrived at Rio, necessary repairs to the ship were made and paid for by Messrs Nathan Brothers. I accepted the liability for the bill on behalf of the partnership, but Mr Masterman refused to pay the amount owing, leaving me to pay all out of my own pocket.

'All in all, I received only £80 of the profits made by the partnership, surely far too small an amount, but Mr Masterman refused to let me examine the books which he was holding. He also refused me access to the premises, and would not account for any of the profits or rents from the business. I had no choice but to write to him dissolving the partnership, but he never acknowledged the letter, instead, he has threatened to take possession of the *Rob Roy* and all her freight now that she has arrived back in England. I would ask that he be prevented from doing so, and that an appropriate person be appointed to divide the assets.'

*

Masterman's Answer

Masterman's answer to these charges told a different tale; and though neither man was shown in a good light, the case was not as straightforward as might be supposed from reading Mills's side of the argument.

He rebutted the claims of Mills, and stated that all expenses had been borne by the partnership. He declared that he had already been trading as a Zinc Worker at No.1 Prospect Row, Dockhead before entering into any agreement with Mills. He had owned this property with a mortgage which Mills, he owned, had redeemed. 'I would like to add, my Lord,' said Masterman, 'that our current premises at Peckham were purchased without my knowledge by Mr Mills, sight unseen by either of us, using partnership funds. They proved to be worth only half the amount paid.

'He told me, convinced me, that there were large profits to be made if we bought a ship for trading purposes, and so the *Rob Roy* was bought and registered. It was registered to me alone for the following reason:

'As you know, my Lord, Mr Mills, is my brother-in-law, he having married my sister. The best understanding existed between us prior to our partnership. I knew that he had been in the employ of Messrs Soames, who are large Ship Owners, as Captain. One of their vessels, the *Subraon*, was wrecked while under his command, and his conduct towards some female emigrants on board the vessel was notoriously bad. The ship having been chartered by the Government, there were penalties outstanding amounting to £500. Now, in August or September last year, he told me that he owed Messrs Soames a large sum of money and that he was determined not to pay them, for if he did so he should be left quite destitute. If Messrs Soames had proceeded to enforce their claim against him, he would have been forced to make use of the Act for the relief of Insolvent Debtors. Therefore, to prevent Messrs Soames from getting his interest or share in the *Rob Roy*, the vessel had to be purchased and registered in my name alone.

'All purchases were made using partnership funds, but just as arrangements for the first voyage of the *Rob Roy* were nearly completed, Mr Mills was arrested at the suit of Messrs Soames, to recover the amount due to them, though he wrote to me that he was absent due to influenza.'

*

A letter from Mills to Masterman was then read out.

October 1st 1849. To William Masterman Esquire— Sir, for your kindness towards me in assisting to fit me out by the aid of your Funds previous to my departure in the *Subraon* I do hereby acknowledge the sum of £400 borrowed money of which I have paid you £200. For the remaining sum I offer you the whole half of my property situate at Bermondsey and Peckham. You are at liberty to have it conveyed over to you at any time you may think fit.

Your humble servant J.P. Mills.

*

Masterman continued: 'I therefore took and sold those properties. Mr Mills was released on bail, and it then transpired, to my surprise, that he owed Messrs Soames an additional £500. He was suffering severely from depression, and so I and some friends offered to raise the sum of £30 to give to Messrs Soames if that company would consider his debts to them to be fully discharged for that amount. We told them, at the same time, of his illness and depression and also that he was entirely destitute. They, fortunately, believed what we told them, for they must have realised that they had little hope of receiving anything more, and they agreed.'

Masterman continued with further information about the voyage of the *Rob Roy* to Rio de Janeiro. Since Mills had been unavailable to captain the voyage, another captain had been found (and paid for). The replacement was Captain John Long Cant. Unfortunately, once in Rio, Cant had died, and the

British Consul there had appointed Captain G. Cook to replace him on the voyage back to England.

The *Rob Roy* was now back in the London Docks with many unpaid financial liabilities which were, according to Masterman, daily increasing. Mills, he said, had been summoned before a magistrate for wages due to the ship's apprentice (£10), and since Mills had defaulted on the magistrate's order to pay him this amount, a distress warrant had been issued against the vessel, and its tackle had been seized and sold for about £100.

The voyage to Rio had been most unprofitable, and the value of the freight—£400—had been absorbed by expenses and there were still outstanding liabilities of £300. Furthermore, the ship had been severely damaged and was now worth less than a third of the sum originally paid for her.

With regard to his refusal to pay for repairs to the *Rob Roy*, he stated that the demand had come from the new captain, G. Cook, who he did not know. He stated that he had never refused to produce the partnership account books, that there were no account books only the rough daybook, nor had he excluded Mills from the premises. He did, however admit that he had kept the profits of the partnership after it had been dissolved, but claimed that Mills had kept the stock in trade.

The case was resolved to the dissatisfaction of both parties, neither being awarded anything at all, and both expected to pay the legal costs.

2
Between Ships

John Powell Mills was tired, depressed and anxious. He tried forgetting his troubles by sleeping, but he was restless and sleep would not come easily. When he did manage to sleep, his dreams were full of those things he wished to forget. He tried forgetting his woes with liberal internal use of rum and brandy, but those made him more depressed than ever, and, when he woke from alcohol-induced fugs of unconsciousness, his head pounded as if large cannons were firing mid-battle. He lay in his bed for days at a time, unwashed, unkempt, bored, angry, uncomfortable, and irritable. Life was not worth living. Knocks at the door of his room got either no response, or a gruff, 'Go away!'

He felt certain his days at sea were over; he would never again be given command of a ship.

As for Rachel, she was furious with him. She hated having him around, and, furthermore, his argument with her beloved brother had placed her in an invidious position. Rachel longed for her husband to go back to sea as much as he did. But time passed without any opportunities, and they were living off their savings. Then Mills, after months of inactivity and slovenliness, suddenly smartened himself up. The motive for this—he had invested money in another vessel, and become a Ship's Master again.

3

Captain Mills of the *Colinda*

1853

With unusual activity, Mills applied for a Master's Certificate of Service, something which had just become compulsory for all Master Mariners; he had been a Master Mariner for some years, so he had no need to sit an examination. He had obtained part-ownership of the barque *Colinda*, and as captain of that ship was chartered to undertake a voyage to the west coast of Canada. An inward breath is needed at this point in the narrative, as realisation dawns on us that despite his previous record he had once again been entrusted with a voyage carrying emigrants to a new life.

How could this be? Why was he chosen? What might be the result of such foolhardiness on the part of the Honourable Hudson's Bay Company who had placed him in charge of this voyage? And there is another point to consider: previously, Captain Mills had been involved with transporting convicts, women and girls, and the starving poor. This time, he was entrusted with carrying burly workers from Scotland and Norway to work as miners on Vancouver's Island just off the west coast of Canada. Perhaps he should have realised that although he might get away with being overbearing and corrupt when in charge of the weak, his position of power might not be so steady when faced with the strong.

'Difficult times are at an end,' he thought to himself as he took charge of the *Colinda*. 'I am Master once more.'

Thus did Captain Mills tempt fate; the result was not as he expected.

✲

The years and rough weather had taken their toll on the appearance of Captain John Powell Mills. He had not become the heroic figure he had hoped to be as a youth, and there was even a noticeable contrast between his appearance at the age of thirty-one when he became Master of the *Subraon* and his appearance at the age of thirty-seven when he became Master of the *Colinda*. Once bright-eyed and with a gaze that could pierce all he met to the soul, his weathered face appeared almost to lack eyes, so small did the droopy eyelids make them seem. Efforts to keep his eyes open by will power had caused his forehead to be lined, and shortsightedness meant that he wore glasses when examining navigation charts which almost made him look professorish. He was still a hard drinker and had become a stern and unforgiving man, embittered by the lack of success and the surfeit of infamy which had come his way. He asked himself many a time what it was that kept him going back to sea where he could not enjoy the small wealth he had built, for when he was at sea he longed to be home, but when at home he couldn't wait to be at sea.

✲

Some of the Crew of the Colinda*:*

Master—Captain John Powell Mills
Chief Mate—Mr H.W. Birt
Second Mate—Thomas Hawley
Midshipmen—Mr Caley, Mr W.H. Bullmore, Mr
    Chambers, and Mr W.S. Holligan

Ship's Surgeon Superintendent—Dr Henry
    William Alexander Coleman
Captain's Steward—Frederick Augustus Luke
Emigrants' Steward—William Feltham
Emigrants' Cook—Mr Honeyman
Apprentices/Cabin boys— Masters Barrett,
    Flude, Darnell, & Ebenezer Lambert
Able Seamen—Wrench, Anderson, Henderson,
    Jones &c.
Ordinary Seamen—Rowland &c

*

Cabin Passengers were Mrs Matilda S. Leigh and her three children who were joining Mr Leigh in Canada, and Miss Williamina Manson Forsyth, a governess from Thurso, Caithness. Miss Forsyth was a very determined lady of twenty-seven, who had decided to leave Scotland to find her destiny elsewhere. One of five children, she remained tight-lipped about the reason she was so anxious to get away as far as she could, leaving behind her parents and her brothers and sisters.

The *Colinda* was towed into the Thames estuary by steamer, and then set sail. The two vessels parted amidst cheers from the sailors. A wind had sprung up, and the sails, gleaming white in the summer sun, seemed to blossom forth like waterlilies in the new Waterlily House at the Botanical Gardens in Kew. The barque had already shaken off the black gloom of London; now the wind whispered messages of hope, bright futures and happy fortunes. The emigrants' hearts sang inwardly; they breathed deeply and thought of new lives ahead. Some looked back at the land they were leaving with regret for those they might never see again, others gazed ahead with determined faces. Many had wet cheeks, though whether from tears of sorrow or joy, or perhaps because the wind had made their eyes water, was hard to say.

The Chief Mate, Mr Birt, stood on the poop deck feet planted firm as he gave instructions to the crew. Captain Mills was nowhere to be seen.

On the quarter deck Dr Coleman stood besieged by a group of Scottish men already expressing dissatisfaction with the arrangements on board.

Henry William Alexander Coleman, Surgeon, was an idealist, young (being twenty-five years old), but determined to make a success of his time—to be efficient and effective, and to get all his charges safely to Vancouver's Island, their final destination. Eager to make a mark, he had impressed the representatives of the Hudson's Bay Company; they selected him because of his fine references which made particular mention of his methodical and modern methods. He had been a house-surgeon at Guy's Hospital, and thought himself ready for a position of responsibility and the world. He had already found Captain Mills to be a demanding and awkward man, but he had decided to be as pleasant and accommodating as possible, so that all might have a peaceful time during the passage. He quieted the passengers down, and organised them into messes. The Scottish passengers were cantankerous and complaining; the Norwegians seemed more peaceable and willing to help.

After the departure it dawned upon the passengers that oceans, of water lay between England and the west coast of Canada, and they murmured troubled words among themselves. A ship crawls across the sea, sometimes cradled, sometimes tossed in its arms. Those on land, looking out to sea on a stormy day, will stand affrighted at the sight of ships in the offing in danger of being dashed to pieces; but the full power of the ocean can only be truly appreciated from the deck or mast top of a vessel once it is out of sight of land, days distant from the shore, when even on a calm day the mighty swell imparts a feeling of deepest awe to all on board. Sailors accept the ocean for what it is: a great heaving monstrosity whose immenseness can best be understood, not during dangerous storms when the mind is busy on other matters, but when the waters are calm.

For it is then that there is time to contemplate the ocean's potential to wreak devastation upon ship, crew and passengers. Let all take this as fair warning, for the ocean cannot and will not be tamed. An insolent man is audacious enough to challenge the great waters of the world to a jousting match. Let him beware! Moreover, there is another danger, for, even if the weather is set fair for a prosperous voyage, weeks and months spent at sea with limited space breed resentment among those on board toward each other.

The ancient Greeks when at sea might have prayed that Zeus and Poseidon would have no argument, for one would hurl thunder and lightning and the other respond by unleashing the great monsters of the deep. The greatest monster is the sea itself. If one could capture any single moment, freeze time and motion, and look at a ship on the surface of the water from a distance, she would appear as a tiny pimple on the vast face of the world, subject to the whims of current and weather. Only the Master can communicate with the powers, interposing himself between the precious lives of those on board and Davy Jones.

The voyage of the *Colinda* began by settling into an uncomfortable routine. The passengers grumbled at their provisions, both quality and quantity; Dr Coleman did his best to ease matters.

Passengers were assigned various duties: taking part in the watch, assisting the cook, helping in the two hospitals (one for women, one for men), or holystoning the deck—a tiresome task involving pushing blocks of sandstone around, on hands and knees, in order to keep the deck clean.

The officers (Chief Mate, Second Mate and Third Mate), had their own quarters. The stewards, midshipmen and cabin boys slept in, or near, the sailors' dormitories, forward. The emigrants were assigned to small family cabins or travelled steerage in the hold.

The Captain had the largest cabin, and beyond it was a large stateroom where he could meet with the ship's officers. On the other side of his cabin was the cuddy which had a dining table and four dining chairs where he and the private passengers would take their meals. There were three other rooms leading from the cuddy: Dr Coleman had one, one of the others was occupied by Miss Forsyth and the last by Mrs Leigh and her small children. They were served at mealtimes by the Captain's Steward, Frederick Luke.

The first meal taken in the cuddy was a convivial affair, with much laughter and talk of a successful voyage. Captain Mills offered the Doctor a cigar, and the two smoked, though the ladies were present. 'Perhaps he isn't so bad, after all,' thought the Doctor.

*

Upon examining his stores, Dr Coleman was shocked to discover that the ship had been poorly equipped with medical supplies. Indeed, they were wholly inadequate for the purpose of a long voyage. He suspected that there had been an attempt to save money by cutting corners, and these suspicions were increased when, every day, passengers went to him complaining that some of their food was rotten. Furthermore, the Captain was unwilling to be of much help in his endeavours to keep the passengers healthy. The emigrants on the *Colinda* had contractual agreements which stated that they would be paid wages monthly from the date of embarkation and fed well, and these matters would prove to be bones of contention—but more of that in its place.

In his cabin, Dr Coleman began to write his medical journal, not as others had done before him with notes of illnesses and a few general comments, but with full entries made every day, detailing the happenings on the *Colinda*.

*

From the (later) Memoirs of Dr Coleman
Notes taken from my journal of events which occurred on board the *Colinda*, barque bound for Vancouver's Island.

Even now that so many years have passed since the voyage of the *Colinda* my blood boils when I think of that time. I have spent sleepless nights rehearsing in my mind the things I should have said and done under the intolerable pressure placed on me by the Captain.

On 4th August 1853, we set sail for Canada. All was confusion on board, and the dissatisfaction of the passengers was made clear to me almost at once. Parties of men were sent up to my cabin from one group or another, deputised by their friends and comrades to complain about the lack of comfort in their quarters, the paucity of food allowed to them and other matters which were totally out of my terms of reference. I had organised the families into groups to make meal times as simple as possible, but this, it seemed, had satisfied none. There were two nationalities on board as passengers, Scottish and Norwegian, and it has to be said that the English language as spoken by the Norwegians was hardly less understandable to me than that of the Scots. After some days, once I had become attuned to the Scottish accent, things became easier.

I soon found it necessary to keep a detailed journal of everything, since the Master, Captain Mills, magnified every piffling and frivolous circumstance into matters of great consequence. His vindictiveness and his mercenary plots became unbearable to me, most of them were, indeed, directed towards me or to those with whom I had established some little friendship.

My examination of the ship's hospital, equipment and medical supplies proved all to be totally inadequate for a voyage of even one week, let alone four months, and I was grossly irritated to discover that all the assurances made to me by the representatives of the Honourable Hudson's Bay Company, which had chartered the vessel, were worthless.

My hopes had been effectively dashed. Young as I was, and inexperienced, I had been placed in charge of one hundred and seventy-five emigrants bound for West Canada, and this responsibility had been the cause of some rejoicing for my parents who foresaw great things for me.

My disappointment notwithstanding, I set to work to make the best of things, and made application to the Captain to have alterations made to the hospital in order to create a dispensary—though drugs being inadequate, there was but little to dispense. Great was the sea-sickness among the passengers. The Scots became impolite, and even rebellious when I refused to prescribe them brandy, though I did allow them some tobacco.

★

August 10th saw the *Colinda* 100 miles due west of Brest; two days later the ship was 100 miles due west of Santiago de Compostela.

The voyage continued with an unhappy doctor and discontented passengers. Regulations dictated that Divine Service was held every Sunday and that all should attend. Usually, the Captain would lead, but on Sunday 14th August, Dr Coleman took charge, and the following day he appointed one Charles Lewis to be schoolmaster to the children and any others who wished for instruction in reading, having observed Lewis to be both conscientious and pious. He also appointed William Sutherland, who had assisted before at a hospital, to be his own assistant, finding in him a willing workman. Dr Coleman was determined to make a success of this, his first voyage, and succeeded in vaccinating many of the children and infants.

Sea-sickness was rife, and in her cabin, Mrs Leigh suffered more than most. Dr Coleman was concerned, for his patient seemed very delicate, and he worried that there was something more seriously wrong. Ellen Sutherland, wife of William Sutherland, volunteered to sit with her. The Doctor gratefully accepted the offer finding Mrs Sutherland to be very well-disposed. He was harried and importuned on all sides by other passengers demanding brandy as a sea-sickness cure; they continued to accuse him of being uncaring when he resolutely refused to prescribe it. Captain Mills looked on with a wry contempt for his passengers, but was happy not to interfere with the Doctor, as long as he had no intention of broaching any casks of brandy.

There were petty squabbles among the emigrants, and there was great alarm when, a few days out, it was discovered that there were rats on board. Women and children screamed in terror so that both the Captain and the Doctor supposed that someone had been set on fire.

*

Thursday 18th August: the *Colinda* was 250 miles west of Gibraltar.

Most of the children had become ill; Dr Coleman diagnosed smallpox, measles, and scarlet fever, and was fully occupied in treating them. It was summer, and, as the ship sailed further southwards, the air became unbearably stuffy below deck. Dr Coleman ordered that the boards around the passengers berths should be removed to supply more ventilation, but this was of little help.

That day, he was visited in the hospital by two of the Norwegians, Berentzen and Johannesen.

'What can I do for you, gentlemen?'

Berentzen looked at him with a fixed stare, which Coleman interpreted as impudence, and without taking his eyes from the Doctor's face laid a small pile of books down on the table which lay between them.

'We won't be needing these.'

The books consisted of religious and educational tracts which had been supplied by the Hudson's Bay Company for the edification of the passengers.

'May I ask why?'

'They are no use!'

'No use?' said the Doctor, restraining himself from showing any signs of anger.

'No use to us,' said Berentzen simply. All the time he had not shifted his gaze. Johannesen, meanwhile, had uttered not a word but had hung back in the doorway as if anxious to get away.

Dr Coleman picked up one of the books and opened it at a random page. He was about to respond, when light began to dawn in his mind. 'Can you read?' he asked.

'Read, yes.'

'Then…'

'Read Norwegian, yes. English, no.'

The Company in its wisdom had supplied only English books. None of the Norwegians could read them. After the two men had gone, the Doctor sat on a chair with his left elbow on the table and his face in his hand, and sighed deeply. Earlier that day, he had discovered that the books in the ship's library were largely unread by the English passengers also, particularly the married ones who had little time to do anything except look after their children (referring to the women), or play cards (referring to the men).

*

Friday came, and William Sutherland arrived in the hospital rather late and looking flustered.

'I'm sorry, Doctor,' he said as he came through the door.

'This is very unlike you, William, to be behind time. What can the meaning of it be?'

'I hardly like to say, Doctor.'

'Oh, come, now, we are already old friends, you can confide in me.'

This last remark was not truly sincere, but Dr Coleman had already learned the necessity of bending the truth in order to obtain information.

'They are jealous of me…' Sutherland could not restrain this from bursting out of his mouth, but then checked himself abruptly.

'But who, William, who are jealous of you?'

'The other men. They make my life a misery because I am assisting you.'

'Yes, I have already discovered that some of them would not be happy unless the ship's surgeon had been born north of the border, or had, at least, studied medicine in Scotland. But don't let them upset you, we have a long voyage ahead of us.'

Later the Doctor noted in his journal the 'ridiculous' behaviour of the emigrants: how the women still grumbled because he would not allow them brandy, and how the Scottish passengers would not 'bow down to an Englishman,' adding, 'Knowing that there is no means of punishment on board they try to be as insolent as they can and whenever I speak to them, they argue the point and then tell me that I do not do my duty to them; they are a most unruly set of people.'

The unruliness of the emigrants was exemplified in his opinion by the quarrelsome nature of the passionate and hasty Mrs Brown, a Scottish lady in her mid thirties, who continually argued with the other passengers and sometimes took out her frustration upon her husband. George Brown became a frequent visitor to the hospital, usually in search of ointment for bruises as well as a refuge. Dr Coleman often found himself reprimanding Mrs Brown, but thought most of the other women to be just as troublesome.

Meanwhile, he was having a hard time keeping the infants on board well. By mid August six children had died. Their parents were, naturally, distraught. Some blamed the Doctor, others understood that he was doing the best he could in difficult circumstances. He had found on further examination that both the mens' and womens' hospitals were full of provisions that should have been stowed in the hold, and that consequently there was no room for any patients, and it took much time to clear space when it was needed. Furthermore, the water casks in the hold had goods stacked upon them, which needed to be lifted off once a day before the water could be got.

One of the adult passengers, Joseph Featherstone, became seriously ill. Dr Coleman found himself in great difficulty—for there was no bedding in the hospital! Since the Featherstones' cabin contained only a double bed, the sick man slept there, and his wife had to sleep on the floorboards. The Doctor gave her some of his own blankets.

*

On the afternoon of Monday the 22nd of August the *Colinda* was in sight of land. The closeness to Palma in the Canaries gave the passengers hope that they might land to get supplies and to get respite from their sea-sickness, but their hopes were soon dashed. In the evening, a comet was observed in the sky. Some of the sailors grumbled for it was a bad omen.

That evening, there were raised voices in one of the mess rooms. The indomitable Mrs Brown, with a fiery temper had become mightily enraged with her neighbour Mrs Hunter.

Mrs Brown: I think you've taken more than your entitlement.

Mrs Hunter: Indeed, I have not. I'll thank you to keep your remarks to yourself.

Mrs Brown: I warned you before.

Mrs Hunter: *[sorely provoked]* I'll not stand that woman any more.

Mrs Brown: Just who are you calling 'that woman'.

Mrs Hunter: You, you evil old witch.

Mrs Brown: You deserve everything I said. I'll not take it back.

Mrs Hunter: Just wait till I report what you have done.

Mrs Brown: Report it? Report away! I'll soon give you something to report.

Mrs Hunter: Keep your hands off!

Mrs Brown: If you need so much more water than the rest of us you had better have this, too.

And with that, Mrs Brown picked up a water keg and a plate and heaved them at Mrs Hunter, who dodged them, and ran out of the door.

*

Early the following morning Mrs Hunter made a formal complaint about Mrs Brown to the Doctor, who promised to investigate.

'I'll see what I can do, Mrs Hunter.'

'Well, if that's the best you can offer: *Seeing what you can do!*— I expect that nothing will come of it.'

Dr Coleman made a mental note to solve the Hunter-Brown problem by separating the two ladies and moving Mrs Hunter to another berth. He was feeling rather distracted at the time, since a seventh child had died, of measles this time, only a short time before. The sailors had spoken meaningfully in whispers about the comet which had been seen in the night. Dr Coleman had worked hard, but in vain, to subdue the child's illness.

No sooner had Mrs Hunter gone, than Mrs Wyllie, the dead child's mother, was standing before him with her husband in tow.

'I'm very sorry for your loss, Mrs Wyllie,' said the Doctor.

'That's all very well,' she replied, 'but you would not let us feed young Robert with jelly and wine, which might have saved him.'

'But, Mrs Wyllie, Robert was not yet weaned, he was still suckling. In his condition it would have been very dangerous to give him those things.'

'He died anyway,' said Mrs Wyllie baldly. 'You're a hard-hearted man!' And she left, taking her husband with her.

The Doctor looked on as they walked away and shook his head ruefully.

Soon after, three of the male passengers went to see him. 'What can I do for you, Ewart?' said the Doctor.

'Some of us feel that you should allow the women and children wine,' said Robert Ewart.

'Gentlemen, what you ask is impossible. I could not allow that unless they were ill and needed it for the sake of their health. I am very busy trying to cure those who are sick. That is what I do. That is what I have been trained to do. Please let me do it!' The Doctor found it hard to control his irritation, pressed as he was with growing sickness on board. 'I'm sorry, I spoke hastily. I will find a way to help. I'll have a cask of stout opened tomorrow, and perhaps distribute some groats to nursing mothers so that they may have milk-porridge.'

The three men, Ewart, Wilson and McMurtrie left: thanking the Doctor as they went.

*

All this time, Captain Mills was noticeably absent from ship life, and unaware of the comings and goings of the passengers. During the day Dr Coleman communicated with him with brief written messages whose responses were briefer still. Mrs Leigh, Miss Forsyth and the Doctor saw him at mealtimes, and Mr Birt saw him when he made his reports and took orders, but otherwise Captain Mills kept himself to himself, speaking little when they sat round the table, except to ask for the salt or other such small matters.

*

Some of the children became ill with the dysentery which followed on from measles. The Doctor despaired of getting even half of them to their destination alive.

The weather had become hot and sultry. There was much rain, but nothing to be done, for the wind had dropped and the *Colinda* was becalmed for two days with much sickness on board. Most of the food supplied to the passengers was very nasty, and the children refused to eat it. By Sunday, the wind had picked up, the sea become rough, and the Doctor was obliged to hold Divine Service indoors, for it was impossible to perform it on deck. Attendance, though compulsory, was poor.

*

Monday 29th August: the *Colinda* was 150 miles west of Portuguese Guinea, West Africa.

Yet another child died that day, this time from hydrocephalus which the Doctor had tried vainly to control with mercury. He himself performed the burial service at 10 a.m.

The following day, all passengers who were carrying firearms were instructed to clean them to prevent their rusting in the humid air. Mr Caley, Midshipman, reported to Mr Birt, Chief Mate, that £5 and some personal papers had been stolen from his desk. He declared that William Feltham, the Emigrants' Steward had been seen near the midshipmen's quarters, but enquiries into the matter came to nothing. Privately, however, Dr Coleman resolved to keep a wary eye on Feltham.

*

The passengers attended to their chores, some dutifully, others not. While travelling through tropic climes the men of the morning watch were instructed to turn the other passengers out of bed at 6 a.m. and make them come on deck to wash themselves, and also to holystone the deck. This was done, but with many curses and groans from those given the task of scraping the planks clean. The Doctor found himself faced with still more complaints from those hardworking emigrants who attended to their duties, that only a few of them actually did the work, while others shirked the tasks set for them.

August passed, September arrived by stealth overnight. There was little relief to be had from the sultry heat, and drinking-water was strictly rationed. One month had almost passed since the sailing of the *Colinda*; early on the morning of 1st September several emigrants went to the Doctor with their contracts from the Hudson's Bay Company in their hands, demanding to be paid, as was the agreement. The Doctor had no money with which to pay them, and told them patiently that they would all be paid by the company upon arrival at Vancouver's Island. There was nothing more to be said upon the matter, but the men were not happy. Some expressed themselves very strongly, and showed their resentment of Dr Coleman, accusing him of favouring some of the passengers over others. It was true that he had allowed a few of the harder workers some grog, but at that accusation, he lost his patience, and ushered them from his presence. His nerves were as tight as a bobstay, and with clenched fists and jaw he paced round the quarterdeck for fifteen minutes with a look of thunder on his brows enough to keep any others who wished to importune him from daring to approach.

On Sunday, 4th September, Divine Service was performed by Captain Mills in the large cabin. He had been seen about more frequently in the last few days, and seemed to take an interest in some of the doings of the passengers as well as the running of the ship itself. The following day, most of the Norwegian men declared that they would not keep watch even though Dr Coleman showed them the clause in their contracts which stated that they were obliged to do so. The Captain on being informed of this told the Norwegians that they would be punished if they did not take their turns, and they promised obedience.

*

And the deaths continued: a child of sixteen months died from dysentery on September the 6th and was buried the following morning. Soon another was dangerously ill from the same cause. On September the 8th, Dr Coleman wrote that he feared the child would die during the night. He found the atmosphere on the *Colinda* oppressive, mealtimes were purgatory to him, for the glowering presence of Captain Mills seemed to pervade every corner of the ship. The Doctor made up his mind to be as pleasant and accommodating to the Captain as he could be. He had no intention of causing any unwanted tension during the voyage, 'and perhaps,' he thought, 'that may allow the passage to seem shorter, for there is much time left.'

Tempers among the emigrants were frequently frayed, the women and children grew peevish, and the men could be violent if not soothed by telling them what they wished to hear. The *Colinda* was now approaching the equator; the passengers suffered from ennui, but some of the crew were beginning to become excited, especially the novices.

4
The South Atlantic Ocean

Friday 9th September: the *Colinda* crossed the equator and entered the South Atlantic Ocean midway between Southern Africa and South America.

That morning Captain Mills sat at the table in his cabin with a glass tumbler within easy reach of his right hand, and a decanter of brandy a little further off. There was not much brandy left in the decanter as most of it had found its way into Captain Mills. He drank because he was depressed, but his drinking only served to increase his depression. 'I won't put up with fools anymore,' he said to himself. 'I'll tell them what they can do!'

He stood, and walked towards the door, muttering with a scowl, 'This doctor thinks too much of himself with his clean fingernails and his wide grin. By Hell! I'll show him a thing or two—if he thinks he can lord it over me, when he's still wet behind the ears, he'll have to think again, I'll soon wipe that smile from his face—Mr Birt!' The last remark was loudly addressed to the Chief Mate, who, standing just beyond the door, turned towards the Captain with a quizzical look on his face, for Mr Birt was not himself that morning and not in a good frame of mind.

'Captain?'

'Are the lads going to perform for us today when we cross the line?'

'Yes, Sir.'

'Kindly see that they do not get too carried away, we don't want 'em scaring anyone.'

'Aye-aye, Captain.' And Mr Birt strode off to have a few words with the Boatswain.

The Captain returned to his chair with a raging headache and in an affable fury—that is an anger which is disguised by an excess of goodwill towards the Despised.

Dr Coleman, though, unaware of the Captain's dangerous mood, had a request to make, and five minutes later arrived at the cabin door to speak about the cleanliness of the emigrants, for vermin were everywhere. The Captain, who had, meanwhile, decided to bide his time, acceded to the Doctor, and the following order was duly posted where all might see it:

*

Notice

1 Every passenger must bring his bedding on deck twice a week.

11 While the bedding is on deck the berths must be washed with a solution for destroying vermin.

111 The Children's hair must be kept closely cut, their heads washed daily & occasionally with a liquid (which will be supplied to them) for destroying vermin.

1V That the adults keep their own skins & heads clean.

V That in every case of default, punishment will be strictly enforced according to the Act of Parliament.

By order of
Henry Wm Alex Coleman, Surgeon
John Powell Mills, Master

*

The emigrants resented these interferences. It would not be the last time this notice would be posted up: each time it would soon be torn down. However, there were occasional distractions from their resentment. That afternoon, as the *Colinda* crossed the Equator and as is customary on board many ships, a special ceremony was performed. The Boatswain was dressed up by the crew as Father Neptune, and then made a tour of the ship with an improvised trident in his hand, commanding as he did so that all sailors who had not previously crossed the line should undergo the ordeal of being shaved. Those members of the crew who were deemed to fall into this category were duly herded up, and, much against their wills, had the hair on their heads crudely clipped and then scraped. Those who did not struggle got away with the least blood lost. The emigrants, on the other hand, managed to avoid this processing of their heads, the sailors being content to douse as many as could be caught with seawater. They took care not to catch any of the stronger or more belligerent of the passengers, but some of the women got soaked. The young boys stripped to the waist, and were duly rewarded with buckets of water upended over them as they danced around the quarterdeck hooting with laughter.

Earlier, below deck, the Hunter family had gathered around the cot in which lay the body of their youngest, for Peter Hunter had died during the night. Dr Coleman entered the death into his journal, again recording the cause as dysentery. At nine-thirty that morning, he read the burial service with the assistance of the Chief Mate, Mr Birt. Mrs Hunter wept, her husband stood mutely next to her. The other passengers felt for them, and even Mrs Brown did not speak roughly to her sparring partner.

*

Up till that time, all on the *Colinda* had merely been uncomfortable; arguments amongst the passengers had, for the most part, been petty; but now a new phase of the voyage was beginning. The full madness was still a while off, the sea for the time being remained calm; the approaching storm was not of the ocean's making.

Whether Captain Mills was sitting in his cabin or pacing the deck, his mind was in a turmoil of contradictory thoughts. He had begun to question the reason for mankind's existence, and, unable to come to a satisfactory conclusion, he had begun a steady spiral downwards into the depths of depression. His head ached, and he dosed himself with brandy. But however much he drank, there was no end to the pain. His thoughts made things worse still: 'I should be captain of a better ship than this. What am I doing here? Herding sheep to the command of others.'

He resented the emigrants and began to devise ways to make their lives a misery. And only the presence of the Doctor stood between him and his desire to do something violent to quench his desire for revenge against those who had plotted, yes plotted, to keep him in his place. Slowly, things began to move to a bitter conclusion. Like a rolling wave he felt the bile rise up within till he choked.

*

The day after the *Colinda* crossed the equator, Captain Mills ordered that only four lamps would be allowed to be kept alight below deck. The Doctor was puzzled, for he was not aware of any shortage of oil; the passengers were most unhappy, and complained of being in the dark. Dr Coleman made application to Captain Mills for an alteration in his decision, but to no effect.

That same day, Miss Forsyth gave a note to Dr Coleman, explaining that it had come from the Captain.

*

Sir,

Have the goodness to allow each member of the crew, including Midshipmen, Stewards, Mates &c. a measure of grog. Remember that, though you hold the supply, I am Master here, and I expect my request to be acceded to. I do have the power to ensure that you comply. If not, I will show who is Master of the *Colinda*.

Captn JP Mills

*

Dr Coleman, as might be imagined, was most dismayed by the unexpectedly sharp tone of the note, and sent back another refusing absolutely to agree to the Captain's demand. The crew seemed to know about the Doctor's refusal, and a most unpleasant atmosphere pervaded the ship's company as a result.

The crew's resentment of the Doctor began to be manifested in various ways. In the first place, Mr Luke, the Captain's Steward, became insolent towards him, Mrs Leigh and Miss Forsyth at mealtimes in the small dining room which they shared with Captain Mills, particularly if the Captain was not present. On Sunday, when the three of them sat down to supper, he refused to give them any beer to drink, and banged the plates of food down before them. They began their meal in silence, eating slowly, until it became necessary for something to be said.

'Luke,' said the Doctor, 'where is the beer we asked for?'

'Not my fault, Doctor, there ain't much on board to be 'ad— Sir!' said Luke impudently. 'If you want anything more, you must be satisfied with some hard biscuit, 'cause there won't be any more beer. You can't expect to live as they do in vessels fitted up for Cabin Passengers; this isn't a First Class Ship, y'- know.'

Miss Forsyth and Mrs Leigh were both shocked by the steward's remarks, and said as much to Dr Coleman once Luke had gone out. The three of them sat at the table unable to eat more, since the meal had consisted of salted provisions and water was scarce.

'I'll speak to the Captain about that man,' said Mrs Leigh.

'Pray, don't,' said the Doctor, 'we have enough troubles at the moment without making things worse.'

'His behaviour is completely unacceptable,' said Miss Forsyth.

The Doctor resolved to have William Sutherland, who was helping him in the hospital, attend him also in his cabin, since the Captain's Steward was evidently going to be of little use.

*

Tuesday 13th September: the *Colinda* was 560 miles east of Natal, Brazil.

Dr Coleman made his rounds among the passengers. He talked to the mothers about their children, and expressed concern about them. But his task was made most awkward by the lack of light to examine them properly. He sent a note to Captain Mills, asking for one extra light be allowed so that he could attend to the passengers better. That day another infant died of dysentery. The Doctor felt overwhelmed by the task before him: that of keeping all the emigrants well until they reached their destination. He wrote of this last death in his logbook, noting his frustration with the young mothers who, he felt, did not understand the management of children: 'I find them now and then doing the most barbarous things.'

*

Wednesday 14th September

All was not death and despair. Ten minutes after the burial of the latest casualty, Dr Coleman found himself attending the birth of another child: 'born to a life of hardship,' he thought to himself.

*

The next few days were comparatively uneventful, and he hoped that all conflict was now at an end. Three casks of stout and a tin of sago were opened; a bottle of lime juice was used. The most dramatic event of that easy time involved allowing the passengers to brew their own tea, as they complained that the ship's cook did not make it well.

*

Dr Coleman went among the Norwegians and made a note of those who had trades.

Tradesmen among Norwegians
Mathias Larsen, Carpenter
Martin Larsen, Blacksmith
Charles Larsen, Shoemaker & Carpenter
Ole Engebretsen, Gunsmith & Watchmaker
Martin Andersen, Tailor

Andrew Neilsen, Carpenter
Niels Ostgaard, Saddler
Frederick Pedersen, Shoemaker
Ole Torstensen, Tailor

'Finally,' he thought, 'all is well and calm, and we can get on with the job,' and he allowed himself the luxury of a smile, the first for some days. Both Mrs Leigh and Miss Forsyth noticed that he was in a better frame of mind, and talked of it as they promenaded together in the late afternoon on the quarterdeck.

*

Saturday 17th September. The *Colinda* was 300 miles east northeast of Rio de Janeiro.

The passengers were bored; tempers frayed easily. An uneasy relationship existed between the Norwegians and the Scots. They tolerated each other, but there was always rivalry beneath the surface of the studied politeness which they used towards each other. There was a good breeze, and that kept the temperature above deck mercifully cooler than might have been expected, even in the early afternoon. Captain Mills stood on the fo'c's'le with Mir Birt; the crew, busy at work, avoided the Captain's gaze not wishing for his attention. At the other end of the *Colinda*, Dr Coleman stood on the poop deck watching a school of dolphins which followed in the ship's wake. It was the first moment he had had for some hours, having recently attended the deathbed of yet another child. The Doctor was having serious doubts about his doctoring abilities, and, knowing there could be no way out of his work for some time yet, those thoughts revolved ceaselessly in his head.

The Captain became aware of a disturbance on the main deck, and instantly he and the Chief Mate moved to find out what the noise was. A ring of emigrants, mostly men, stood blocking their way. Mr Birt elbowed his way through the crowd.

The passengers, initially objecting to being jostled, called out, 'Find yer own place,' 'Who do you think yer pushing,' 'Get out of it,' or other phrases of that sort, but they fell back when they saw who was thrusting them aside. The Captain followed the Mate, eyes flashing but with a deadly calm. At the centre of the ring, two men faced each other each with fists clenched. Scottish miner Thomas Easton, and Norwegian shoemaker Frederick Pedersen, neither of them built large, were both the worst for wear, one with a badly bruised eye, and the other with blood running along his jaw. Mr Birt strode between them, and with one gesture of his arms and fists drove them apart. Both men sprawled upon the deck. Mr Birt summoned the Boatswain who laid hold of Pederson, while he himself stood over Easton. The crowd dispersed somewhat, though a few, more curious than the others remained not too far off. The Captain directed that the two fighters should be taken onto the quarterdeck, where they were joined by the Doctor who had been made aware of matters by other members of the crew who had hurried to assist or to gawp.

On the quarterdeck the two men stood, breathless and wild. The Captain and the Doctor, for once in agreement, both berated them soundly, though without inquiring into the cause of the argument. Easton and Pedersen both promised not to repeat their bad behaviour, and were allowed to go each to their own berths.

Once they had gone, and the crew were all back at work, Captain Mills looked hard at Dr Coleman. 'Is this how you look after the welfare and discipline of your charges, Doctor? If so, I can't say that I admire your methods. Do better in the future, or I will be forced to make a report of the matter accordingly.'

The Doctor began to remonstrate, but before he had uttered two words, the Captain interrupted him, 'Remember who is Master here!' And with that, he strode off leaving Dr Coleman fuming.

*

For the next few days, the passengers kept themselves to themselves, and the Captain observed wryly that he kew how to keep control of his own ship. On Tuesday, it began to rain hard, and the passengers and children were ordered to stay below deck. The rain continued incessantly; the passengers fretted and the air below became close and unbearable.

Dr Coleman was tired to the bone, but, unable to sleep even when he found that his time was his own, he began to take stock of his own supplies, and discovering that two sheets and two blankets were missing, asked Mr Hawley the Second Mate to instigate a search for the missing items. There was no sign of them, and the Doctor resigned himself to their loss, promising himself to take better care of his property in the future. He felt disturbed about it since it meant that someone had been rummaging around in his cabin.

The rains stopped after a few days as suddenly as they had started. Once more the passengers were allowed above deck, and the Doctor noted in his log that they were all very much amused by catching some birds and then cooking and eating them. The cantankerous Mrs Brown, meanwhile, had suffered an epileptic fit, and was put under his care for a short time.

*

Sunday 2nd October: the Colinda was 300 miles northeast of the Falkland Islands.

Dr Coleman kept a careful note of all that happened: the emigrants continued to complain about the quality of the food supplied to them, some of the tinned meat had become unfit to be eaten as the tin had been carelessly soldered, and a baby girl had been born the previous day. The weather was growing noticeably colder day by day. The Captain held Divine Service in the large cabin where a swinging stove had been hung for a while; the smoke it produced had proved unbearable, so it had been moved to the hatchway where its warming effects were little felt. The service was very thinly attended, and even those who were there longed for it to end so that they could try better to keep warm.

The Captain had ordered the main topsail to be reefed, and the crew busied themselves with this and other matters. They were all supplied with warm clothing, and that, together with the activity of rolling the sail up kept them far warmer than the passengers, even though they were above deck and the passengers below.

The weather became still colder, and the sea friskier. Mrs Brown and Mrs Hunter renewed their old enmity and began to find excuses to argue. Their husbands left them to it, for it made their own lives easier if their wives were taking things out on each other rather than themselves. The Doctor was forced to intervene, upon which the two women rounded on him and warned him that there would be dire consequences if he did not keep out of their affairs. This he was not prepared to do, and finding their husbands enjoying a smoke together while watching their cronies playing cards, he lost his temper and ordered them to set about controlling their wives. Andrew Hunter and George Brown left to do as the Doctor ordered. For a moment, the Doctor gazed at the men who were still at their game before striding off himself. The card-players burst into roars of laughter once he had gone. The Doctor heard them, but disdained from giving them a piece of his mind, though he thought about it.

*

On Wednesday, another child died.

The sea was by now very rough. All the passengers stayed below. The crew worked mightily to keep the ship on course led by the Chief Mate, Mr Birt, for the Captain was rarely to be seen.

Captain Mills gave orders for a temporary fireplace to be installed in the dining cabin shared by the Doctor, the two ladies and himself, but the smoke it gave off was intolerable, and all but Captain Mills choked at each breath. Mrs Leigh suggested opening the cabin door, but the icy draught thus produced was worse than the smoke.

The Doctor tried to remonstrate with the Captain, 'Perhaps it might make things a trifle easier for the ladies if the carpenter installed a chimney to carry the smoke from the fireplace.'

'Damme, sir,' replied the Captain, 'do ye think that I can spare my carpenter's time for trifles such as that, or indeed any pipework to create a chimney for *your* comfort? No, Doctor, the wood on the Colinda is required for more pressing things than your requirements. The carpenter will make pipes at my command only, and that to keep the smoke clear of the spanker and the mizen mainsail. Do not presume on my good nature to think that you may command my crew. Remember who is Master here!'

The Captain left. Mrs Leigh turned to Miss Forsyth and shook her head. 'This cannot be permitted to continue,' she said.

Miss Forsyth would have answered her, but the Doctor silently motioned her to keep quiet, for he saw Captain Mills returning.

'I'll leave the cabin door open for you ladies,' he said, keeping his eyes firmly fixed on Dr Coleman. 'Don't feel that you need shut it.' Which was as good as saying that it must be left open and not shut on any account. And he left again.

*

Saturday 8th October: the *Colinda* was 280 miles south of Cape Horn, approximately one third of the distance between Cape

Horn and the South Shetland Islands, the northernmost islands of Antarctica, sailing due west through Drake Passage; weather, intensely cold—all the passengers, particularly the children, suffered badly: many were quite ill from it. The Doctor devoted much time and effort to keep them warm. Hot stones were suspended from the ceilings in order to produce some radiated heat, but they had little effect, and gave off sulphurous smoke which made everyone feel worse.

And in the private dining cabin, Miss Forsyth and Mrs Leigh felt the need for warmth more than most, for the Captain would rarely permit the door to be shut. The Doctor hung a blanket and quilt over a rail to help keep out the draught, but their teeth still chattered and their bodies shook no matter how many layers they wore.

Captain Mills had become more than unpleasant to those who shared this room with him. His behaviour disturbed them both mentally and physically. Sleeping was hard in the desperate cold, but the moment they managed to get some sleep in their own private rooms which led off the cabin, the Captain would start to make loud noises—bellowing for his steward to attend him, or slamming heavy books down onto the cabin table.

That evening, Dr Coleman boiled some water over the cabin fire to make hot rum and water for himself and the others. 'This will warm us all,' he said to the ladies. They were looking forward to it with great anticipation. As his preparations came to an end, Captain Mills entered together with a blast of icy air and slammed the cabin door shut.

'Would you like some fresh grog, Captain?' asked the Doctor, thinking of making peace between them all.

'Aye, I would,' replied the Captain, and taking the container from the doctor he drank it all down without pause for breath. 'That's mighty good,' he said coarsely, 'I'll have more of that.' and the Captain took to himself the bottle of rum and the small cask of water which served for them all, and proceeded to make more grog drinking it all as he did so, glass after glass until he was more than tipsy.

The others were quite disgusted with him. It was now 10 p.m. and they retired to bed, leaving him to his own devices. Captain Mills sat in a chair and drank on, heedless of the growing storm outside, for the *Colinda* had now entered into the most dangerous part of her voyage.

Half an hour later, there was a loud crash from inside the cabin. At almost the same moment came a loud knocking and calling from outside. Dr Coleman rushed into the cabin from his room. Mrs Leigh came out of her room a moment later. The Captain had fallen from the chair against Miss Forsyth's door, so she could not get out of her room. Urgent knocking from outside continued; the Doctor opened the door. The Captain's steward Luke stood there soaked to the skin and looking very shaken. 'If you please, Doctor, the Captain's wanted up on deck.'

The Doctor turned to Captain Mills who still lay sprawled on the cabin floor among broken glass and spilled grog—dead drunk!

5

The Inebriation of Captain Mills

The frightful noise and the dreadful pitching and tossing was beyond any experience or expectation of the passengers below. To a person they were horrified. Wails of distress were heard from all, man woman and child. None expected to last the night; all longed for the end, even Death itself would have been welcome to many. The sea crashed over the deck and found its way down to where they lay in their berths, clutching on to whatever they could find and to each other as the ship groaned and creaked.

Up above, Mr Hawley, the Second Mate, was in charge. Mr Birt, exhausted, had gone to his quarters to snatch a moment of whatever rest he could find. Hawley called out to one of the crew to summon the Captain, and that man had roused the Captain's Steward to fetch his master. And so, it was that Mr Luke had come upon the scene in the private cabin. With great difficulty, he and the Doctor together with one of the young midshipmen heaved the Captain up from the floor, and then carried him as best they could to his bed. The Captain lay there snoring, while the Doctor and Mr Luke tried to rouse him with slaps and shakes.

'This is no good at all,' shouted the Doctor over the thunderous noise outside, 'we'll have to let them know what's going on.' He grabbed at a piece of paper from the Captain's table, and hurriedly wrote a note in pencil. 'Here, he said to the boy, take this to the officer on the watch.'

The midshipman took the note, and staggered out of the cabin. The blinding rain lashed along the deck. He handed the note to Mr Hawley who was standing on the quarterdeck. 'Note from the Doctor, Sir,' he said loudly.

Hawley could not read the note where he stood. 'Mr Holligan,' he shouted, 'rouse Mr Birt, I'll look to this.' The boy went to fetch the Chief Mate, and Mr Hawley went himself to the Captain's cabin.

'What's happening, Doctor?'

'The Captain is unfit for duty just now, Mr Hawley. I'm afraid you'll have to do without him.'

'Damn!' said Hawley, leaving at once to take charge until Mr Birt came back on deck.

*

The *Colinda* was being carried further south by the Antarctic current. The temperature dropped still more, but the weather became somewhat calmer. There was no service on Sunday since the weather was still very bad. The Captain kept to his cabin the entire day nursing a headache. The ship was now closer to the Southern Shetland Islands than she was to Cape Horn, and had still not entered the Pacific Ocean. Yet another child died on Monday 10th October. The Doctor felt that she might not have done so had the parents followed his directions. Every death affected him, and there had been many, too many.

But the working life of the *Colinda* continued, though the behaviour of Captain Mills still troubled the three who shared his table. Something strange seemed to have happened to him. Always a difficult man, some of his decisions were now hard to explain, and he had the power to make himself unpleasant, very unpleasant, to anyone he chose.

On Tuesday morning the Doctor opened his cabin door and walked into the shared quarters. The quilt and blanket he had hung to keep out the draught had been taken down during the night, and an icy wind had made the room very cold. The Captain was sitting in a chair picking at his fingernails with a penknife, the quilt and blanket lay in a pile on the floor where they had been negligently dropped.

'I'll hang them again later, with your permission,' said the Doctor to Captain Mills, and he went out on his rounds.

When he returned some time later, the Captain was nowhere to be seen, but Mr Luke was standing on a chair just inside the doorway attacking the rail from which the coverings had been hung with a hammer and chisel.

'What are you about, Luke?' said the Doctor, more astounded than angry.

'Captain's orders, Doctor. The rail is to be removed so that nothing can be placed over it which might block the entrance,' replied Luke. 'I hope you'll enjoy the nice fresh air,' he added impudently under his breath but loud enough for the Doctor to hear.

And each day brought fresh niggles to the lives of the three who shared quarters with Captain Mills. On Wednesday evening the Captain ordered that the cabin fire be put out at 7 p.m., despite the freezing cold, and even though it had been kept lit every night up till then until 10 p.m. Dr Coleman and the two ladies did not know what to do, for 7 o'clock was too early to go to bed, and yet it was too cold to sit in the cabin. Mrs Leigh had the largest room, for she had her three very young children staying with her, and they suffered greatly. The Captain, though, seemed rather to enjoy the bitter temperature.

It was a burning cold which benumbed every limb. Below deck, the emigrants did their best to keep warm with vigorous movements and rubbings. The crew, though, seemed not to care too much. The Captain saw to it that they regarded him favourably by treating them to grog and other warming things. It must be said, though, that it seemed likely to the Doctor, who harboured great suspicions of the Captain, that the treats given to the crew came from the stores which had been marked out to be specifically for the passengers who did not seem to get enough of what was due them.

The Doctor had further complaints against the Captain, for he discovered that the latter was in the habit of interfering with his medical treatments of the passengers, asking them as he went round the *Colinda* how they were, how often they saw the Doctor, and if they were satisfied with him.

'I'm certain there is a better way of dealing with your trouble…' the Captain might say, and then explain his own medical theories, which always differed greatly from those of the Doctor. Since he was the Captain, and an impressive presence therefore, and since he always took great care on these occasions to express himself as if he were truly concerned, the other party would be convinced that the Doctor was wrong in his methods. The Doctor began to find himself quizzed by his patients who would express their opinions that he should be doing better for them.

Dr Coleman determined to have it out with Captain Mills, and duly sought him. 'Captain, I should care to know upon what right you interfere with me, my diagnoses and my treatments of my patients. The passengers are under my care, not yours. If I have need of your advice I will ask for it, but I do not need your advice. That is all.'

The Doctor's righteous indignation burned deep within him, and yet he felt unsatisfied by this confrontation. The Captain uttered not a word, and the two men stared at each other for a moment, after which Dr Coleman turned his back upon the other, and walked smartly away, feeling that he had put paid to the Captain's interference.

Captain Mills was a tactician, and, deeply resenting the way he had been spoken to, determined to be revenged upon Dr Coleman. 'I'll find proof of his incompetence, and then he had better watch out for squalls.'

6
Mary Seal's Leg

Between decks, the emigrants tried their best to lead normal lives, though normality for them had become perverted into a strange parody of existence. The children played with each other, and their shrieks and yells combined with the scoldings from their mothers. Captain Mills walked there on his own rounds of the *Colinda*. His steely eyes searched everywhere in an effort to find fault where he could.

Friday morning, the 14th of October—the sea was comparatively calm. Between decks, little Mary Seal was playing with a rag doll while her mother looked on as she sat mending a hole in her husband's spare trousers. The bitter cold made her task the harder as she could barely hold her needle. The Captain sat beside Mary and watched her for a moment.

'How did you get that graze on your leg, child?' Mary remained silent.

'Answer the Captain, Mary,' said her mother.

'I fell over and scraped it on the floor.'

'Did it hurt much?'

'Yes, I cried, didn't I, Mother?'

'She did,' said her mother to the Captain.

'How long ago did it happen?' he asked.

'The day before yesterday, I think,' said Mrs Seal.

'And what did the Doctor say when he saw it?'

'Oh, the Doctor hasn't seen Mary's leg, it's nothing at all, I shouldn't like to bother him with a trifle like that. I'm seeing to it myself.'

'Please take Mary to see the Doctor today,' said the Captain mildly, adding with affected concern, 'I shouldn't like there to be anything seriously wrong… I'm quite certain there isn't, but I should like him to see her, just to be on the safe side.'

Captain Mills stood, and took his leave of Mrs Seal and her daughter, walking away with an interesting twisted smile upon his lips.

William Sutherland, Dr Coleman's assistant, heard of this conversation, and reported it to the Doctor. Dr Coleman hardly knew what to do with himself when he heard what Sutherland had to say. He turned very pale, and then flushed with suppressed fury, but he was in the middle of examining another of the sick children, and though he burned with a desire for an instant confrontation with Captain Mills, he had no choice but to delay.

'I'll see the Captain later, and I'll need you to come with me,' he said to Sutherland. 'I may find you useful.'

So that afternoon, Dr Coleman, with Sutherland in tow, sought out Captain Mills to have another word with him. The Captain had not felt the need to seek the Doctor, being content to bide his time—knowing full well that the Doctor would soon hear of his conversation with Mrs Seal and little Mary.

On his way to see the Captain, the Doctor became aware of shouting from inside one of the messes. Others were there before him, and the fight which had broken out had already been stopped when he arrived at the scene. Two men stood glaring at each other, Alexander Watt, a thick-set Scottish man, and Honeyman, the emigrant's cook.

'What's the meaning of this?' said the Doctor loudly to Watt. 'I'm really tired of this kind of behaviour. It's bad enough looking after everyone's health on this tub without having to check you for violence.' He had lost his temper, which was unusual, but he was under great stress at that moment.

'It's that sodding idiot there giving us food that a pig wouldn't eat if it was starving!' said Watt, vigorously rubbing a large bruise which was appearing on the side of his face.

Honeyman, a small man was trembling all over. Somehow, he had managed to get the better of the fight, though the other man was so much more powerful. 'It's just not true, Doctor, and it's not my fault, I only cook what is given me.'

Dr Coleman left with these words, 'I'll look into this later. Don't let this happen again, or I'll ask the Captain to put you both in irons.'

*

The Captain was standing by the cabin table examining a large chart of the Pacific Ocean and was apparently concentrating deeply. The Doctor marched boldly in, and stood before him. Captain Mills continued to gaze down as if unaware that anyone else was present. William Sutherland remained just outside the cabin.

Eventually, the Doctor spoke. 'Captain Mills, I thought we had agreed that you were not to quiz my patients or indeed any of the passengers regarding medical matters,' he said with studied restraint.

'Did we?' responded the Captain, 'I have no recollection of such an agreement between us, or, indeed, any agreement.'

'Did you or did you not speak to Mrs Seal about her daughter?' persisted the Doctor, choosing to ignore the Captain's remark.

'Dr Coleman, I must tell you that it has become necessary for me to take a firm hand upon matters with regard to your practice on the *Colinda*. You have not done your duty! In the case of the Seal girl it is evident that you have been sorely remiss. How is it, Doctor, that you were unaware of her injury? You carry on your little visits oblivious to what is happening about you. You have now heard of the incident in which this child was injured. Go now and do your duty better!'

'I do not know, sir, how you can have such effrontery to speak to me in this tone of voice. I am not under your command, but I am in charge of the welfare of the passengers on this vessel. Your charge against me is most unwarranted. The nature of this case as has now been reported to me is of such slight importance according to the mother that to make issue of it in this fashion is quite ridiculous.'

Dr Coleman signalled for Sutherland to enter, and instructed him to fetch Mrs Seal instantly. While he and the Captain waited, an icy silence was maintained, broken only by the crew calling to each other as they worked. The sea was becoming more boisterous now. Mrs Seal was brought in by Sutherland; she stared at the Captain and the Doctor in turn, not knowing the reason she had been summoned.

'Take note of everything, William,' said the Doctor to Sutherland, handing him his notebook and a pencil. 'Mrs Seal,' he then said, 'with regard to the graze on Mary's leg, does it bleed?'

'No, Doctor, it never did.'

'Has it caused her much discomfort?'

'No, sir.'

'Were the other passengers aware of it, aside from your husband, I mean.'

'No sir, for it was covered by her dress.'

'Would I have been aware of it if I had seen her.'

'No, sir, for it was covered.'

Here the Captain interjected, 'But I saw it, though it was covered.'

'Yes,' said Mrs Seal, 'but Mary was sitting with her dress not pulled down over her knees.'

Mrs Seal stood for a moment, and then, realising that the interview was at an end, left. Dr Coleman took his notebook from Sutherland. 'Understand, Captain,' he said, 'I have made these notes so that I might be protected from any false charges you might choose to make against me. Sutherland here will sign his name to them as witness.'

The Doctor left with Sutherland following. The Captain looked thoughtful. 'Protected... Is that what you think, Doctor?' he said to himself, 'We will have to see about that, won't we?'

7
Cheese and Biscuits

Captain Mills sat at his desk in his own cabin. His sleeping quarters were comfortable, though basic. Before him lay a sheet of paper, an inkwell and a pen. He stretched his arms out wide and expanded his chest, and then with a sigh of satisfaction picked up the pen, dipped it into the ink, and began to write.

*

Notice is hereby given that no meals are to be taken after 8 p.m. and furthermore that cheese is only to be eaten at dinner which must end no later than 8 p.m.

Signed JP Mills, Captain of the *Colinda*

*

He copied the notice out twice more, and then called for his steward. 'Luke, kindly see that two of these notices are posted up in the messes, and that the other is posted in my own dining cabin.' It was a small thing, but he calculated well that these small annoyances would rebound more upon the head of Dr Coleman than upon himself. And so his campaign had begun.

*

Sunday 16th October, the *Colinda* had almost rounded Cape Horn.

Dr Coleman wrote in his logbook of yet another death among the children. It had been an unpleasant and lingering illness, and no one was surprised. The parents, however, had a few sharp words for the Doctor regarding his treatment of their son, and he, though he felt that he had truly done all he could, kept quiet and listened to what they had to say.

It had become evident to him that the emigrants were losing their respect for him, and he laid this to one cause only, namely the open disrespect shown to him by Captain Mills, who now made a habit of undermining him at every opportunity both in his presence and out of it. Once more, the Doctor sought out the Captain, with the intention of forming a more pleasant relationship.

The two men stood before each other in the cabin, and the Doctor began. 'Captain, may I request that you do not overstep your duty or have words with me on any professional subject? I say this with all due respect to your natural authority on the *Colinda*. You must know that should I be anxious for your assistance on medical matters, I will write you a note to that effect. I hope after this, we may remain on more friendly terms than heretofore.'

Dr Coleman offered the Captain his hand in friendship, and Captain Mills took it, saying as he did so, 'I thank you for your condescension in this matter'. The two men parted: Dr Coleman feeling somewhat relieved, the Captain with other thoughts. Dr Coleman's naivety in this may, perhaps, be excused on account of his youth.

*

Captain Mills walked between decks examining everything he pleased. Talking to the women, chucking the children under their chins and ruffling their hair, opening boxes, looking into the passengers' rooms, and generally making it known that he was a most benevolent leader, but that he was, indeed, the Master of the *Colinda*. Many tried to avoid his notice, the women in particular, for he had a way of speaking to them which made them uncomfortable with his suggestiveness, for his language could be lewd and loose.

'Good day, Ellen,' he said to Mrs Sutherland, one of the younger women aboard he found more attractive than most. Her husband was not present, as he was assisting the Doctor in the hospital at that moment, Ellen Sutherland was still attending the needs of Mrs Leigh and was on her way to see her. She looked around her for moral support, but found that all the other women seemed to have disappeared.

'Good day, Captain Mills,' she replied, 'I'm just on my way to see Mrs Leigh.'

'Wait a moment,' said the Captain. 'I wonder that you feel the need to attend to her, you were surely made for better things.'

'Now really, Captain, I must go…'

'Tell me Ellen, you have no children? Have you thought about how many you might like to have?'

Now this last remark was said with a kind of twist in the voice which held an implication that was unmistakeable, and Ellen Sutherland flushed with anger and embarrassment.

'I think that's enough, now,' she said. 'You can have nothing to say to me that my husband should not be able to hear,' She pushed past him, and quickly left. Captain Mills smiled sardonically; at that moment two others came into view, and he went back up on deck to smoke his pipe.

★

The freezing weather continued. The Scottish passengers in particular were having a very hard time of it. Many had bad feet and complained bitterly that they had not felt any warmth for weeks. The Captain's orders regarding cheese and eating times were adhered to with ill grace by most of the passengers, and matters were not helped by the observation that the ship's crew seemed to be treated far better than they were. The deck was often slippery with ice and slush, which returned almost as fast as it was cleared; some of the crew had torn the skin from the palms of their hands after they had torn them from the ship's rimy rigging. Between decks, the passengers were deeply unhappy.

Dr Coleman once again bore the brunt of complaints, this time regarding ship's biscuits. He was in the hospital busily tidying his tools when there was a knock at the door and two of the emigrants, John Miller and Jacob Wilson entered.

'What can I do for you gentlemen?' he asked with little enthusiasm, for he was tired after a hard day, and he was tired of hearing nothing but complaints wherever he went.

'It's like this, Doctor,' said Jacob Wilson, 'we have noticed that we, the passengers, are given only small and broken biscuits for our rations, whereas the best and whole biscuits get selected out and are given to the crew.'

'Are you certain of this, Jacob? I was not aware that the crew are fed out of the same stores as the passengers. Who is it that sorts them in this fashion?'

'The stewards, Doctor,' said Miller. 'Not only food, but the water which supplies your cabin is meant for us passengers alone.'

This too was a surprise to the Doctor, for it was laid down in the ship's charter that the water for the Captain's cabin, and by extension for himself, Miss Forsyth, and Mrs Leigh and her children, were to be from a separate supply so as not to deprive the passengers.

'Thank you for bringing this to my attention, though I am not sure if I can be of much help. Is there anything more?' said the Doctor, regretting the question as soon as he had asked it, as he felt certain there would be more, and he would rather not hear anything else just then.

'Indeed there is,' said Wilson. 'The rice we are given to eat is quite spoiled, and we cannot eat it.'

'That is unacceptable if true,' said Dr Coleman, 'I will look into that at once.' He went to the stores to examine the rice sack currently open, and found that the contents were mildewed and fermenting as the bottom had become wet. He ordered the sack to be thrown overboard and a fresh one to be opened.

Then, hoping for a moment's rest, he went back to his room to lie down if only for a minute. It was not to be, however, for there were so many other passengers with complaints of their own regarding rations of one sort or another, that it was fully two hours before he could rest.

The matter of the biscuits came to a head the next day, for another passenger, James Frew, declared to the Doctor that he had seen Mr Luke going into the store room, open kegs of bread belonging to the emigrants, and pick out the whole biscuits so that they might be served to the Captain. Dr Coleman informed the Captain of this. Luke was questioned, but denied any wrongdoing. The accusation was proved against him, however, and the Captain berated him in the Doctor's presence. Dr Coleman's mind was put to rest by this; the Captain only regretted that Luke had been caught.

Dr Coleman soon found that his satisfaction was premature. Robert Ewart and John McIntyre came to him to say that the crew were now being served with all their provisions out of the passenger's stores. The Doctor felt overwhelmed by it all, and longed for the voyage to end.

The two men stood there looking at him.

'We know it's not your fault, Doctor,' said McIntyre, 'It's that de'il of a Captain. I'd soon tell him what I thought o' him if I had the chance.'

'Take no notice of him,' said Ewart afraid that someone else might have heard. 'He's always braggin', he's a real bugger!'

They left Dr Coleman to his own devices, all three feeling that there was no solution to their problems on the horizon.

★

At 7 p.m. that evening, as dinner was served in the private cabin, the Captain asked a question of the Doctor in the most ingratiating manner. 'Tell me Doctor, are you supposed to be taking the same rations as the emigrants aboard this ship, or are you indeed supposed to be eating here with us?'

This was so unexpected that Dr Coleman did not know for a moment what to say. He was instantly on his guard, for the question was couched in unfriendly words however pleasantly put.

'No, Captain,' he responded eventually, 'I am not supposed to be dining with the passengers, and it was the company's express intention that I dine here.' Underneath this, his thoughts were different:

'Crafty bastard! He wants to take over my ration for himself!' and the Doctor nodded and smiled pleasantly at Captain Mills.

★

The next morning there was another fight. This time it was a quarrel about the fire and cooking arrangements, for the passengers were allowed to take turns at cooking some of their own meals. The Captain had arranged it in such a way that it would always be known who had been cooking last and what they had cooked. This had been done because some beef had been stolen and eaten .

Andres Hansen and John Paton each wanted to cook, but could not agree who should be first to do so, both having arrived there at the same moment, and neither willing to defer to the other. The argument was brought before Dr Coleman, who promised to speak to the Captain about it, feeling that in this case he could not overrule the current system. In point of fact he had no intention of speaking to the Captain about this matter, and that for two reasons: firstly because there had been enough conflict between them already, and secondly because he thought the system to be for the best.

There were other problems on his mind which he felt to be far more pressing. The ship had been supplied with a salt-water distilling apparatus, which was supposed to produce fresh water from seawater. In theory this was a wonderful idea, however, the mechanism didn't work. The steam produced would not condense effectively because the refrigerator was too close to the boiler, and the water produced was almost as saline as that which was put in. Fresh water for drinking was strictly rationed as a result; even so, supplies were rapidly diminishing. All passengers and crew felt thirsty most of the time.

In the afternoon, up on deck, a punishment was in progress. One of the ship's apprentices, Master Barrett, was being flogged with a rope's end by the Boatswain by order of the Captain. Some of the male passengers had gathered round to watch. Barrett, jaw set in a grimace at the end of his ordeal, stood before Captain Mills.

'Keep your hands away from your eyes, boy,' said the Captain, 'and think on before you try your monkey tricks on anyone else. Now, up with you to the top of the mizen mast, and be quick about it. That'll teach him a lesson he won't forget in a hurry, eh, Mr Birt?'

Barrett began his ascent, his crime a mystery to the onlookers. The emigrants seemed to sympathise with the lad. 'If that boy falls, he'll kill himself,' said John McIntyre loudly to Archie Galloway.

'Who said that?' said the Captain, whirling round to face the emigrants.

'I did, and what of it?' said McIntyre who was a burly fellow and refused to be cowed.

'Get below to your cabin now!' ordered the Captain.

McIntyre left, but the Captain followed him down to his cabin.

'I will not have you interfering with my crew and discipline on my ship,' he shouted at McIntyre with his face in the other man's face. 'That is an offence for which you will be fined £2 and perhaps put in gaol.'

*

Sunday 23rd October, the *Colinda* was in the Pacific Ocean— about 500 miles west southwest of Cape Horn.

More food was discovered to have been stolen by persons unknown, for a ham was found to have been half-eaten. Everybody suspected everyone else of being the thief, and tensions ran high. Dr Coleman was frantically trying to resolve another situation, for it had come to his attention that the passengers were not being allowed any of the poultry which had been intended for their meals, but that the cabin steward, Luke, was helping himself to that supply since he had a key to the storeroom. Tension between passengers and crew was running high, and the Doctor seemed to spend most of his spare time trying to pour oil on troubled waters, though with little success.

Captain Mills, meanwhile, gave every appearance of enjoying the discomfiture of Dr Coleman, relishing every opportunity to best him, heaping irritation upon irritation. That evening, Mrs Leigh drew the Doctor aside in order to have a private conversation with him.

She began in a whisper, but at that very moment, there was a disturbance outside the cabin, and she was obliged to raise her voice so that the Doctor could hear her.

'Doctor, the Captain is saying wicked things about you, you can't imagine,' she began.

'I can indeed,' interrupted the Doctor. 'What's the latest?'

'That you would not allow the passengers any wood to make fire, though the weather is so cold. He is telling them all that the cold they suffer is your fault.'

The Doctor became most indignant at this intelligence. 'It is a lie…'

'I know it is,' said Mrs Leigh, 'but there are many who believe it to be true.'

The conversation might have continued further, but neither of them had noticed that Captain Mills had entered the cabin. He had overheard most of what had been said, and was determined not to let any chance of undermining the Doctor to be missed.

'What's all this?' he bellowed. 'How dare you, madam, repeat such falsehoods? You know, Doctor, this lady has such a contempt for you, that she herself told the cabin boy that you were not to be trusted. Deny it if you will, madam!'

'I do deny it,' said Mrs Leigh, almost in tears. 'It is you yourself, Captain, whose behaviour creates antagonism among us all. How can you say such things?' She turned to the Doctor, 'Don't believe him,' she said, 'call Lambert, and ask him if I said any such thing to him.'

Lambert the cabin boy at that moment happened to enter, but the Captain sent him away with a wave of his hand. 'I'll not have you question my authority,' he bellowed at Mrs Leigh. 'You need to know your place.' Then, lowering his voice somewhat, 'In future, madam, you shall not have your meals at my table, but with the steerage passengers. You may cook your own food, madam, and let that be a lesson that will teach you not to bandy words with me. I will give directions that the steward will supply you your rations uncooked. Your children, madam, may eat food with you.'

The spitefulness of this last remark was not missed by Mrs Leigh, who stood stock still, aghast at the awful thought of mucking in with the other passengers at mealtimes.

'You think yourself too much the fine lady to eat with the rest,' said Captain Mills, understanding what was going through her mind. 'You will soon learn better.'

Dr Coleman felt dizzy. Unable to utter a word of protest at that moment, he felt himself to be clutching at air. The Captain's aspect and demeanour were so intimidating that he could only gulp and splutter. Mrs Leigh gave an inarticulate cry, and left the cabin to seek Miss Forsyth who she felt certain would offer support and sympathy; Captain Mills turned to Dr Coleman.

'Have the goodness to follow my instructions in this matter,' he said with a fixed look at him, 'I will not be crossed or accused of lying; my word is as good as anyone else's. You, Doctor, have been too busy fostering discontent among the passengers who now mutter against me. Do not think that I have not heard the women muttering after I speak, "it's a lie, it's a lie, it's a lie." That is your doing, and I will not have it.'

At that moment Miss Forsyth entered the cabin.

'What is going on?' she demanded.

'As for you, madam,' said the Captain disdainfully, 'I counsel you to mend your lascivious ways, (oh yes, I have noticed your behaviour), and mind your own business in the future!'

'This is too insulting, Captain, I will not stay here a moment longer. I certainly will not be taking any more meals in your company!' and she rushed out of the cabin, calling out as she did so, 'I don't know how you can stay, Doctor!'

'Do as you please, madam,' said the Captain to thin air. 'I, for one, will not care. There will be no females at my table on this ship at any rate, and that will be a comfort.'

The Captain looked at the Doctor, and then turned on his heels and made to leave the cabin, stopping at the door and turning to the Doctor to make one last remark: 'Remember, Mrs Leigh is to take no food or drink here.'

8
'The Doctor is a Vagabond'

It is a matter of common experience that one only thinks of a reply to unjust remarks when it is too late. Dr Coleman was left fuming. With pounding heart and a bitter taste in his mouth he began rehearsing in his mind all the things he could and should have said and done, murmuring some remarks out loud, crescendoing to loud exclamations, and then dropping his voice in case he should be heard. He retired to bed early that evening, so as to avoid any confrontation with the Captain, or the embarrassment of being forced to meet the resentful gaze of Mrs Leigh who he felt certain would hold him, in part, responsible for her downfall. Mrs Leigh returned to her room, for she still had access to that, with her children once she was sure that the Captain was not in the cabin. Miss Forsyth had been sympathetic and indignant, but had offered little advice. When the Captain returned to the cabin, only Miss Forsyth was there, and she, as soon as she saw him enter, retired to her room.

'Good riddance,' said Captain Mills out loud as he sat down. He pulled a bottle of brandy towards him and poured himself a large tumblerful.

✶

Dr Coleman spent a sleepless night arguing, in his mind, with Captain Mills about his treatment of Mrs Leigh and of himself.

The following day dawned; he had decided to try again to make peace with Captain Mills, and to offer his cooperation. With freezing hands he wrote a note to the Captain to that effect. That note went unread, for Captain Mills, upon being handed the letter by Mr Luke, tore it into tiny scraps, and allowed them to flutter away in the wind.

Dr Coleman, meanwhile, began his duties, though he felt unwell that morning. The wind up on deck was more than usually biting, and his tiredness due to lack of sleep put him out of sorts. On reaching the hospital he dragged a chair from a corner and sat near his dispensary cupboard wishing that it had been better supplied so that he might dose himself with a tonic that would not send him to sleep. He poured a small amount of lime juice into a glass and drank it. The acid taste made him wince, but his head still pounded, and he held it in his hands with his eyes shut. On opening them, he was not best pleased, therefore, to find William Sutherland standing before him staring at him as if he were out of his mind.

'What is it, William?' asked the Doctor tersely.

'Only this, Doctor: my wife has told me, begging your pardon, that she and some of the other married women on the *Colinda*…'

'Out with it man, for heaven's sake! And stop shuffling around as if you had scabies.'

'It's the Captain, Doctor. He speaks to the women in a most disgusting way, even to my own wife.'

Sutherland related details of the conversation the Captain had had with Ellen some days before. She had only just been able to bring herself to tell him of it, he said, and that only because other women had been made to feel uncomfortable by the Captain's importuning of them.

'I know, William, that the Captain calls the woman by their Christian names, and it may seem too familiar, but surely that is just his way.'

'Doctor, you may think he is simply joking when he speaks in such a way, but I tell you there is more to it. Many of the men will not speak to the Captain, and that cannot be natural. I will not speak to him either. My wife would have struck him if he had not been who he is.'

'Thank you for sharing this with me, Will,' said the Doctor, 'I know that was hard. I'm not sure what can be done about it at the moment, but I will take note and keep my eyes open.'

*

Dr Coleman had a number of patients to attend to, some in the hospital, and others in their cabins. Both Mary and Joseph Featherstone, husband and wife, married only three days before the *Colinda* had embarked, were suffering with syphilis. The Doctor had separated them as soon as this had become known to him; they had been fighting like cat and dog, for each blamed the other.

It was reported to him later that day that three of the Norwegians had berths which frequently were soaked by seawater. The Doctor wrote a note to Captain Mills requesting that the ship's carpenter be asked to make the necessary repairs, for despite their dislike of each other, they were obliged to work together, and the Doctor in particular was determined to avoid quarrels with the Captain if at all possible. The carpenter reported to Captain Mills that the repairs would be impossible, and the Captain relayed this back to the Doctor in a haughty note stating that more advance notice of such matters was required.

*

On Tuesday morning there was news that almost a whole sheep, and a large piece of cooked pork had been stolen from the poop deck where they had been kept in a locked cupboard,

225

and a cask of biscuits which was kept in the cabin had been half emptied.

The Captain told the Doctor of it over breakfast. 'The padlock securing the meat store was rudely broken, and for this the emigrants are to blame,' he said. 'You must find out who the guilty parties were and report their names to me, for I will not have such behaviour on my ship.'

The biscuits, though, were more worrying to him because it meant that someone had been in their cabin when all were asleep.

'And now I have something else to say, Doctor. I wish you would not have Sutherland attend on you now that these things have happened.'

Dr Coleman felt this merely to be an excuse to inconvenience him as Sutherland had become of enormous help to him, tidying his room, carrying out and emptying his slops, as well as helping in the hospital. Luke was supposed to do these things, but had been of little use.

'Very well, Captain, with your approval I shall ask Lambert to attend me.'

'There is more, Doctor. I wish Ellen Sutherland to be prohibited from attending Mrs Leigh, for she cannot need her any longer.'

'I cannot allow that, Captain. Mrs Leigh is in a more difficult position than ever now that she is no longer permitted to eat with us. She has two children and a suckling baby with her, and you have insisted that she prepare her own food from its raw state. No, Captain, she has every need of Ellen Sutherland.'

Later in the morning, the Doctor took a casual stroll to the poop deck to look at the store room and the padlock. 'There is more to this than meets the eye; it is most curious,' he remarked to himself, 'the padlock was broken, but there is no damage to the staple to which it was attached or to the surrounding wood. Furthermore, to break the lock and to carry off a sheep must have taken some time, and it is strange that the culprit was not seen by the officer on watch, the man at the wheel or the midshipman who is always there on duty.'

There had been no moon the previous night, and that, thought the Doctor might account for the success of the thievery from the poop deck, but he still felt uncomfortable in his mind.

Lambert, the cabin boy, was in the cabin, setting the table for lunch when the Doctor entered.

'Did you see anything last night?' the Doctor asked him.

'Well, sir, I did go out at one time last night, because nature called, and on my way back from the head I did see a man in the cabin who rushed past me and knocked me over onto my back.'

'Indeed,' said the Doctor, 'can you describe him?'

'Well, he was half a head taller than me, wore a short coat, woollen trousers, heavy boots, and a black sou'wester.'

'It beats me how could you have seen all that, Lambert, seeing as the night was so dark, and that you were knocked over onto your back.'

'I could feel the material of his trousers as he went by me, and, and, and…'

But at that moment the Captain called out for Lambert, and the boy left quickly, relieved at avoiding the Doctor's further questions.

*

The Doctor once alone, made the following note in his journal:

Everything is now presenting a most painful aspect, the cabin is a perfect Hell. The table is deserted, formerly it was occupied and enlivened by the ladies' society, but now every face there is long and serious. The Captain, myself and Mr Birt are the only ones there, scarcely a sentence is uttered by anyone. If I make a remark I am just answered and that is all. Each one appears to be wrapped in his own mysterious reverie and shows an annoyance to be unearthed out of it.

⋆

Towards noon, Captain Mills took two pistols into his room where he handled them gently as if they were objects of great beauty. Going out onto the deck, he pointed one purposefully over the side and fired it. Everyone nearby froze at the sound, but the Captain merely turned and went back inside. The male passengers there began to talk animatedly among themselves, scowling all the while, and with occasional glances towards the cabin door. They had all conceived a great hatred for Captain Mills, but felt helpless. Dr Coleman, arriving on deck soon after, was met with a barrage of questions regarding the Captain's erratic behaviour. 'Does he mean to shoot us?' 'Is it his intention to act as a tyrant over us?' 'Does he accuse us of stealing the meat?' The Doctor could answer none of them, and hurried past.

Greater disturbance still was created when one of the men reported that he had seen Lambert in the Captain's cabin, walking about with a loaded pistol on his shoulder. Over the next few hours the men continued to meet together in groups of eight or nine. Dr Coleman found that whenever he approached to find out the subject of such vehement conversations, all talk would suddenly cease, and the men disperse in various directions. He dreaded the outcome of the unrest.

⋆

The very next morning The Doctor was on the main deck talking with three of the men who were drawing provisions out of the hatchway and doing his best to allay their fears, though he felt like a hypocrite to be doing so.

'We can hardly credit your explanation of the situation, Doctor,' said Thomas McMurtrie. 'The man must be out of his mind.' The others nodded in agreement. 'He thinks it would be better that the ship should sink,' he continued, 'I heard him say so, and I was not the only one to hear him.' The Doctor was about to answer, when, from on the quarterdeck, the voice of Captain Mills, speaking in fierce answer to the Chief Mate, could be heard.

'The Doctor is a vagabond, Mr Birt. He hides up all day with that gal, and has let half the children die with his neglect.'

9
A Spy

Dr Coleman flushed upon hearing the Captain's words. The three passengers stood stock still, the Doctor immediately left them and hurried into the cabin. Captain Mills could only have been referring to Miss Forsyth as 'that gal', and Dr Coleman was determined to warn her of this accusation.

But here we must pause a moment to consider the Captain's words. For, though we surely cannot doubt that Dr Coleman was truly dedicated to the welfare of the passengers, is it possible that he had formed a less than professional relationship with Miss Forsyth? They were, after all, often in each other's company and a long way from home and home comforts. It is true that in private they called each other by their Christian names, though Dr Coleman had asked her to use his third name, Alex, but perhaps we should not judge too harshly two lonely people who found themselves thrust together.

Mina Forsyth took great exception to the Doctor's revelation of the Captain's little speech.

'How dare he say such things, Alex? I've a good mind to tell him what I think of him!'

'Don't even think of it. I wouldn't have told you, but I think he may be dangerous. He certainly would be if crossed.'

Dr Coleman resolved to have a written testimonial signed by some of the passengers, in particular those whose children had died during the voyage, stating their satisfaction with his treatment of themselves and their families. 'I must have some way of guarding myself against any future accusations the Captain might make against me,' he told Miss Forsyth.

But deep down he worried more about the Captain's intentions towards the emigrants, for if he truly believed that it would be better if the ship should sink, that could only mean that he was considering defrauding the insurers; and worse still, it might mean that he set the value of life at nothing.

★

The Captain continued to make himself unpleasant at mealtimes, finding any excuse to pick an argument; his temper had worsened to such a degree that no one dared approach him. However, he kept himself to himself for much of the time, and that was a great relief to all.

Dr Coleman, meantime, continued his work. In the evening he was visited by Mrs Hunter. She seemed upset, and though the Doctor was not, in point of fact, an approachable person, being too conscious of his position of authority on board and the need to maintain it, he listened to what she had to say with a convincing pretense of sympathy.

'About six weeks ago,' she said, 'I cannot positively state the day, I was sitting on the quarter deck between eight and nine o'clock in the evening; I was crying. When Captain John Powell Mills came up to me and laid hold of my head, and enquired of me what was the matter, I told him that I was unhappy because I had lost my baby. He then said, "Oh! Never mind that, If you come into my cabin any night after ten o'clock when the lights are out, I will soon get you another." I was quite disgusted with his speech, but since then, I see him watching me, and it makes me very uncomfortable.'

'Why do you only tell me this now, Mrs Hunter?'

'I am afraid that my husband may do something foolish; I told him what happened, and he is very angry about it.'

'I know this is difficult for you, so I will talk to your husband, and persuade him to do nothing.'

'Oh, would you, that will be a relief? Thank you, Doctor.' And she left.

Dr Coleman added this new task to his list. This latest intelligence of the Captain's behaviour didn't surprise him, but it added to his worries. 'Just let us get safely to Canada,' he thought, 'that is all, and then I can be away from the wretch.'

The following evening found him inside his own cabin writing in his logbook. It was the only place he could find privacy, though it did mean balancing the book on his wash stand. Miss Forsyth sat in her cabin with the door open, reading her bible, stopping every so often to rub her hands together for warmth. Mrs Leigh and her children were nowhere to be seen. The Captain was in his own room.

A little later Lambert went into the Captain's cabin. They spoke to each other in low voices.

'Just go and see will you, Lambert,' said Captain Mills.

'Aye, aye, sir.'

A noise outside his room caused Dr Coleman to open the door slightly to look into the main cabin and see if anyone was there. As he did so Lambert came out of the Captain's cabin and peeped into Miss Forsyth's room surreptitiously. He then returned to the Captain, and the Doctor heard him say from just outside the Captain's door, 'No, sir, he is not.' From this, he assumed that Lambert had been sent to find out if he (the Doctor), was ensconced with Miss Forsyth in her cabin: for the Captain had surely hoped that they would be discovered canoodling together.

Not willing to countenance someone spying on his movements, the Doctor called out to Lambert in a brave voice, 'Are you looking for me, Lambert?' And then without waiting for an answer added, 'Miss Forsyth, did you see young Lambert peep into your cabin just now?'

Lambert was so embarrassed by this that he made good his escape as quickly as he could. The Captain merely closed his own door and chose to ignore the Doctor's indignation.

Very much later that evening, Doctor Coleman and Miss Forsyth might, indeed, have been found together in Miss Forsyth's cabin and in her bed where they made great effort to see that their lovemaking was quiet. Mina had told her lover that she had left her home to escape an unbearable life, and he had determined to make it more bearable for both their sakes.

'How will this end?' she asked him.

'Everything will be fine as long as no one finds out,' was his answer.

He slept, and she lay awake for a long time. After a while he stirred and she woke him.

'You must go back to your own room now,' she said, and he left her silently.

*

Sunday 30th October dawned. During the night a pig died. The ever decreasing livestock on board had been a bone of contention throughout the voyage as the passengers were all convinced that the food intended for them was feeding Captain and crew. Captain Mills declared that the pig must have been poisoned out of spite by one of the emigrants, and had it thrown overboard before the Doctor was able to carry out a post mortem.

'I must tell you, Doctor,' said the Captain, 'I myself am certain that someone has been trying to poison me also. My tea tasted most strange the other day. Do you ever leave your medicine chest open?'

'Never! If it happens again you must let me know at once so that I can make a proper diagnosis from examining any symptoms you may have.' Dr Coleman could not understand why the Captain had made such a statement, unless it was part of another scheme to discredit him.

That day, only one person attended Divine Service, and that because the passengers were all busy cooking. Until recently, they had cooked their Sunday meals the previous day, but the Captain, in order to annoy them, had forbidden this practice.

*

Was it a need to control or just bloodymindedness that gave rise to the Captain's behaviour, obsessed as he was with making everyone uncomfortable? Surely this arose from an unhappiness with his own life and a need to make others as unhappy as he. An obsession amounting to a monomania was exacerbated by continuous reliance on alcohol which he used to supply anaesthesia for the mind—to dull the heaviness that existed within. He drank without tasting the liquor, for the taste was of little interest to him. Moreover, though he would never have admitted to himself that he could be envious, his belief that the Doctor had formed an amorous connection with Miss Forsyth made him wild with envy, for, unusually, he had found no solace himself in female company on this voyage.

Captain Mills presented a wild and unkempt appearance. His beard which he had previously kept clipped and neat was wild and tangled. Mr Birt came to see him in his cabin shortly before one o'clock in the afternoon, for he had been summoned there. The Captain was sitting at his desk. He spoke tonelessly of strange things.

'Last night I dreamed of Death. Not of being dead or of the act of dying, but of Death as an entity, a being I could not escape. Wherever I ran, I saw him. Finally, I was cornered, and he spoke to me with a voice smooth as silk. "You see me; only the Dead can see me. If you see me, then you too are dead, and you must come with me." He reached out his hand to take me, and I woke. I tell you, Mr Birt, I fear no man nor no thing, not even Death itself; but my heart went cold as stone. Pass me that bottle.'

'Don't you think that's unwise, Captain?'

'Pass me that bottle, I say. Mr Birt, I do not appreciate your manner towards me. Your time here may be coming to an end.'

The Chief Mate made no response, but watched the Captain glumly. Captain Mills was silent for some time; his hands wandered idly over the desk top as if mapping out some fantastic course for the *Colinda* upon a sea of mahogany.

Eventually he spoke again, his voice hoarse after gulping down a glass of brandy. 'Mr Birt, I wish to know if, in your opinion, passengers who are not ill should be permitted to take their meals in their private cabins.'

'I should say not, Captain.'

'Thank you, Mr Birt, that will be all. Should you see Mr Luke, kindly send him to me.'

Mr Birt left, and Luke, who was waiting close by, duly appeared.

'Mr Luke,' said Captain Mills, 'you will see to it that Miss Forsyth does not take her meals in her own room, but only at table with the Doctor and me. You are to carry no dinner into her cabin, you understand. If she wants any, she must come to table.'

'Aye, aye, sir.' And Luke, too, left.

'And that will put paid to your high-and-mighty ways, Miss!' said the Captain to himself as he poured himself another glass.

*

In his determination to air his grievances and to show his superiority, Captain Mills summoned the Doctor to his cabin for an interview which he intended to make as unpleasant as possible. At five minutes past eight o'clock in the evening, therefore, Dr Coleman presented himself to the Captain.

'Now, Doctor,' began the Captain quietly, 'Lambert tells me that you have accused him of spying for me… say nothing, I am speaking. I will have you know that I do not resort to such petty means as that to achieve my ends. Do not presume to reach too high, Doctor. Remember, people who soar up in the clouds sometimes receive thunderbolts!'

'Captain, I do not wish to argue with you, I only go by facts. I saw Lambert leave your cabin, and look in Miss Forsyth's cabin. If you both deny this, what is the use of my saying anything? You can make the boy say anything you like, after all, as you often remind us, you are the master here.'

'And I'll not have you forget that, Doctor.'

Doctor Coleman felt out of his depth. He was dealing with a man in authority, who was a good deal older and far cannier than he. He knew that the denial of events by Master and Apprentice was a lie, but was powerless to do anything about it.

'Doctor, I have it in my power to do a great deal; if I chose to be wicked, I could do so. I could run the *Colinda* into port, say she was unfit for sea and sell half her cargo if I so chose. But I believe in integrity. God is my witness that I am an honest man; my right hand may drop off if it is not so.'

'Captain, I am sure I have never doubted you,' said Dr Coleman, and with that statement which was no more a lie that that of the Captain's that he was an honest man, he left, rather bewildered.

*

The Doctor found it hard to understand the Captain's intentions, and matters were made more puzzling later that evening, when he was handed a letter by Robert Ewart. The Captain had written Ewart a letter which read as follows:

Ewart
You were very grateful to me at one part of the passage, but at present you appear to be a very mutinous character; on your peril mind how you behave yourself with respect to me, my person is as sacred as any magistrate of the land on board this ship. Worst of all you have styled me a bugger. As my ship sails, you shall explain yourself, rely on that. I am placed here to do justice between the Honourable Hudson's Bay Company and the Passengers. The Agent at Victoria no doubt will see that I am doing justice between Man & Man, but don't run away with a notion that because I am slow to anger, that I am prohibited from punishing you.

JP Mills

*

Ewart watched the Doctor as he read the letter. 'I shall write to him and tell him I care nothing for his threats. I have done nothing wrong, and I shall tell him so, if necessary to his face.'

Dr Coleman spoke quietly, 'Don't do anything you might regret. I don't know why he sent you this, but I advise you to ignore it for the moment, and be careful what you say, he has spies.'

10
Defamation

Monday 31st October: the *Colinda* was 325 miles west of the coast of Chile, and 1000 miles southwest of Valparaiso.

When at lunch Miss Forsyth did not appear at the table, Dr Coleman called Lambert to tell him to take some food in to her; Lambert refused. Soon after that Miss Forsyth sent Ellen Sutherland, her maid, for some butter. The Captain prevented her from going near the food and said abruptly, 'She shall have nothing unless she comes here to eat.'

Dr Coleman was shocked by this harsh behaviour, and having bottled up his antagonism for so long came out with a well-rehearsed phrase: 'You will have to answer for your brutality!'

This did not have the dignified result that he had supposed it would. Captain Mills's fury at being crossed was all too plain. 'I am Master here, and can do as I like!' he shouted indignantly. 'What ever you say! Yes, Master over you,' he said, 'and I can feed you all on whatsoever I choose. If you are insolent to me, who am Master, then I will have you put in irons as happens in other ships, and I will make you answerable for your conduct before the authorities.'

The Doctor said nothing but rested on the hopes of justice being done at some future time. Lunch continued in silence. Miss Forsyth went hungry that day.

Captain Mills had worked himself up into such a passion that nothing could now satisfy him except to see the complete downfall of Dr Coleman. His mind was in such a frenzy that he could barely keep up with himself as plot after plot and web after web occurred to him with the sole aim of achieving the utter disgrace of the Doctor.

In his cabin he set to composing a letter to all the passengers on the *Colinda*. He wrote in such a fury that even he realised that the letter was illegible.

'Come on, man, this'll never do!' he said out loud, and he set to again, but this time in a more studious and focused manner. He summoned his steward, and upon Luke's appearance, handed him the document directing him to fix it up where all the passengers could see it.

*

To the Passengers on board the ship *Colinda*, John Powell Mills, Master.

I have been directed to carry you all to Victoria in Vancouver's Island. You are quite aware that I am Master. Now within this last few days a great many of you have had a very angry feeling towards me, but I have been placed here by the Honourable Hudson's Bay Company to do justice which I am determined to do cost what it will. Now, I suppose you all know good from evil and right from wrong, while I am known to be a man that has discipline and good feeling towards all on board. You are not blind, I know, to the Doctor's neglect towards you all and the poor little children for the first part of the passage, which I several times called his attention to them. I have told him often that he was not doing right towards you, nor as Doctors had done for the many Thousand Emigrants I have conveyed across the seas to various parts of the World.

Shall I tell you the difference that exists between the Doctor and Myself, it is I will not allow him to go into the young Lady's Cabin in the dark, this Lady being under my charge? Now I am quite determined that these things shall be made known to the Honourable Hudson's Bay Company. I ask you as fathers and mothers to give me letters from you that knows what is right stating how badly you have been attended to by the Doctor who is well paid for his attendance to you. I address this to the whole of my passengers both male and female & should I have committed anything detrimental to any one of your welfares I should candidly like to know what it is, and you may rely upon it, I will endeavour to rectify it at the risk of my life.

Yours Truly
J.P. Mills, Commander and Master

*

Dr Coleman, upon being made aware of the Captain's letter, could not prevent himself from trembling uncontrollably, though whether from rage, despair or the helplessness of his position cannot easily be known. There was no one he could turn to for advice or commiseration (for he was embarrassed to mention his feelings to Miss Forsyth), and no one to whom he could complain of such libellous treatment. He wanted to roll himself up in his bed and sleep for the rest of the voyage, but he knew that sleep would never come so easily to him while he churned matters over and over in his mind with pounding heart and temples. He hid himself in the hospital's little storeroom and tried to calm himself down. Finally, he walked to the large cabin, hoping that the Captain would be occupied on deck and would therefore not notice him. In this he was lucky, Captain Mills was on the poop deck. Dr Coleman entered the cabin, and found himself face to face with Miss Forsyth.

'Everything is ruined,' he groaned, 'all my ambitions, crumbled into dust. It is quite plain that he has been speaking ill of me to the passengers during the entire voyage.'

'It is true,' replied Miss Forsyth.

'I know what it is,' said the Doctor bitterly. 'He wants to ruin me for the money he can make by selling the passengers' stores for his own profit. He knows I would never allow that. But by discrediting me, he will make it impossible for me to convince the authorities that he is corrupt. But by Hell, I will show him!' (suddenly shouting out the last remark), 'I know there were not enough supplies brought onto the ship in the first place. I shall bring proof of it all.'

'You must hold your nerve, and be steady,' said Miss Forsyth. 'I fear there will be more for us all to go through on his account before our time on the *Colinda* is over.'

'You are right, Mina. I must gather up all my evidence so that I may present it later. But what should I do about the letter?'

'Ignore it,' said Miss Forsyth—the Doctor looked puzzled. 'For the moment ignore it,' she continued. 'There will be time enough to show your hand. He has too much power at his command while we are at sea for the crew will do as he tells them. For the moment ignore the letter and wait for the right time.'

'Thank you,' said the Doctor. 'You are right, and you have suffered at his whims as much as any. Thank you.' He went into his room and shut the door. Miss Forsyth looked wistfully after him.

11
Dr Coleman's Plan

That evening another infant died. Dr Coleman sat up all night by her beside, but had been unable to help. He had known for weeks that the child was in danger, and had tried hard to keep her alive; matters had been greatly worsened by the dreadful cold. The parents were, naturally, distraught, the Doctor was deeply depressed.

His depression was exacerbated by the unhappy situation in which he now found himself. The following morning, his suspicions were aroused upon noticing the Captain in deep conversation with six or seven men, but he persuaded himself that this meant little as it might have been entirely about the voyage—and yet, he wished very much to ask the men about the subject of that conversation. All the talk among the passengers was about their wish to put into port at Valparaiso that they might have some relief from the privations of the passage, and also to make some complaint about their treatment to the British Consul there. From Valparaiso, Chile to Victoria, Vancouver's Island would be a voyage of another seven-and-a-half thousand miles, and they felt a desperate need for a change of scenery. Everything rested on the Captain's decision, and the passengers awaited that with bated breath

Dr Coleman, though, felt that if the passengers were allowed off the *Colinda* at Valparaiso, it would be likely that few of them would return to the ship to fulfil their contracts with the Hudson's Bay Company, and this was of some concern to him as he felt the weight of responsibility rest upon his shoulders. In point of fact, he was drawn both ways, as he realised that the emigrants would find a continued voyage without a stop might place the health of all in even more danger.

He thought hard until his head hurt, but could formulate no plan other than to try to make peace with the Captain. With that in mind he resolved that morning to go to Captain Mills and ask him to shake hands so that he might see he had only friendly feelings towards him. By doing so, he thought he might be able to restore peace among the emigrants in general, and bring Miss Forsyth and Mrs Leigh to their former place of favour in the cabin.

His thoughts, though, were duplicitous, in that he reserved in his mind the right to make complaint to the authorities about the Captain's behaviour at the earliest possible opportunity. The realisation that the Captain might sink the *Colinda* for the insurance money he would receive gave the Doctor great anxiety, and this, he felt, compelled him to take the odious step of appearing to submit to a man for whom he had nothing but scorn.

To allay bad feeling, he decided to treat everyone on board, passengers and crew, to a glass of grog. The Norwegians would not accept this attempt at reconciliation, so dissatisfied with their situation did they feel. The unmarried Scottish men felt the same. It was not Dr Coleman they resented, however, but Captain Mills. Their refusal to accept the grog was a confused attempt at showing their support for the Doctor.

On the main deck the Captain accepted the Doctor's hand when it was offered and shook it, though with no enthusiasm. Dr Coleman's hopes of peacemaking were disappointed. The Captain went onto the poop deck; Dr Coleman went into the cabin.

Once inside, he found the room empty. Nor were Miss Forsyth or Mrs Leigh in their own rooms. He swallowed, and bit his upper lip, for a thought had occurred to him that he might take advantage of being alone there. After moving to the door of the Captain's room, he listened intently in case the steward was inside. Then he gingerly opened the door and looked in.

The room was tidy, nothing out of place. Dr Coleman looked behind himself and then stepped inside. Heart pounding, he turned round looking everywhere, but not knowing what he should be seeking. He went over to the Captain's bed and gazed at the pillow. Something was not right. He reached a hand out and felt underneath. His hand closed upon a cold, hard object. Carefully, he drew it out. It was a pistol, and loaded! There seemed to be a noise outside. Realising that he might now be in some danger, for he had already been there too long, he carefully replaced the pistol under the pillow and left the Captain's room quickly.

Dr Coleman moved over to the door of his own room, then turned and stood as if he were just coming out of it. At that moment, Mr Luke walked into the cabin. He looked suspiciously at the Doctor, but said nothing. The Doctor realised how flushed his face must look, but was determined to brazen it out. He nodded at Luke, and left the cabin, hoping that his activities had not been discovered or suspected. The cold air gave his hot face some relief, but his heart pounded furiously. 'What dreadful suspicions must lurk in the Captain's mind—to sleep with a loaded pistol!' he thought to himself as he made his way to the hospital.

12
A Petition

On board the *Colinda* there was a general feeling of suppressed anger. Resentment among the passengers, however, could usually be deduced only from looking at their hard set faces. The crew mostly went about their business, but even they could not feel comfortable. It was still bitterly cold, though not so much as it had been when the ship had been south of Cape Horn.

Wednesday morning, the 2nd of November, dawned. The Captain had been up and about for some time. He arrived back inside the cabin for his breakfast and sat at the head of the table like a princely potentate surveying his dominions.

Dr Coleman entered from his room and shortly after Miss Forsyth entered from hers. Their conversations even when alone had become more formal, and they had agreed to stay away from each other. Mrs Leigh was already up and dealing with her meal with the other passengers. The Doctor, in order to promote the false peace he wished for, had persuaded Miss Forsyth to partake of breakfast at the table with him and the Captain; she had reluctantly agreed to do so. It was, therefore, a silent and dreadful atmosphere which dominated their eating. Mr Luke and Lambert the cabin boy served them, behaving deferentially to the Captain, but carelessly to the others. Lambert, believing himself to be highly favoured by Captain Mills, could hardly hide his glee at discovering himself to be in a position of apparent superiority to the Doctor.

*

Meanwhile, the passengers continued to grumble among themselves and to Dr Coleman who noted their complaints in his records; the catalogue increased daily. Mouldy biscuits, bad rice, sour flour and insufficient water numbered among them. Additionally, the men who slept for'ard were in great difficulties as the continued wetting of their beds by the salt water which leaked into their berths was not only uncomfortable, but also caused the bedding to become rotten.

The Doctor asked the Captain to help them, but Captain Mills had his own agenda. He found in David Shaw a passenger who was willing to sign a document complaining of the Doctor's neglect.

The following day the emigrants petitioned the Captain to put into Valparaiso that they might acquire more provisions, and generally make themselves more comfortable. They placed such hope in the good will of Captain Mills that they had no doubt he would see their great distress and comply with their request.

The Captain's answer to them was as shocking as it was unexpected, though, had they truly divined his character, they might have known the manner in which he might answer.

*

To the Passengers on the *Colinda*

You say the Rice, Bread, and flour are bad, but in none of the ports between here and Vancouver will you get provender as good as you have on board the *Colinda*. Furthermore, should you imagine that once at Valparaiso you would be at liberty to go on shore you would soon be disappointed, for the ship would have to be put into quarantine. Therefore, I think you should be satisfied for things to continue as they do, remembering that we must get to Vancouver as quickly as possible so as to fulfil your contracts with the Honourable Hudson's Bay Company. If we should, perhaps, chance on an island, and these seas are studded with them, then we might stop to barter for some fresh meat.

Yours very truly
JP Mills

*

That the passengers were dismayed by the Captain's refusal to put into Valparaiso would be greatly to understate the case. Half an hour after receiving his reply a large group collected themselves around the cabin door with the purpose of telling Captain Mills directly to his face that it was their intention to put into Valparaiso come what may.

13
A Refusal

Led by Thomas McMurtrie, the passengers were filled with such confidence in themselves as a group, that they were prepared to declare themselves ready to take charge of the *Colinda* and *make* the Captain acquiesce if necessary to their demands.

Captain Mills walked out of the cabin and faced the passengers assembled. They had been talking loudly and bravely until that moment, but there was a sudden hush when the Captain appeared before them, looking, for once, like a commander whose clear-headedness as a great tactician should be given instant respect.

'How can I help you?' he said. His voice was steady, and his countenance showed no trace of emotion.

There was a moment of silence, and then McMurtrie stepped forward. He had vowed not to be cowed by the presence of Captain Mills, but he was aware of the great step he was about to attempt, and though he did his best to keep his voice from faltering, he found it hard.

'Captain, we have determined that it is vitally important that the *Colinda* should call into Valparaiso for the good of all on board.'

'Is that so?' replied the Captain. He uttered not another word, compelling McMurtrie to take the lead again.

'Captain, we know our rights, and there are matters which must be settled before we can continue this voyage.'

'Are there, indeed?' said Captain Mills, holding himself erect in as statesman-like a pose as he could manage bearing in mind the few glasses of brandy he had already drunk that morning.

'Captain, if you will persist in not listening to us, we will be compelled to authorise Mr Birt to stand in your place and to take the *Colinda* into Valparaiso.' McMurtrie said this with a degree of confidence, and two of the Norwegian men standing by him slapped him on his back in appreciation. The rest of the crowd stood close by listening to all that was said with stern faces.

'You wish me to put into Valparaiso, do you?' The crowd began to murmur their assent. 'Mr Birt!' called the Captain suddenly. The Chief Mate appeared. 'Follow me!' And the two men went into the cabin leaving the passengers standing where they were.

'He may do it yet,' said McMurtrie. 'Let's see what happens.'

In the cabin Mr Birt was informed of what had been said. 'I warn you now,' said the Captain, 'If I find that you have had anything to do with this plan of theirs, I will see that you are charged with mutiny. You understand me.'

14
Captain Mills's Plan

Friday 4th November. Captain Mills strode the deck with a dark look on his face and all kept out of his way if they could. Two of his crew had been put in irons for stealing food, a crime for which he had accused the passengers. He, feeling that he had been made a fool of, was determined to make quite certain that respect for his position as Master of the *Colinda* was intact.

He called to the Chief Mate to gather the officers and follow him into the Captain's cabin. Mr Birt did so with a feeling of dread.

'Mr Birt,' said Captain Mills, 'I have determined to put into Valparaiso after all.'

'Aye, aye, Captain, but…' Mr Birt's voice trailed off. He looked troubled.

'But what, Mr Birt?'

'I thought you had intended to sail straight for Vancouver.'

'You see very little of what is before your eyes. Do you not see what sort of men we are carrying? Have you not realised their intention? We will put into Valparaiso, which is their desire—not mine, and I will charge them all with mutiny.'

The others present looked uncertain.

'Well,' said the Captain looking at them, 'have any of you something to say on the matter?'

No one made any response, and after being dismissed, they all filed out.

*

Captain Mills was the *Colinda*; the *Colinda* was Captain Mills. His personality filled the ship until it seemed to burst with it. None could go anywhere on board without feeling the Captain's eyes gazing at him.

The Captain had not been idle. He had made sure of those of his crew he felt he could trust; Mr Birt, the Chief Mate, was not one of them. Later that day Mr Holligan and Mr Bullmore, midshipmen, were put into custody for speaking to the Doctor, probably warning him of the plan which should have been kept secret.

As the day progressed, an ominous silence descended upon the ship. The crew worked and called to each other as they did so, but the passengers sat glumly for the most part—cold, tired, bored, frustrated, angry.

Saturday 5th November— Captain Mills still moved round the deck, speaking to some of the passengers, asking questions about the Doctor and his doings. He interviewed Charles Lewis for almost two hours. Lewis, who had been schooling the children when it was not too cold and they were not unwell, felt a kind of loyalty to Dr Coleman, but he was a thin, scrawny man who seemed to wither in the Captain's presence, and Captain Mills looked satisfied once Lewis had left him.

He called to the Chief Mate who went over to him. 'Mr Birt, have it entered in the log book that I have been forced to abandon the ship, that the emigrants have forced me to turn the ship towards land, and that it is now under the protection of the underwriters for it will not be my fault if the *Colinda* is lost.'

The Doctor, meanwhile, worked on in the hospital, for there was plenty to keep him busy. His work there lasted some hours, as many were unwell. Just before 4 p.m, a note was delivered to him, by whom he could not say, for he did not see it arrive, but it was from Mr Bullmore in his place of confinement. It confirmed the Captain's plan to charge some of the passengers with mutiny, but added the information that the Doctor dreaded—that he himself would also be charged.

Dr Coleman destroyed the note, crumpling it in his fist, his face creased in anger. He left the hospital and went onto the main deck. Robert Ewart saw him arrive there and went over to speak with him.

'We have just been told that the Captain has decided to go to Valdivia instead of Valparaiso, he says it is nearer.'

'He is afraid,' said the Doctor. 'Valdivia is safer for him, for the authorities are at Valparaiso, and he is being cautious. He is afraid—but Valdivia is not far from Valparaiso, so it will make little difference.'

'The crew have been told to look out for land,' said Ewart.

15
The Madness of Captain Mills

Mr Hawley, the Second Mate, lay ill and in pain in his berth. It was not within Dr Coleman's remit to treat the crew if they were unwell, but Hawley had not been seen about for some days. The Doctor asked Mr Birt about it, but he only shrugged his shoulders in a non-committal sort of way. It was not that Mr Birt had anything against Mr Hawley, or that he was an unfeeling man, but merely a wish to keep a low profile at that time. Treatment of any members of the crew who were sick was the prerogative of the Captain, and he guarded his rights jealously.

Dr Coleman felt his duty to mankind keenly, but he was aware that any approach he made to Captain Mills directly would be met with a rebuff. He wrote a brief letter to the Captain and gave it to Bullmore, who had just been released from the hold, to deliver.

Later, while at work in the hospital, writing notes about his patients, he was very much taken aback by the sudden and unexpected appearance of the Captain himself.

'What is the meaning of this, Doctor?' he said roughly, at the same time banging the letter down onto the desk.

'Merely an offer of help for one of your crew who is unwell. I realise it is not my place, but I thought I might take the liberty…'

'Liberty! I'll give you a liberty! Too damn right, it is not your place to encroach on my command. No, sir, I will have you communicate with none of my men, and if you don't hold your tongue I will put you in irons. I'll not forget that you refused to doctor the crew when I asked before.'

The Doctor was most surprised by this last statement, for he had never been asked to examine any of the crew, and would never have refused to do so if the situation had demanded it.

'Must Hawley, then, suffer in pain, Captain? You are not a medical man. Remember what happened when you treated Anderson with calomel, it nearly killed him.'

Anderson, an able seaman, had been dosed early in the voyage at the Captain's orders.

'Damn your impudence!' said the Captain with gritted teeth, shaking a finger in the Doctor's face, 'I'll not have you criticise me.

"Captain Mills,' said the Doctor as calmly as he could, though with raised voice, 'If I had not prevented your treatment of Anderson on that occasion, you might have found yourself charged with manslaughter.'

'In any case,' said Captain Mills, 'you shall not see Hawley.'

*

Affairs were becoming desperate. That evening, the Doctor sat in his cabin writing in his journal, 'I believe the Captain to be out of his mind, but I am powerless to do anything about it.'

A rumour was going about that the ship's chronometer was wrong, and that the Captain did not know the current position of the *Colinda*: that land ought to have been seen by now, and there was a danger of striking some rock or other. The passengers began to be afraid for their lives, and much wailing was heard from below deck.

Mr Birt, in a state of some excitement, knocked at the Doctor's door and on being admitted, asked his opinion of the current state of affairs. There was no time to make an answer, for it was the hour of the evening meal, and the Captain arrived in the large cabin. Upon seeing Mr Birt standing inside the Doctor's room, he called to him peremptorily.

'What is the meaning of this, Mr Birt? Do you not know that that man is not to be trusted? Even the passengers do not trust him, and he is their own doctor. It is quite shameful.' This last remark was pointed directly at Dr Coleman who blanched at such a direct insult.

Mr Birt spoke before the Doctor could answer. 'Why, Captain, I have no doubt that you will sell everything for your own advantage once we come into port, and I myself will not allow that to be done.' This was said in an authoritative voice which was intended to cow the Captain into submission, but that intention failed miserably, for Captain Mills was now white with fury. In a controlled voice, the like of which cast fear into all who might hear it, he made the following pronouncement: 'Mr Birt, consider yourself under immediate arrest. You will go to your quarters now and wait there for my decision as to what is to be done. You, Doctor, are not to speak to any of my officers on any pretext whatsoever.'

The Chief Mate left followed by Captain Mills. Once Mr Birt was in his cabin his door was locked from the outside, and the carpenter was instructed to secure it further with a padlock.

Miss Forsyth, who had seen only the last part of the above scene, was left with the Doctor.

'What has happened? Why has Mr Birt been arrested?'

Dr Coleman found his voice with difficulty. 'It is a plot. A plot to discredit me. He was arrested for speaking to me. I think we may be in some danger, for the passengers will not accept his arrest. They may try to take the Captain prisoner and give command of the *Colinda* to Mr Birt because they trust him.' He rubbed his hand over his face for a thought had occurred to him. 'We must not allow a mutiny to take place, that would be to play into the Captain's hands. I must go to the passengers and prevent it.'

'Tomorrow,' said Miss Forsyth. 'Go to them tomorrow, you look exhausted.'

And although it went against his better judgment, he decided to take her advice.

⋆

The following day was Sunday. The passengers were so restless that no service was held. Some of them were so alarmed by thoughts of what might happen to them, that they could not be prevented from loudly bewailing their thoughtlessness at embarking on such a wretched voyage as this.

Dr Coleman had thought better of his plan to go among them fearing that such an action might be misinterpreted as sedition. He was, however, surprised to find that the carpenter had not found a way of supplying more air to the passengers below. He had asked for this to be done the previous day. He made his way to the poop deck in order to speak to the Captain about the matter.

'Good morning, Captain Mills,' he began, but the Captain moved away as if he had not heard. Dr Coleman followed. 'Captain, I have a request to make…' Once more the Captain moved away. The Doctor was not to be put off, and followed a second time. 'Captain…' But Captain Mills looked beyond and through him as if he was not there. Instead of acknowledging the Doctor, he spoke calmly to one of the crew. 'Captain…' began the Doctor a fourth time.

Upon this, Captain Mills turned on him in a fury. 'This vessel is busy going into port. Do not speak to me, but address your remarks elsewhere!' Flecks of spittle flew from his mouth as he spoke.

Dr Coleman immediately turned on his heels and left the poop deck. The Captain grinned; 'One victory to me, I think, Doctor,' he said to himself.

*

Captain Mills had other matters to think upon. It occurred to him that the ship's logbook might reflect matters he would not wish to be discovered. In particular, there was the matter of the ship's arrival at Valdivia instead of Valparaiso, for the winds had been favourable for the latter destination.

He had been wary of the scrutiny under which he would have been placed had the *Colinda* arrived at Valparaiso and had considered this carefully upon making his choice.

The logbook was kept by Mr Birt, and Captain Mills feared that the Chief Mate would find some way to secrete it until an official inquiry might be made. Mr Birt, confined to his cabin as he was, would have little opportunity to place the book where it could not easily be found, and so, together with Mr Hawley (who had recovered a little from his indisposition), Feltham and Lambert, he marched off to Mr Birt's cabin with a loaded pistol, unlocked the door, and strode in. Mr Birt, who had been asleep, awoke with a start, and stood.

'The logbook, if you please!' the Captain demanded of Mr Birt with outstretched hand.

'I cannot give it to you, Captain, it is my duty to keep it safe and in good order.'

But the Captain, seeing the logbook lying on the table, snatched it up and passed it through the door to Lambert. 'Take this to my cabin and then wait there till I return, for no one else must take possession of it, and I have a few more words to say to Mr Birt.'

Lambert left, and Captain Mills spent some minutes searching the Chief Mate's cabin for any copies of the logbook. Finding none, he left locking the door behind him, went to his cabin, where he gave some instructions to Lambert who was still there, and who received his orders quietly.

★

Lunch in the cuddy was taken in absolute silence but for requests to the steward to pass certain items. At the end of the meal Dr Coleman finished the wine in his glass, and began to speak to Miss Forsyth, but suddenly finding that he did not feel well, he stopped speaking abruptly.

'Whatever is the matter, Doctor,' asked Miss Forsyth.

'I feel a little strange,' came the drowsy answer.

'Let me help you to your bed.'

Miss Forsyth assisted the Doctor to his cabin and shut the door behind them. 'I don't know what the matter can be, Mina. I was fine a moment ago.'

Miss Forsyth began to feel alarmed. 'Suppose something had been but in your wine…'

But the Doctor was already in a deep sleep.

Captain Mills, meanwhile, had left the cuddy and was telling some of the men that the Doctor was dead drunk. This rumour had soon spread all over the ship.

'Frankly, I'm not surprised,' said one of the women. 'There was always something unpleasant about the Doctor's ways. Always prying into everyone's affairs he was.'

'I think you'll find that it was his job to know about us,' said her friend.

Some of the passengers spoke up for him, others against him, though most had positive feelings towards him.

When at last he awoke, he found Mrs Leigh and her son shaking him. Thomas McMurtrie stood close by. 'How are you feeling now?' he asked.

'Not too good, thank you, Thomas.'

McMurtrie told him what had been going on. 'Some of us think you were poisoned,' he said.

'I'm sure that cannot be so,' came the response, and Dr Coleman got up and walked unsteadily onto the deck.

Several passengers were waiting to see him. He presented a very sorry picture: bloodshot eyes which seemed to roll in their sockets and a fuddled appearance which seemed to give the impression that the Captain had been telling the truth. All eyes were upon him. No one made a judgement to his face, but after he had passed them by, knowing looks were passed between some of them as if to say, 'there I told you so'.

He had a brisk walk around the deck for some time before returning to the cabin for some tea. His mouth was so dry that he could barely speak, his head throbbed so much that it was almost impossible to articulate words. He retired to his room, but lying down was torture, so he sat up and forced himself to write in his journal.

'When the Captain made known to the emigrants that I was dead drunk he showed them a brace of loaded pistols saying at the same time that he always carried them about with him, this threw them all into much anxiety and alarm as they thought that as he was such a desperate man that he would shoot any-one on board who offended him.'

16
Valdivia Harbour

Monday 7th November. There was great excitement on board, for as morning dawned, land was sighted. Crew and passengers joined in congratulating each other. Dr Coleman had mixed feelings, but relief predominated. Only the Captain felt an oppressive weight on his shoulders. He had much to think about, for he needed to present a convincing argument to the authorities which would justify all he had done during the voyage. He knew that he needed to save face, and that this would be a time of great personal danger. Not wishing the embarrassment of disgrace, and wishing to further enrich himself at whatever cost, might have been enough to think about, but now he had other issues to deal with. It was necessary to demonstrate that there had been a mutiny on the *Colinda*, and this, he reasoned, should not be too difficult. Furthermore, he felt a vindictive rage towards the Doctor, that could only be assuaged by managing his absolute downfall. This he had plotted over and over again: rehearsing in his mind every word that he might need to say to convince both the Hudson's Bay Company as well as a jury. But he realised that he must be careful not to overplay his hand, and that, however difficult it might be, he must remain in control of himself, never allowing himself to be riled whatever the provocation.

Captain Mills knew well the procedure for arrival in port, and in order to present as respectable appearance as possible he ordered that the *Colinda* be cleaned from top to bottom. The decks were holystoned, something which had not been properly done for some time, and he himself made certain that he was as well presented as he could be. As noon approached, he sent a boat to carry a letter of invitation to the captain of another vessel lying in Valdivia Harbour. That officer arrived on board the *Colinda* soon afterwards.

'Captain Mills, I am here and ready to assist you,' was his opening remark, but after a short time he was overheard remarking to Mills, 'I pity your case, it is hard to know how best to proceed when faced with matters such as these.'

Mills, realising that they were in too public a place, conducted his visitor to his cabin where they continued their discussion.

At one-thirty, the Captain of Valdivia Port, Don Luis, and his lieutenant came on board. Captain Mills began making his way to where they stood, but not before the other had walked up to Dr Coleman with hand extended and addressed him.

'Captain Mills, I believe.'

'You mistake me,' said the Doctor. 'Here is the Captain.' They all smiled at the mistake, though Captain Mills's amusement was feigned, for it would have been his last wish that such an error should have been made.

*

Dr Coleman sat in the hospital alone. Even those passengers who felt unwell were not there, such was their excitement. He looked up as Mr Luke entered with a letter for him. Luke delivered it with a smirk on his face and then left. The contents of the letter were greatly worrying.

*

Monday Nov 7th 1853.
Doctor,

As you procured bottles of Rum from my Steward without my sanction and glaringly carried them in your pockets down among the Mutineers on the evening of the same day that the ship was taken at sea, purposely and cruelly to glut and excite the Norwegian mutineers into this diabolical mutiny, for the Interest of the Hudson's Bay Company, for the preservation of my valuable cargo and ship, as the anchor touches the bottom, you are under arrest and I beg you to keep in your state room. I am under a heavy penalty to be at sea with so many persons without a medical person otherwise you certainly would have been arrested before and have saved this mutiny, now we are in port, I can obtain any medical treatment I may need.

JP Mills, Master

*

The accusation was false, for the Doctor had neither obtained rum from the ship's Steward nor encouraged mutiny; but now the Captain had these officials in his cabin and was telling them lies. Dr Coleman, knowing he must tell his side of the story, went to the Captain's cabin and knocked at the door. Mills opened it himself and appeared surprised to see the Doctor there.

'You are a prisoner, sir, leave this place immediately!' and Dr Coleman left.

Captain Mills's visitors left shortly afterwards; communication with Don Luis had proved very trying since he spoke almost no English. The Doctor, felt he must approach Captain Mills again. He had made up his mind to visit the British Consul and lay the whole history of the case before him and also his defence for the men who were to be charged with mutiny. In an attempt to ameliorate the situation he went to the Captain together with Miss Forsyth.

'Captain, I request permission to take a boat on shore that I may search out food supplies, particularly fruit which we greatly need.'

The Captain was not to be fooled by so obvious a prevarication, and if the Doctor thought that the presence of a lady would help, he was sorely mistaken. Captain Mills answered with evident delight:

'You shall not be permitted to have any of my boats to land in. You are under arrest, and are my prisoner. You are to remain in your quarters and that is that! You will soon know who is Master here! You must know, sir, that I have two loaded guns and that I will shoot the first man who steps off the side of this vessel.'

A crowd of had gathered round. As the Doctor and Miss Forsyth turned to leave, the Captain called out, 'Miss Forsyth, I will blast your character forever!' Then speaking to those nearby, 'We shall be here for some months, I fear. Some of you men will, no doubt, find yourselves at the wrong end of rope. You won't be much use to your women once your necks have been stretched. Mind what I say, I am Master here, and you shall all soon know it!'

Miss Forsyth flushed with embarrassment at the Captain's words, and hoped that no one noticed. Dr Coleman walked back to the men who were looking dangerous. 'Keep cool and hold your tongues. This is not the time or place to make trouble.'

'Is that you interfering again, Doctor?' said the Captain. 'Perhaps it is as well this time, for these men will make things worse for themselves if they carry on as they have been doing.'

But the last remark was barely heeded, for the crowd was already dispersing, having taken the Doctor's advice: otherwise Captain Mills might have been torn to pieces.

*

A little later Don Luis and his lieutenant arrived on board again, this time in the company of Captain Stewart whose ship was also in the harbour. Captain Stewart spoke Spanish well, and had agreed to act as interpreter. Dr Coleman attempted to have Sutherland take a note to Captain Stewart telling him that Mills's accusations were part of a villainous plot. Captain Mills saw to it that the note was not delivered.

*

Deep down inside, Dr Coleman was afraid. He sat in his cabin with his hands on his cheeks and the tips of his little fingers against the corners of his eyes. 'Think, you idiot, think!' he murmured to himself.

'Point one—the crew are all loyal to the Captain, but on the positive side I think that the passengers will for the most part side with me. If they try anything by force, there may be bloodshed, and they may do something stupid if they find that I am molested.

'Point two—'

At that moment, there was a rapid double knock on his door. He stood and opened it; Sutherland was standing there with an expression of urgency on his face.

'Your presence is requested in the Captain's stateroom. I couldn't deliver your note, but I got the message to Captain Stewart anyway.'

The Doctor passed through the cuddy and alongside the Captain's cabin into the stateroom, which, to tell the truth, was a rather shabby place. The two captains and Don Luis were sitting round the table. Don Luis's lieutenant stood by the window gazing out.

The Doctor, unable to restrain his deep feelings any longer, for he felt he would burst otherwise, began to speak, intending to lay his complaints clearly before Don Luis through the intermediary translation of Captain Stewart, but after uttering only three or four words, he was at once interrupted by Captain Mills.

'I desire you to hold your tongue, sir. You are not here on anyone's orders but my own, and you will kindly observe proper decorum where it is due.' Then turning to the others, he remarked, 'You see what I have had to put up with, a whippersnapper for a doctor who does not know his business, neglects his duties, and creates such dissatisfaction among the emigrants that I have had nothing but trouble from them since we left England.'

'Thank you, Captain,' said Stewart, 'pray continue, Doctor.'

'I really must refute all that...'

At this he was again interrupted by Mills. 'Remember who has brought you here and commanded your presence.'

The Doctor was, this time, not to be cowed, and continued regardless. 'I would be happy to give you a full list of the passengers, and you may inquire of any of them whether or not I have done my duty.'

Captain Stewart interpreted this for Don Luis, who seemed unperturbed by all that was happening as he was busily smoking a large cigar, inhaling deeply, while taking occasional sips of brandy from a glass which had been poured for him by Mills himself.

Mills then spoke as if considering every word, 'It would suit me if you were to leave the *Colinda* now—today.'

'You wish to separate me from the passengers?' said the Doctor brazenly. 'I am their protector, they will not wish to see me go. I must stay on board to keep them safe.'

'Then you must be answerable for yourself and the behaviour of your charges,' said Captain Stewart.

Doctor Coleman sighed, for he knew that there would be more trouble. 'I must look to the *safety* of my charges,' he said pointedly. He left the stateroom and returned to his own cabin, where he lay down with a crushing headache.

'That man wants to be captain in my place,' observed Captain Mills, 'he has plotted to take the ship from me. My sole desire is the preservation of peace on board.'

Captain Stewart, Don Luis, and Don Luis's lieutenant left the *Colinda* and were rowed back to shore.

17
Loaded Pistols

The tension on board the *Colinda* was so terrible by this stage that conversations were, for the most part, held in whispers. Captain Mills was to be seen striding round the deck with every appearance of a martinet. His eyes seemed to be everywhere and none dared speak to him.

Dr Coleman had determined not to leave the ship until it had reached Valparaiso, for it was there that justice might be sought from the British Consul. 'Oh! What plotting what new things every day produces,' he wrote in his journal. His misgivings for the future were not unjustified, and he found himself walking a very narrow and dangerous path.

Many on the *Colinda* spent an uneasy night. The following day dawned bright, and the weather seemed set fair. A balmy breeze blew and the crew seemed to work with a will at their various tasks, mending sails and cleaning equipment. The Captain stood on the poop deck surveying his territory as if it were a kingdom. 'None shall take this from me,' he thought, and he breathed the air deeply and with great satisfaction.

Miss Forsyth sat with Mrs Leigh in the cuddy looking at a note received that morning. The Doctor entered and saw them there; they looked disturbed, so he asked what was troubling them. Miss Forsyth handed him the note and both ladies looked anxiously at his face as he read. It was short and very much to the point.

*

November 8th 1853
Miss Forsyth

Since you are so dissatisfied, I guarantee to refund you the money you have paid for your passage, but I will not allow any further improprieties to be carried on aboard my ship between you and the Doctor. These have been recorded by the Chief Mate in my logbook.

JP Mills, Master

*

'How dare he?' said Miss Forsyth with quavering voice. The Doctor was silent for a moment, but then he spoke with a croak in his voice, for he was tired after a sleepless night, and was developing a cold which made him hoarse.

'He has told Mr Birt to write this, but his logbook is not evidence. Mr Birt will not support him in his accusations anymore, for he hates him. He can write whatever he wishes, it makes no difference.'

This was somewhat disingenuous of the Doctor, for he himself had noted events in his own journal which he hoped to use as proof of the Captain's wrongdoings. The ladies were silent.

'He has become a most desperate man,' he went on. 'I often think he is out of his mind. Yes, he is desperately infamous, the plot he is now adopting is one which could only be thought of by someone out of his mind.'

'What is he trying to do?' asked Mrs Leigh.

'He wishes to discredit me,' came the answer. 'You and Miss Forsyth are merely figures in his plot. I don't know why he wants to do this, but he does, and that is the end of it.'

'What will happen to us?' said Miss Forsyth.

'We must be strong and resist his attempts to bully us into submission, but we must wait for him to make the first move.'

Above and below deck all seemed to be normal. In fact, the most unusual aspect of that day was the outward ordinariness of everything.

Captain Mills, though, realising the necessity of keeping the crew on his side, had ordered the release of Mr Birt from his confinement, and allowed him to resume his duties as Chief Mate, but with a warning that he must be careful with regard to his behaviour and his speech.

*

That evening after all had eaten, the passengers were summoned aft; the Captain had decided to address them all from the poop. They stood below looking up at him; many had puzzled expressions on their faces. Captain Mills had decided to adopt a dignified and commanding bearing. On arrival at Valdivia he had cleaned himself up, and no longer presented the drunken, dishevelled appearance seen during the second half of the voyage to date. He had, of course, stiffened his resolve with a tumblerful of brandy, but that was nothing to him. He thought he knew how to manipulate opinion when necessary, and his crafty mind had devised a subtle plot.

'We have now been two days in port. It had been my intention that you should have fresh meat today, but you shall have it tomorrow. I did not realise that there was a shortage of meat, that should have been told to me by the Doctor when we arrived here…'

'He was under arrest then,' called William Sutherland from below.

'Enough!' said the Captain, 'I did not ask for your thoughts on the matter.' He then continued: 'Some of you have been causing trouble with libellous talk. I know who you are, and you will be sent on shore tomorrow.' Then, aside to Sutherland, 'You will be going with them.' There was some scowling among the men, but the Captain went on regardless. 'The Doctor may have told you some untruths about me, but I wish you to know him by his true colours. He is a scoundrel who does not do his duty, although I have reprimanded him about this a number of times.'

As he said this Dr Coleman came out of the cuddy, and looked up at him. The two men stared at each other hard. The Doctor had heard everything said up till that moment, but had been disinclined to say anything unless it reflected on himself personally.

'That is a falsehood, and you know it,' said the Doctor as loudly as he could.

'This Doctor,' said Captain Mills, still looking at him, 'has insulted you all while we are at table, calling you dirty rabble.'

'That is also untrue,' said the Doctor.

'You are a liar, Dr Coleman, it is noted in my logbook. Furthermore, Mrs Leigh told me how she came upon you and Miss Forsyth canoodling in the hospital dispensary.'

'I never said any such thing,' said Mrs Leigh with red face.

'Hold your tongue, woman!' shouted the Captain. Then controlling himself: 'At the start of this voyage I was made protector of that young lady,' (indicating Miss Forsyth).

'Persecutor is closer,' said Miss Forsyth quietly.

'All this has come about because I would not allow my rooms on this ship to be turned into a common brothel.'

There were shocked expressions among some of the passengers at this. By now the crew were also beginning to gather round.

'I would not allow anyone' (looking towards the Doctor) 'to enter her cabin after dark or to cohabit with her. But this is what they have contrived to do.'

Some of the passengers turned away and would have left in disgust at the Captain's speech.

'Mind sir take care what you say, for you shall have to answer for it and dearly pay for it,' said Dr Coleman from below.

'You, sir, are a brave fellow indeed!' said the Captain disdainfully. 'You are no gentleman, you are nothing but a damn scratchdick. Since you are so brave,' he went on, 'perhaps you would like to come with me on shore and fight it out…No? I thought not!' And Captain Mills made his way off the poop deck and walked into the cuddy.

*

Question: how could it be that two men at such odds should still share the same table? Answer: because there was no choice. Captain Mills was determined to make the Doctor's life a Hell on Earth and absolutely refused to allow him to take his meals anywhere else, insisting at the same time on the presence of Miss Forsyth.

The crew grinned at each other. Some of them had sailed with the Captain before. 'He's really got it in for them now,' said one. 'I wouldn't be in their shoes for anything.'

Most of the passengers, on the other hand, were horrified by what they had heard. 'The man's out of his mind,' said McMurtrie, 'there's no knowing what the end of this will be.'

*

This was only the beginning of a long night of irritation and dread. In the cuddy, Captain Mills refused to let any retire to their rooms, and so the Doctor, Miss Forsyth and Mrs Leigh were forced to stay awake in the gnawing silence that ate into the darkness of their thoughts.

The light that burned was dim and gave an amber cast to everything. Finally, the Captain called for Lambert the cabin boy to fetch his pistols. Once they had been brought to him and he had loaded them, he put them on the table before him and toyed with them in a manner calculated to disturb the minds of the others. He stood and pushed one towards Dr Coleman who was standing on the other side of the table trying to appear unconcerned.

'There you are, Doctor. Perhaps you will take one and I the other, and we can shoot at each other across the table.'

Dr Coleman turned without a word and began to walk away. Infuriated, the Captain followed him and quickly caught him by the wrist. Then he turned him round with a twist of his arm so that they were face to face.

'It is time for our duel, Doctor. I'll wager you're itching for it. Choose your weapon now.'

The two ladies were standing and began to speak simultaneously.

'Silence!' commanded the Captain.

Horrified by this turn of events, for he was not a fighting man, the Doctor stepped back with his palms held out before him.

'I know we have our differences, Captain, but I feel we would be better settling them at Valparaiso when we arrive there.'

'You snivelling coward, do you think for one moment that I have any intention of taking the *Colinda* to Valparaiso? My contract with the Company lies in tatters, and you think I will submit to an Inquiry. No, sir, not on your life. Not if we stay here for twenty months. I will do as I please, you will remember that I am Master here, not you, though I have no doubt that you would choose to take my place at the drop of a hat if you could. I will have you put in irons and confined in the hold.'

The Captain snatched up the pistols and left the cuddy in a fury and went onto the poop deck where he could be heard shouting commands to the Second Mate.

The Doctor and the two ladies looked at each other. 'Go to your room, Doctor, and lock yourself in,' said Mrs Leigh. 'Whatever happens do not come out, for he will kill you if he sees you.' They then immediately went into their cabins and secured their doors. No sooner had they done so than the Captain re-entered the cuddy. He had worked himself up into a murderous rage.

'Where is that damned Doctor?' he shouted. Then, pistol in hand, he rushed to the door of the Doctor's cabin and battered hard upon the door, causing no little damage to the door and to himself. By now his face was as dark as the night, and having hurt his hand he swore fiercely. The Doctor, though had barricaded his door, and made no noise from within his room.

Captain Mills moved quickly to Miss Forsyth's door and called out, 'Miss Forsyth, is the Doctor there?' She said nothing. 'Is Dr Coleman with you?'

'No!' came the answer.

'Open the door at once!'

'Why?' said Miss Forsyth with a trembling voice.

'I insist that you open your door!'

'I am half undressed, and I cannot open the door.'

Mrs Leigh ventured to open her door and looked out of her room. 'Please calm down, Captain.'

'Shut up, bitch!' he hurled back at her. 'You'll leave the *Colinda* tomorrow morning.' And then calling: 'Lambert, fetch me a boom, I will break this door down.'

Mrs Leigh instantly went back into her cabin and began to cry.

'Open this door or I will break it down. Be quick about it!' called Captain Mills to Miss Forsyth.

'But I am undressed.'

'Lambert, where is that boom?'

At this, Miss Forsyth opened her door, and the Captain rushed in expecting to find the Doctor there.

18
A Steamer

Once in her cabin, Captain Mills made Miss Forsyth open everything—even her box, though it was barely large enough to hide a grown man. The Doctor, of course, was not there.

While this search continued, Dr Coleman hurriedly opened his door and closed it again as silently as he could. Then, leaving the cuddy, he made his way to the women's hospital to take refuge there. A few minutes later, Captain Mills, having finished his search of Miss Forsyth's room, went back into the cuddy and sat before the Doctor's cabin door to lie in wait for his reappearance, unaware that his intended victim was safe down below under the watchful guard of some of the male passengers who had been alerted by the noise to all that was going on.

*

When the dawn came, all the passengers and crew did their best to affect the appearance of normality, trying hard to make it appear as if nothing had happened to disturb their ease of mind. All were deeply shocked by the events of the night, though there were several versions of what had actually happened circulating around the vessel. Most of the passengers agreed that the Captain's behaviour was despicable, but that there was nothing that could be done, since his position as Captain of the *Colinda* would undoubtedly be defended by the authorities. Just before midday, Don Luis arrived on board together with a Danish captain. They toured the ship below deck, and so it was that Dr Coleman was able to speak with them.

'After what happened last night no one feels safe here,' he concluded.

They heard what he had to say with a mixture of shock and disbelief, for surely, they reasoned, such behaviour on the part of the captain of a ship was impossible to credit. Finally, they came to the conclusion that the passengers must be carried on to Valparaiso as soon as could be arranged, and that for this purpose a steamer must be procured. In the meantime, Don Luis promised to send men to guard the safety of the passengers.

So it was that in the afternoon two custom house officers and an interpreter came on board. But no sooner had they arrived than they were whisked away into the Captain's cabin and were soon in deep conversation with him. Miss Forsyth, from her cabin, heard her name mentioned several times, followed by much laughter. Feeling upset, she left, and went to the ship's hospital to see the Doctor.

Dr Coleman was busy at that moment, but even so he took her into his dispensary so that they could speak more privately.

'Something is wrong,' said Miss Forsyth, 'I am sure that they are plotting some harm to us.'

'Don't worry too much,' said the Doctor, 'those gentlemen are here to protect us from the Captain.'

'They seemed to be too friendly with him.'

At that moment a voice was heard from the deck calling to Dr Coleman. He left Miss Forsyth and went up. The interpreter was standing on the poop deck, and the Doctor, on the deck below, looked up at him.

'They would like to know,' said the interpreter, 'if you were laughing earlier in the cabin with your girly girl.'

The Doctor was greatly taken aback by this uncouth language. Just then, Miss Forsyth appeared from below.

'Are you referring to this young lady?' he asked in as dignified a manner as he could muster, bearing in mind the anger which he felt rising up within.

'Yes indeed. We have had such information from Captain Mills.'

'The implication is false,' said the Doctor, and then turning away as if disdaining to hold further conversation with the interpreter, he went with Miss Forsyth back below, remarking to her quietly as they went, 'You were right. Something is going on; this is part of a plot to discredit me to justify my arrest by the authorities.'

'What will you do?'

'I don't know yet, I need to think. But this cannot be allowed to go on any further.'

*

In the afternoon Captain Mills left the ship and went on shore. He was away for some hours and arrived back on board at nearly six o'clock with a small bunch of flowers. Once on deck he appeared to be in an unusually happy mood. McMurtrie, who was lounging on the deck with Sutherland, called a greeting.

'Good evening, Captain Mills, have you had a good day?'

'Indeed I have, McMurtrie. I have been kissing girls, and they gave me this nosegay.' And he went whistling a hornpipe into the cuddy.

'I'll wager he's been doing a good deal more than that,' said Mr Birt to Mr Hawley, both of whom had overheard this exchange.

'I have no doubt about it,' said Hawley. 'Just shows that even the old man can have a happy time.'

'It'll never last,' came the reply.

*

In the evening, Dr Coleman went below to visit the passengers. They were not happy, but he did his best to calm them by telling them that he would do everything that he could to ensure their safety, and that their arrival at their final destination would be without incident. They would not be reassured, but it was a long time since any had given much thought to the mining work in Vancouver's Island. Some expressed a wish to leave the *Colinda* there and then.

'We can surely find work here in Chile.'

The Doctor became concerned. 'You all have contracts; you cannot leave the ship.'

But the idea was beginning to take root in their minds, and he realised that the problem which he had foreseen only a few days before, that once allowed ashore they might refuse to return, was a real risk.

'Yet another burden for my mind,' he thought, as he made his way to the hospital where several sick passengers lay abed.

By this time, Dr Coleman no longer felt that his cabin was a safe place, and had arranged to sleep in the men's hospital and for Miss Forsyth and Mrs Leigh to remove their quarters to the women's hospital; despite the Captain's command, Mrs Leigh still remained on board. He felt a headache coming on, and went over to the dispensary where he had set up a bed for himself. Mr Birt was standing by the entrance when he got there. The two men had not spoken for some days, and the Doctor, who had always felt a liking for Mr Birt, would have been pleased to see him were it not for the ache in his head.

'Would you join us for some red wine in my cabin,' said Mr Birt, 'just Mr Hawley and myself?'

'Thank you, Mr Birt, I am afraid that I have a bad headache, and I fear wine would make it worse, but thanks all the same.'

'Those men sent by Don Luis have been asking lots of questions, Doctor. I think the Captain has put it in their minds that something untoward is going on now that you and the ladies have changed quarters. I told them that you spent your time in the hospital as there are several sick people here, but something is in the wind, I don't know what. I just wanted to make certain that you were all safe, and to invite you to our small gathering.'

'Thank you, perhaps another time.'

Mr Birt went up onto the deck and Dr Coleman sat on his bed and held his palms over his aching eyes.

*

Thursday 10th November. Time on the *Colinda* always passed more pleasantly when the Captain was not on board, though there were always niggling doubts about what he might be getting up to. He left the ship just after 1p.m. and returned three hours later. At about five he left again to go on a duck-hunting cruise. In his own mind, Captain Mills was so sure of himself that he had become slightly careless. When one has a plot to carry out, watchfulness is the order of the day, so he was unaware that on the first of these expeditions Don Luis arrived on board in the company of the Danish captain who was able to act as interpreter.

Dr Coleman was thus able to take advantage of the Captain's absence, and he told Don Luis of all their troubles in great detail. Don Luis became serious, for he had not been aware that the problems on board were as critical as the Doctor presented them. He spoke briefly, and the Danish captain interpreted.

'A mail steamer will be ready tomorrow to take all the passengers to Valparaiso where they will be able to make formal statements.'

19
Mr Birt is discharged

When Captain Mills returned from hunting duck, he went directly to the cuddy over which he now held solitary dominion, and drank several glasses of grog served by Mr Luke who stood nearby heating it. Then, drunk almost senseless, he went to bed and snored all night long, not waking until almost midday.

*

Friday 11th November. The mail steamer was to depart at nine in the morning. The passengers were prepared to board the vessel and to proceed to Valparaiso. All looked forward to being out of the jurisdiction of Captain John Powell Mills, Master of the *Colinda*.

The steamer arrived and Dr Coleman received a request to go on board for the captain of that vessel wished to speak with him.

'You understand, Doctor, that the passage to Valparaiso, though not troublesome, will involve some expense,' said that gentleman.

'I naturally supposed that it would, and I am certain that any amount will be met by the Honourable Hudson's Bay Company upon receipt of your bill to them.'

'Doctor, you must understand the way we do things here. We will need to be paid in advance for the voyage.' The captain of the steamer mentioned at this point the price, and Dr Coleman made a mental calculation.

'Why that is over three hundred pounds sterling!' he exclaimed. 'We have not such an amount on board between us.'

He was surprised because the decision to offer the passengers transportation had been made by Don Luis and had nothing to do with him.

'I am sorry, but I can have nothing to do with this,' said the Doctor.

Once back on the *Colinda*, Dr Coleman wrote two letters: the first to the English Consul to ask for his assistance, the second to Captain Mills asking him to arrange supplies of fresh meat and vegetables, for they were beginning to run seriously short.

Captain Mills was up by this time, and, after drinking some brandy to assist with a powerful hangover, dressed slowly with the assistance of Lambert and many curses, and walked out to find the Doctor.

'I will not arrange anything for this ungrateful rabble,' was the first thing he said on seeing him. 'If they need fresh food, you must get it and draw bills on the Company. That is all!' And he left the Doctor who stared after him, mouth agape.

Without delay, Dr Coleman left the *Colinda* and went on shore where he ordered meat and bread at his own expense, intending to bill the Company later. The crew were having a good time ferrying the Captain and themselves to the shore and back, for it meant that they had plenty of free time on land. The Doctor climbed back into the boat which would take him back to the ship, and the two sailors began to row him back. Another boat had been lowered from the *Colinda* and was coming towards them. Seated within were Captain Mills and Mr Birt. The two boats passed without a word exchanged between them, but the Doctor was most curious to know what was afoot.

Upon boarding the *Colinda*, he sought out Mr Hawley, the Second Mate, and asked him about it.

'The Captain and the Mate have had words,' said Hawley.

'Words?'

'Words.' Hawley would have left it there, but the Doctor held him back.

'Captain feels that the crew are spending too much time ashore—taking advantage of his good nature and coming back drunk so's they can't work. Mr Birt said it was necessary for morale, and Captain shouted at him. Said he was a treacherous cur. I heard it all. Mr Birt, he's a gentle soul mostly, but the Captain don't know him, and he gave as good as he got. Mr Birt's been discharged from the *Colinda*, and they've gone off together to book his passage to Valparaiso. Shame really, I liked Mr Birt, but I'll be Chief Mate now.'

20
Captain and Crew

Saturday 12th November. Mr Birt's dismissal worried Dr Coleman greatly, for he had regarded him as an ally. But since there was nothing to be done about it, he resolved to behave as if everything was normal. Consequently, upon discovering that the fresh meat he had ordered had not been sent on board, he went to see Captain Mills to ask permission to take a boat so that he could fetch the supplies himself.

'There is only one boat available at the moment, and I will be using that myself to go ashore. You may travel with me, though,' said the Captain, adding, 'and I will load a musket for you once we are there.'

The Doctor took this as a threat of violence, and decided to remain on the *Colinda*. The day was warm, but dull, and the passengers were restless. They had all been given chores to do, but they carried them out listlessly. The crew, on the other hand, gave every appearance of satisfaction and worked with a will. Few of them resented the disappearance of the Mr Birt from among them, for all unjust commands regarding their work had been issued from his mouth, though they originated with the Captain.

As the day went on, however, the crew also began to give the appearance of dissatisfaction, and Mr Hawley, now Chief Mate, began to find them tiresome. Upon the Captain's return from shore he reported this to him, and in the evening all hands were called up onto the poop deck.

Captain Mills looked at them silently for some minutes, until they began to feel uncomfortable. Eventually he spoke, though in a voice so low that those at the back found it hard to hear what he said.

'Now, my fine fellows, we have come a long way together: halfway round the world. I trust you are looking forward to the continuation of our voyage.'

None of them knew what to say and all looked puzzled, for the Captain did not usually address them in such measured tones.

'Tell me,' he continued, 'are you all content? I hear that some of you have some complaints. If you have any against me, then perhaps now would be a good time speak out, and we can see how best we can put things right.'

The crew began to feel at their ease, for, though during the course of the day a rumour had circulated among them that the Captain had been at the root of their discomfort during the passage, he seemed to be offering them a chance to air their grievances.

The first to speak was Able Seaman Wrench. 'Capt'n, you'll excuse me for saying it, but the men here feel that we have not had as much in the way of vittals as we have been used to previous, like.'

'It's hard to have such long hours without enough meat,' said Able Seaman Anderson. The rest of the crew shuffled uncomfortably, for they were not used to being given the freedom to speak their minds, and they were a little embarrassed by the whole conversation.

Three or four of them nodded in agreement. Captain Mills looked serious, but few realised the danger they were in.

'Then there was that boy Barrett who was hit so hard,' said Able Seaman Jones.

'Happen he deserved it,' said Anderson.

'Maybe he did, but he should not have been made to climb up the mizzenmast afterwards,' said Jones, 'he might have fallen and been killed.'

Barrett, who was there, squirmed at the recollection and hid behind one of the burlier sailors.

'Is that it?' said the Captain.

Then poured forth all their resentment at being made to work long hours without rest in freezing weather, the lack of grog, the lack of food, the condescension shown to them by the Captain and the officers, and many other matters which they had stored up till that moment.

Captain Mills, who had expected, or hoped, that his mere presence would be enough to cow them into expressions of support for him, became infuriated by this talk, and striding up to Able Seamen Jones and Henderson (though the latter had uttered not a word), struck them both in the face with his fists. The two, who were the least muscular of the adult crew, were sent sprawling on the deck; the rest of the crew became silent.

Captain Mills took two pistols, both loaded, from the pockets of his coat, and held them across his chest. 'This is the last time I will say this to you—all of you. I am Master here, and you are all under my command. If you wish to return to your homes untrammelled by chains, then you will heed what I say and re-member it. I will have none of this kind of talk on my ship.'

Had Mr Birt been on board, it is possible that none of this would have happened, for he had a knack of calming the Cap-tain, or at least deflecting his anger. Mr Hawley, though, had none of his predecessor's skill in that capacity, and, though he regretted the outburst they had all witnessed, was too pleased with his own promotion to do anything to ameliorate the situa-tion—did he not owe his new position to Captain Mills?

*

Sunday 13th November. In the early part of the afternoon, three of the passengers took it upon themselves to speak to the Captain. George Brown, Thomas Easton and James Newlands stood before him deferentially and asked for permission to go on shore.

Captain Mills stood for a moment saying nothing. He appeared to be thinking things over, as if trying to work out in his mind whether it would be an advantage or a disadvantage to allow them to go. Unable to come to a conclusion in the matter, he shrugged his shoulders.

'I will not give you permission, neither will I stop you.'

The men thanked him, and went away. A little later, they were seen with a washing tub on the main deck. Others were there also, and there were signs of furtive joking amongst them.

The three rapscallions undressed themselves and put their clothes into the tub to which they had attached some fishing line. The tub being lowered into the sea, they jumped overboard. George Brown held the other end of the line as they did so, and they then swam to the shore towing the tub behind them.

Mrs Hunter who had seen all went off to tell Mrs Brown what her husband was up to. (The other men were unmarried.) 'You would have thought that a grown man would know better,' said Mrs Hunter.

Mrs Brown laughed. 'That's George for you. But wait to see what he brings back with him.'

'If he comes back.'

'Oh, there's no doubt about that, he knows which side his bread is buttered,' said Mrs Brown knowingly.

Later that afternoon, and before the three adventurers had returned, Dr Coleman was surprised to find that a number of the male passengers, Scottish as well as Norwegian, and some of the crew appeared to be drunk. On enquiring how the men could be drunk, Mr Hawley told him that brandy had been brought on board by local traders, and that the men had exchanged their clothes for spirits.

Captain Mills, on being informed of this latest incident, seemed unsurprised and remarked to Mr Hawley, 'I see a great many things, but I do not wish to see them.'

The Doctor determined to prevent any more traders from coming on board, but his efforts failed. In any case, the damage had already been done, and as evening drew on the men soon became noisy. The noise grew and grew until a great uproar prevailed throughout the ship as those who had drunk the most danced, sang and yelled. Arguments broke out among the sailors, and Jones, who resented the Captain's ill-usage of him the previous day, was egged on by his shipmates until he became so violent that he broke a number of the cuddy windows.

The Norwegians sat drinking among themselves, growing gloomier by the minute. There were occasional raised voices among them, but as they spoke entirely in Norwegian, their arguments were ignored by the Scots who began a ceilidh and went stamping around the main deck with their wives (whether they were willing or not).

This continued until the early hours of Monday morning when most had become too exhausted to continue. Dr Coleman, who had found it impossible to sleep because of the noise, left his quarters in the dispensary and went up on deck. Wrench stood by the foremast smoking his pipe seemingly lost in thought.

'Evening, Doctor.'

'Good evening, Wrench.'

'Fine night now that it's all quieted down.'

'It is.'

'Men seem happier, mostly.'

'But the passengers have bartered away their clothes, and they will regret that when they have nothing left to wear.'

'Captain said that the traders were allowed on board, so we never stopped them,' said Wrench.

The Doctor sighed. 'They're not really happy, it was the brandy, that's all. They'll wake with sore heads and blame me for not being able to cure them. The Norwegians are complaining that they get poorer food than the Scots, because they are all single men and the Scots have got women and children with them, so the best of it goes to them, you see.'

They became aware of a small boat approaching the *Colinda* from the shore. There were five men inside. Two sailors had clandestinely taken the jolly boat out and rowed it to the shore to fetch the three adventurers, and it was only now that they all deemed it safe enough to come back.

'Wrench, you knew about this,' said Dr Coleman with a half smile.

'You know, Doctor, I always think that since time passes without any possibility of stopping it, everything is bound to come to an end eventually, and that includes our time on this ship. Why, this time next year, you'll look back on your time here and wonder what all that fuss was about.'

'Why, Wrench, you're a philosopher,' said Dr Coleman.

'You see if I'm not right, and then when that time comes round, you'll remember what I said just now.'

'Thanks, Wrench,' said the Doctor, 'I think I'll go back down now.'

Wrench watched as he left, and after he had gone gave a low whistle. That was the signal for the five men to board the *Colinda* with their finds. 'Man's an idiot!' he said to himself, though whether he meant the Doctor or Mankind in general is impossible to say.

21
Life on the *Colinda*

Rumour spread among the passengers that a man-of-war would soon be arriving at Valdivia to conduct them all to Valparaiso. Their joy at this news soon changed to despair when it was contradicted. All were impatient for a change in their lot; arguments and fights became commonplace. Daily, they looked towards the shore with hope and longing, but the Captain forbade them to leave the *Colinda*. In this he was supported by the Doctor who was certain that any who left would abscond. The traders who came on board told the passengers that agricultural labourers were much needed, and that they might be well paid. Many longed to abandon their contracts and to make their home in Chile.

The following morning, the passengers were surprised to find that their breakfast provisions had not been supplied to them. Up on deck there was an unusual lack of activity. None of the crew were to be seen going about their usual tasks. Dr Coleman went searching for an explanation, and soon discovered that the crew had decided not to work any longer as long as they were under the command of Captain Mills.

The Captain was in the cuddy eating his own breakfast when the Doctor and five of the emigrants walked in to see him.

'Captain, since the crew are not working, I would like to ask you to appoint a replacement cook and steward for the passengers.'

The Captain made no reply, but carried on with his meal as if there had been no interruption. John McIntyre stepped forward and opened his mouth to speak, but the others held him back. Eventually, the Captain finished his meal, and then looked up at the men standing before him.

'Your troubles are nothing to me, I have no intention of mixing myself up in them.'

'Captain,' said Dr Coleman, 'it is for you to command the crew and to select a cook and a steward.'

'I will not do so, neither will you be permitted to do so. There it is, gentlemen, and now I have work to do. I will send a midshipman, perhaps, to see to your needs.' He stood and walked into his cabin, closing the door behind him.

This was most unsatisfactory. All five of the emigrants made a movement towards the cabin door, but the Doctor stepped before them and shook his head. 'That will not help, we must find other ways of rectifying the situation.'

They left, and returned to their comrades. All were now in a highly disturbed frame of mind and might have been prepared to do the Captain some ill. A short while later Don Luis arrived together with four soldiers, and the crew were summoned to the poop deck where he addressed them in broken English, asking if they would return to their duties. All refused, stating their reason was ill-usage of them by Captain Mills. As a result of this, all the crew were taken on shore with the exception of the two stewards, the four cabin boys and Mr Hawley. The four Chilean soldiers, though, remained on board. Mrs Leigh and her children left the *Colinda* with the crew to find accommodation in the town.

The days passed uncomfortably. All were nervous. Only the Captain seemed unconcerned. He walked among the passengers speaking to groups of them in calm and measured tones, telling them of his great concern for their well-being, and at the same time accusing the Doctor of infamous behaviour that was at the root of all their troubles. Some were soothed by him and believed his words, others did not, and this itself added to the excitement and led to further quarrels.

The health of all on board became a matter of concern. Many were showing signs of scurvy, but still, the Captain refused to allow fresh provisions to be brought on board. Dr Coleman wrote a letter to Don Luis asking for provisions to be sent on board, and the Captain of the Port agreed to this as long as he would be able to bill the Company for the cost. When the food arrived, Captain Mills forbade Feltham, the passengers' steward, to serve anything to them. The passengers helped themselves, though with what organisation and decorum can be imagined!

When Sunday came, the Captain held Divine Service in the cuddy. Only two passengers attended, and this displeased him. He held another service in the afternoon for those members of his crew still on board. Mr Hawley, the mate, did not appear as he was busy, and the Captain went to look for him. Finding him on the poop deck looking out to sea, he told him of his displeasure at his nonappearance, and ordered that he remove his quarters from his comfortable cabin to the crew's quarters in the fo'c's'le.

'Make your bed there any way you please, Mr Hawley.'

Hawley, muttered something beneath his breath as the Captain left and scowled blackly.

Cases of scurvy continued, and the Doctor was hard-pressed treating so many. His life was not made easier by the impudence of Feltham who was now in charge of food stores, but who refused to cooperate with any of his requests to allow the passengers sufficient supplies. Captain Mills, naturally, refused to have anything to do with it.

Many of the men were now greatly anxious to go on shore. Dr Coleman refused to sanction anything of the sort, but, in any case, it was not within his power to organise such a venture. Six of the passengers attempted to take the lifeboat and leave the *Colinda*, but were prevented from doing so by the four soldiers. Captain Mills, though, allowed himself to go duck hunting, and also gave permission for the four midshipmen to go on similar expeditions.

Miss Forsyth and Dr Coleman had by now returned to their previous quarters for the hospital was now full, and patients were sleeping in the dispensary. The danger from the Captain's violent behaviour seemed to have diminished, but Captain Mills was ready to take advantage of their return.

22
Feltham, Luke and Lambert

William Feltham was a scrawny individual who was not popular among the passengers. It was not his fault, he felt, that he had been placed in the lowly position of Steward to a bunch of dimwitted emigrants, when he was surely fitted for far better things. Mean-mouthed and small-eyed he weighed out provisions mathematically and found ways to profit from any scrapings left.

On Tuesday 22nd November he was summoned for an audience with the Captain. Dr Coleman was on shore at the time, attending in medical capacity to Don Luis's wife who had bad toothache. Feltham had no qualms about ingratiating himself with the Captain; indeed, it was, he felt, most necessary to do so, for though the Captain's own position might be sticky, any chance of advancing his own person was not to be missed. When Feltham left the Captain's presence, there was a look of satisfaction on his face. Mr Luke, on his own way to take orders remarked upon it.

'Can't say anything yet,' said Feltham, tapping the side of his nose, 'but all will be revealed soon.'

In fact, it was not until the following day that the reason for Feltham's smile was made known. In the morning Captain Mills called for Dr Coleman to attend him. That day the Captain was suffering mightily with asthma, something which had not troubled him much for some years, but which had returned to plague him in recent months. This weakness made him irritable with himself and others.

Dr Coleman was as sympathetic as he could be towards a man he loathed, but there was little he could do to help. As he made to leave, the Captain called him back.

'Doctor,' he said with wheezy voice, as if about to make a comment of little importance, 'just one other matter occurs to me which I should tell you.'

Doctor Coleman was not to be deceived by the gentle way in which the other spoke. He saw the sardonic smile which flickered across the Captain's face, and mistrusted it. He waited for what was to be said.

'As you know, Mr Birt is no longer with us, and Mr Hawley has been sent for'ard and is to act as Chief Mate for me no longer.' The Captain picked up his pipe and stroked the bowl as if in deep contemplation. 'I have decided to appoint Feltham as Chief Mate, for otherwise there will be no officers on board. That is all.'

This was intended as the signal for the Doctor to leave. Instead, he remained rooted to the floor.

'That is all,' repeated the Captain.

'Surely Feltham is not capable to act in that capacity. He has never been to sea before. If there should be an accident while you are on shore, he would not know what to do.'

'You admit, then, the necessity of my presence? In any case, the decision has been made. That is all.'

Dr Coleman left and went to speak with Miss Forsyth to tell her this latest news.

*

In the afternoon Captain Mills left the ship to go on shore, and at supper time he had still not returned. Miss Forsyth and Dr Coleman sat at the cuddy table eating a poor meal. They conversed in hushed tones, for Mr Luke and Lambert were hovering close by. They seemed impatient for the meal to finish, and did not disguise their attempts to overhear what was being said.

'… two services last Sunday and none the previous two—it can't be right, God will punish him for it,' Miss Forsyth said quietly.

Lambert, overhearing, although it was not his place to comment on this remark, said aloud in sarcastic tones, 'Yes, he will turn his toes up and die in convulsions!'

The Doctor looked sternly at him and told him to hold his tongue.

Half-way through their meal Feltham arrived without knocking at the door. He was carrying two plates of boiled beef, and spoke a moment with Luke. And then, without a 'by-your-leave', both men sat at the cuddy table and began to eat their own suppers while Lambert served them. Miss Forsyth affected not to notice, but Dr Coleman felt grossly insulted at this impertinence.

'You should not be starting your meals here while we are still eating,' he protested.

'Well, as to that, Doctor, I have a position of authority now, and I intend to take advantage of it,' said Feltham. Luke sniggered. 'Mr Luke is my guest, and if I choose to invite him he may eat with me.'

'Might I have some water, please?' asked Miss Forsyth, for there was no more in the cuddy at that moment.

The Doctor looked at Lambert, for it was his duty as cabin boy to fetch it. Lambert looked uncertain, and made a half-hearted attempt to go. Feltham stopped him.

'You will have to wait till we have finished—unless you choose to fetch it yourself,' he said, and he laughed mockingly. Luke began to laugh too, while the Doctor and Miss Forsyth looked on incredulously.

★

The next day Captain Mills kept to his cabin at mealtimes with the understanding that he would take his own meals there, as he claimed to be unwell. He was attended by Mr Luke and also by Lambert who at one point in the afternoon spoke with him for some time.

Such little care was taken that evening with the preparation of their food, that Miss Forsyth and the Doctor found themselves presented with cold, almost raw, meat. The Doctor had it taken back to the galley to have it cooked properly. Shortly afterwards, Luke brought them a message from the cook to say that it could not be done, for the meat was already half-eaten.

At this, Miss Forsyth began to scream and Dr Coleman lost his temper. He sent the food back again demanding that it be cooked. Luke left the two of them fuming with rage. He kept them waiting for over an hour, and finally returned with two plates of meat. But, horror! It was more raw than that which they had sent away in the first place.

Their resentment at their treatment increased still further when they were told that Feltham was to be placed at the head of the table to take his meals with them. They were both disgusted, for Feltham's eating habits were revolting. The Doctor's indignation knew no bounds, for he had been expressly told, before the voyage started, that he should consider Feltham to be his servant. Dr Coleman and Miss Forsyth both stood and left the table in protest, and refused to eat with him.

Feltham was so pleased with himself that he went strutting round the *Colinda* with his hands either in his pockets or, when he really wanted to make a show of himself, clasped behind his back. Lambert, the cabin boy, managed to ingratiate himself with Feltham and was encouraged to be a cheeky as he liked.

*

Mr Hawley, who had been made to stay in very poor accommodation for displeasing the Captain, had become very ill with a fever. He sent a message to the Captain asking for medicine, but was refused. Dr Coleman, though he was not supposed to treat crew members, examined him, and supplied him with what medical comforts he could, though he suspected malaria, and had nothing that might give proper aid.

*

The food continued to be inedible, leftovers were dished up over and over again, cooking utensils, crockery and cutlery were left unwashed, and Feltham, Luke and Lambert continued to be impertinent. Feltham, though, seemed to have a degree of remorse, or perhaps he felt that since matters might go the Doctor's way if there was an inquiry, he felt it necessary to make peace.

In the afternoon he approached the Doctor and said meekly, 'I hope you won't think badly of me, sir. It is not my fault that I sit at table with you—the Captain insisted I should take the head of the table.'

'You have no business to be there unless you choose to be there of your own volition,' said the Doctor spikily, and he stalked off.

At the same time Miss Forsyth was feeling faint and in need of some water. Mr Luke had been serving the Captain with a late lunch, and having done so entered the cuddy.

'Please bring me some water, Mr Luke, I'm afraid I am not feeling well,' said Miss Forsyth.

'I would not fetch water for you if you were Queen Victoria,' he responded. 'I am not bound to wait on you, you must find another to do your bidding.' This last remark was said with a

knowing and offensive tone laden with implication of improprieties. Miss Forsyth would have reprimanded him once she
had recovered from her shock at being thus addressed, but by
that time he had gone.

On Friday, a letter from the Captain to the Doctor and Miss
Forsyth was posted up where the passengers might all see it.

*

The Captain presents his compliments to the Lady and Gentleman Cabin Passengers, *[a reference to Dr Coleman and Miss
Forsyth]*. He would like to inform them that he is not afraid of
turning his toes up nor dying in convulsions he has an honest
conscience and all the hypocritical sayings will not deter him
from keeping the Sabbath as he has done the whole passage.
The Captain is perfectly aware that you would be glad if his
toes were turned up.

*

Captain Mills had vowed to himself to bide his time, but when
Lambert told him of his sarcastic reply to Miss Forsyth's remark that he (the Captain) would be punished for holding ir-
regular services, he had not been able to resist writing his letter
to demonstrate his knowledge of all that was said or done on
the *Colinda*, and to imply that, confined to his cabin though he
was, he sat spider-like at the edge of a web which reached all
corners of the ship.

23
Mr Hawley

At noon on Sunday, Don Luis and an interpreter arrived having been invited by Captain Mills for lunch in the cuddy. Captain Mills was all smiles, and his politeness, for a moment, even extended to Miss Forsyth for whom he held the door as she entered.

'This is a nice room,' said Don Luis.

'It would be very comfortable if we had a few *respectable* passengers here,' came the reply. This pointed remark implied that the current cabin passengers were not respectable, and Miss Forsyth bridled at it.

'I really cannot eat here when I am subject to such insults,' she burst out. 'I will have my meal in my cabin,' she added haughtily, 'with your permission, of course.' She went into her cabin and closed the door after herself.

'Shall I take her a plate?' said Lambert, who was there to serve the meal.

'No indeed!' said the Captain. 'She must come to the table if she wants any food.'

The Doctor, deeply embarrassed in front of the guests, began to remonstrate, but was silenced by a look from Don Luis, who muttered something to the interpreter.

'He say he would do the same as you, Captain. Such rudeness, it cannot be permitted,' said that gentleman.

They ate the meal, the conversation was stilted and over-formal, but when it was finished, and after a few glasses of wine, the Captain became less careful.

'That lady displayed herself in no good light at all,' he said. 'Loose morals, that's her all over.'

At that moment Miss Forsyth opened her door and rushed into the cuddy. She had been listening to the conversation from within, certain that the Captain was bound to say something against her.

'It is not so, indeed it is not. How can I possibly stay in your company when you insult me so grossly before everybody?'

Dr Coleman began to speak in support of her, but the Captain interrupted him at once.

'You are a liar and a damned rascal,' and with that, he picked up his glass of wine and flung the contents in the Doctor's face. 'Come on then,' he continued abusively. 'Come and strike a blow at me now, if you dare.'

The Doctor backed away.

'I thought not,' said Captain Mills. 'You damned coward, come and fight me now! I will get my pistols, and we will shoot it out.'

Don Luis sat at the table, grinning, while his interpreter told him the meaning of all that was being said.

'I challenged this *gentleman* before, but the coward refused.'

'One of the pistols is broken,' said Dr Coleman, trying to appear braver than he was.

'You're a liar and a coward!' said the Captain. 'I will happily take the broken one myself and still shoot you before you can shoot me.'

This stand-off might have continued longer, but at that moment Feltham entered the cuddy to inform Captain Mills that a boat was approaching the *Colinda*. The Captain left to greet the latest arrival together with Don Luis and the interpreter who both had to return to shore.

The new arrival came to tell Captain Mills that one of the passengers had swum to the shore and was walking about with a musket. Dr Coleman was summoned into the Captain's presence, and berated for allowing this to happen.

He, upon looking towards the shore with a telescope, saw at once that it was not one of their men, and said so.

'It is your duty to see that this kind of thing does not happen,' said the Captain, ignoring the facts of the case.

'I am not Chief Mate here,' said the Doctor.

'No, you are an ignorant boy, and you do not do your duty!'

'Kindly do not insult me in this fashion.'

'I will insult you in any way I wish. I am Master here, and I can say and do as I please on board my own ship.'

The Doctor might have answered, but at that moment Mr Hawley came up to them. He seemed to be in a very poor state, clutching his clothes around him as if he were cold, though the weather was quite warm.

'Excuse me, Doctor,' he said, 'I feel most unwell.'

Dr Coleman, forgetting all but his duty to aid the sick, went to Hawley and asked to examine his tongue.

'Do you intend to doctor my entire crew?' said Captain Mills impatiently.

The Doctor made no reply but continued his examination.

'Who do you think will pay for your treatment?' shouted the Captain. 'You shall not be permitted any medicine at my expense, or at the expense of the Company.'

He took hold of Mr Hawley, and wrenched him away from the Doctor's care and forcibly marched him to his quarters. Mr Hawley, who was suffering from influenza and was too ill to put up much of a struggle, found himself thrust down onto his poor bed, handcuffed and coatless. The Captain marched off in a fury, leaving him shivering. Dr Coleman found him there shortly after, and did what he could to make him comfortable, covering him with blankets and dosing him with smelling salts.

When he left, he found himself face to face with Captain Mills.

'You are to have nothing to do with my crew, not Hawley, not any of them. If he requires medical treatment than I will take charge of it. He will be taken on shore tomorrow and locked up in prison until further notice.'

'Captain, if that happens he will die. He is in no fit state to go to prison.'

'If he dies I will be answerable for it,' said the Captain.

'What use will that be if he is already dead?'

'By Hell, I am Master here! Do not presume to interfere with my crew.'

The two men parted with great animosity.

24
A Petition

The last days of November dragged out unmercifully. There seemed nothing for the passengers to do but wait for something to happen. The weather was temperate and warm, and fresh breezes blew in from the west. By the time December arrived a number of further changes had taken place on board the *Colinda*.

Miss Forsyth had left the ship and taken rooms on shore; Dr Coleman had remained on board. He kept to himself as much as he could, documenting all that happened with a sharp, though partial, eye. He had on one afternoon, at the request of Don Luis, gone on shore to treat a badly injured worker, a carpenter who had fallen from a roof and injured his arm severely. Since Midshipman Bullmore was the son of a surgeon, he had taken the lad with him so that he might assist in the event an amputation might be necessary. Mr Bullmore had then been arrested on his return for leaving the ship without the Captain's permission. Captain Mills had made a great show to Don Luis of his own magnanimity by showing him the stores on board of chickens and tobacco. Dr Coleman made note of the irony of this demonstration, since the passengers had been allowed none of these items. The passengers had been commanded by the Captain to wash below deck against the Doctor's wishes, as he had hoped they might take full advantage of the fresh air on the deck. The cantankerous Mrs Hunter, now a shade of her former self, was given an empty cask to store some goods in, but this had been roughly taken from her at the Captain's orders, broken up and thrown overboard. Captain Mills continued to be obstructive, doing all he could to impede the Doctor from treating the injured carpenter by denying him access to the boats to take him on shore, and the man, therefore, became seriously ill and nearly died as a result. Ordinary Seaman Rowland, only a young boy, was thrashed on the deck one evening by the Captain for an unnamed misdemeanour. The passengers became aware of this only because the boy had called out, 'Murder!' at the top of his voice. Mrs Sutherland tried to intervene, but was soundly abused by the Captain, who was inebriated to the point where he was completely out of control. He called her a whore, and accused her of sleeping with the Doctor. Doctor Coleman, infuriated by this denounced it immediately.

'Hold your tongue,' shouted the Captain drunkenly, 'or I will punch your nose!'

Many heard this altercation, some were shocked, others laughed, the Doctor was simply mortified. William Sutherland led his wife, who was crying with vexation, away. Captain Mills staggered back into the cuddy and collapsed in a drunken stupor onto the table. No one went near him for some time, but eventually Mr Luke and Lambert managed to get him into his bed.

Dr Coleman wrote all of this down, and observed that something else was not quite right, for the Captain now seemed anxious for all the passengers to leave the *Colinda*, and was spending some time in the company of Don Luis who was a frequent visitor. 'I suspect he is trying to sell the ship and its contents for his own profit,' he wrote. 'I will not allow the passengers to leave, for they have a contract to fulfil, and I have a duty to the company.'

On Friday 2nd December, the officers, crew and passengers sent a petition to the Governor of Valdivia complaining of their treatment at the hands of Captain Mills. The document had been drawn up by the Doctor, and all had signed.

*

To the Governor of the province of Valdivia,

We, the officers seamen and passengers on board of the British ship *Colinda* from the Port of London bound for Vancouver's Island do petition assistance from your Lordship.

Captn Mills having brought us into this port entirely against our wish and absolutely and in the presence of all, refused to carry us on to Valparaiso where we can have the differences existing between Captn Mills and your Petitioners, terminated by the British Authorities there.

And in consequence of his actions, despotic and tyrannical, and his propensity to liquor which causes a complete aberration of his mind, he is quite incompetent to act as Master to navigate the vessel and have at his charge and responsibility over two hundred souls.

The Chief Officer having been discharged by the said Captain and at the present moment the Second Officer being under arrest, we have no officer to navigate the vessel.

On the 7th November we entered this port and from that time to the present moment no decisive steps have been taken either to terminate our differences or towards the furtherance of our voyage. Sickness in the shape of scurvy and rheumatic fever have already presented themselves among the passengers and are daily on the increase making our situation still more deplorable.

We, your humble petitioners, finding no other means to expedite our departure from this Port appeal unanimously to your Lordship to please nominate a navigator to take charge of the vessel, to whom we all oblige ourselves obediently to submit and comply with any orders which he may think proper to enact during the short voyage between this port and Valparaiso placing the vessel under the immediate control of the British Admiral.

We, the under signed petitioners, supplicate that your Lordship will grant our humble and just request, and for the health of your Lordship we shall ever pray.

*

Captain Mills, however, had other ideas, and refused point-blank to countenance any disturbance of his plans. His mind was a hive of contradiction. Thoughts buzzed around in all directions, and he could not see the illogicality of his behaviour. Perhaps this should not be surprising; to a madman all are mad except himself.

He wanted the passengers off his ship so that he could proceed to Vancouver's Island with the cargo, but refused to let them go. He wished to take the cargo to its destination, while at the same time desiring to sell it for his own profit. He insisted that the ship should be closely guarded by the soldiers who had been sent on board for that purpose, but chose to ignore the fact that it was not guarded. His animosity towards the Doctor had grown into an obsession which he believed perfectly reasonable. Gathering the four midshipmen around him, he declared that the Doctor was a fiend, and not to be trusted.

'If I once had hold of the Doctor's papers I would scatter them overboard, and him with them.'

He gazed at them, looking from one to the other as if expecting a midshipman would volunteer to fetch him Dr Coleman and his papers, but seeing only blank and puzzled faces before him, he retired to his cabin to nurse with brandy a shooting headache which had suddenly manifested itself above his right eye.

*

Dr Coleman, meanwhile, had other matters to worry about. On Sunday, he discovered that several of the Scottish men had made their way on shore, and were refusing to return to the ship. He found them and tried gently to persuade them to return, some of them did so, but he felt that he was fighting a losing battle. Even the faithful Norwegians began to take advantage of the lax security on the Colinda.

*

Monday 5th December. Captain Mills went ashore for several hours and the crew took advantage of his absence by drinking several bottles of port. Even the Boatswain became intoxicated, and instead of remaining aloof from the other men, as was usual for him, he joined in the merriment, and, encouraged by some of the more troublesome crew members, vowed to obtain his discharge papers from the Captain once he had returned. Captain Mills refused to entertain such a thing, and the Boatswain returned to his duties in a somewhat surly fashion and with a raging headache.

Tuesday came, and more of the male passengers began to leave the vessel without leave. Dr Coleman recorded their names, but he had little hope now of controlling the comings and goings of those under him.

Wednesday, and two visitors came on board. Both were captains, one English and the other Spanish. Captain Mills invited them to take some wine while he and Dr Coleman were having an afternoon tea. An uneasy state of peace existed between the two. Dr Coleman, for his part, was glad, and hoped it might remain so. Captain Mills, on the other hand was unpredictable, and the Doctor knew that this unofficial truce could not last long.

Feltham came to the table, to the Doctor's annoyance, and once seated with the others began to pour out a cup for himself.

'Pass the sugar, Feltham,' said Dr Coleman.

At this, Captain Mills held out a hand to prevent Feltham from doing as requested, and turned to the Doctor. 'Pass the sugar *Mister* Feltham,' he said reprovingly.

Dr Coleman flushed, but affected not to notice the reprimand. Captain Mills grinned sardonically, but the other captains seemed not to notice the stiff atmosphere in the cuddy.

The English captain turned to Mills and put his wineglass down. 'I have no doubt,' he said, 'that you will hear some news tomorrow that a naval officer and some marines will be detailed to take the *Colinda* on to Valparaiso.'

'Nothing,' responded Captain Mills, 'not even God Almighty can make me take the *Colinda* to Valparaiso. Not if Christ himself were to appear on earth would I allow my ship, my property, to be taken from me. I should like to see who will dare to try! Did you know I have been informed against for selling tobacco and clothes, I'll sell every damned stick in the ship to find fresh meat for my crew. I intend to stop here till every passenger has gone out of the vessel, and then I will proceed on my voyage.'

The others present were somewhat nonplussed by this reply, and quickly found excuses to leave. Dr Coleman slipped out first, feeling greatly stressed by the proceedings.

Captain Mills, after restating his order that none belonging to the *Colinda* should be permitted to leave, went himself on shore in the evening, and the Doctor took the opportunity to be rowed to the shore himself in order to fetch some of the men who had absconded and were lying tipsy close to the water's edge.

25
The Return of Mr Birt and Miss Forsyth

Thursday 8th December. Early in the morning, the mail steamer was observed in the harbour. Captain Mills went onto it and returned a short time later with Mr Birt. All hands were summoned onto the poop deck and told that Mr Birt was once more chief officer.

All this was keenly observed by the passengers whose natural curiosity had caused them to arrive uninvited onto the scene. This event was followed almost at once by the arrival onto the *Colinda* of some marines who were escorting a number of official-looking gentlemen. One made a brief announcement to the passengers:

'Captain Mills, having now abandoned command of this vessel, the er… *Colinda*, in consequence of the considerable demands made upon him by certain persons here present, the underwriters of this voyage, under the authority of Admiral Fairfax Moresby, Commander-in-Chief of the Pacific Station currently at Valparaiso, have commanded that the vessel should proceed to Valparaiso without delay.'

Captain Mills stared on, stony faced, as this declaration was made, and then turned on his heels and walked smartly into his cabin, followed by the official gentlemen. The marines remained on the deck, where they were subject to the scrutiny of the women.

An hour later, the officials, Lieutenant Lowther, Dr Moore, Mr Ling (agent to the underwriters), and Captain Mills, left the ship to go into Valdivia in order to obtain money to pay the ship's expenses. Knowing that they would be away for some hours, Dr Coleman took full advantage by allowing the women to go ashore in order to wash their clothes. He observed them from the deck as, once they had landed, they proceeded about their business, while the Chileans crowded around as if completely astonished at the sight of so many strange señoras.

'It's like a great village fete,' he remarked to Mr Birt.

Many of the children and men had by this time also arrived on shore. Some sat in groups on the grass playing, others lay in the sun, stretching their pale but weathered limbs while the women slaved away at their task. Some of the men had, unsurprisingly, managed to acquire alcoholic beverages and were quite insensible from drink.

The good-natured conversation and play could not last for long, though, and eventually scuffles and fights broke out among the men. They were brought on board, one with a broken nose. This was an unpleasant brute of a fellow who, as soon as he saw Dr Coleman, clenched his fists and said, 'I have a score to settle with you'. He lunged at the Doctor, but missed and went sprawling onto the deck.

Dr Coleman had him carried below, and then looked at Mr Birt. 'I have no idea what that was about,' he said. 'I have hardly spoken to the man before.'

Friday came, and Miss Forsyth and Mrs Leigh, having been informed that the *Colinda* would now be proceeding to Valparaiso, returned to the *Colinda*. They kept out of the way of Captain Mills when he returned a little later, and for the moment, things seemed to be comparatively calm. The day passed without incident. The *Colinda* was scheduled to depart Valdivia the next day, and Captain Mills, having paid the port expenses, the passengers were mustered on deck and counted. All being present, at three o'clock in the afternoon, the anchor was weighed, and the *Colinda* started to Valparaiso.

For once, the Captain was polite to everyone. The passengers were all delighted to leave Valdivia where they had been for so long and where they had their constitutions so much injured. The next few days passed without incident. Dr Coleman put the Captain's good manners down to the fact of the marines having remained on board for the duration of the voyage to Valparaiso, noting in his journal:

'All is quiet, for, now that Her Majesty's officers are on board, the Captain's talk is so soft and angelic that one would hardly suppose him capable of even thinking of anything wrong.'

The passengers began to feel cheerful, and entertained themselves after their daily chores by singing in the evenings.

On Tuesday land was sighted. The *Colinda* had arrived at Valparaiso. Dr Coleman felt such a feeling of relief, that he went about grinning from ear to ear. He and Miss Forsyth were alone in the cabin as the anchor was dropped, and they held each other tightly. Their tears of joy mingled. 'It'll soon be over,' she whispered to him, and they went out onto the deck to look at the harbour.

The Doctor still had a number or sick passengers to treat; Mrs Lewis, wife of the ship's schoolmaster, had become dangerously ill, but the Doctor was prevented from seeking assistance ashore by the Captain until the following day (Wednesday) when he was able to summon two English doctors based at Valparaiso to come aboard to give their opinions. Matters were grave, and, despite their best efforts, the lady died on Thursday evening. Dr Coleman decided that a postmortem would be necessary, but this the Captain refused to allow. Matters came to a head at suppertime, just as the soup was being served in the cabin. The Doctor began to protest at the Captain's stubbornness, but was at once interrupted.

'You still do not do your duty,' bellowed the Captain.

The Doctor held up his hand to stop the inevitable stream of invective he expected to follow this remark.

'Damn your eyes!' continued Captain Mills hoarsely. 'If you shake your hand at me, I will throw the soup tureen at you, though it should cost me a thousand pounds.'

*

A frustrating few days followed for Dr Coleman as he tried in vain to have an interview with the British Consul. He did, however, manage to have the ship's provisions surveyed by the port authorities, and was gratified when the Captain was reprimanded for his neglect of these matters. Captain Mills left the ship with bad grace to buy provisions, but the Doctor did not hold out hope that things would improve much. They did not. The Captain was his usual difficult self, putting up obstacles to all Dr Coleman's reasonable requests, and refusing him permission to leave the *Colinda*.

On Monday 19th December, Captain Mills sent a note to the most senior naval officer then present at Valparaiso complaining that the crew were deserting the ship. Captain Morshead of HMS Dido arranged for the matter to be formally heard in court, and sent an official request to the British Consul.

*

'Whereas Mr John Mills Master of the Ship *Colinda* has represented by letter received by me this day Sunday a charge of Mutinous and Piratical conduct and threats against persons on board the *Colinda*, it is my direction that you proceed on board the *Colinda* at 9 o'clock a.m. on the 21st December and hold a Court to investigate the said Charges in Compliance with the Mercantile Marine Act 1814. Given under my hand on board Her Majesty's Ship Dido at Valparaiso 19th of December 1853. (Signed) N.H. Morshead, Captain of Her Majesty's Ship Dido.'

*

The following day Dr Coleman was left in no doubt as to the direction things were likely to take.

A representative of the British Consul, Mr Taylor, arrived on board and read to the Doctor the charges that Captain Mills had laid against both him and the passengers.

'The proceedings against you will commence tomorrow morning at the British Consulate,' said Taylor. 'That is all,' he remarked, stopping with a gesture the protestation that Dr Coleman had been about to make.

26

The Case against Dr Coleman

Wednesday 21st December. The Court met at 10 a.m. to consider the case against Dr Coleman and sixty-two of the passengers. The Doctor felt unaccountably calm, all his nervousness seemed to evaporate from him as soon as he entered the large room where the proceedings were to take place.

Behind a long table on a dais at one end of the room sat Mr Lowther (Lieutenant of the Port), Mr Rouse (Her Britannic Majesty's Consul in Valparaiso), and Mr Cumming (Master of the merchant vessel Briganza). Mr Taylor acted as Clerk of the Court. Since many of the defendants were Norwegian, the Norwegian Vice Consul was present to act as interpreter. Twenty-seven of the passengers were Scottish, thirty-five were Norwegian.

The passengers were charged with mutinous and piratical conduct, and Dr Coleman was charged with aiding and abetting them. The Doctor, on behalf of the passengers, made his own charge against the Captain: that the latter had failed to provide enough food for the passengers.

Captain Mills had appointed a solicitor, Mr William Corde, to act for him, the Doctor represented himself, and the passengers were represented by the Doctor and Robert Ewart.

The case against the Norwegians was disposed of quickly. Witnesses were heard, and the charges were dismissed. Then came the charges against the Scottish men and Dr Coleman.

Captain Mills had summoned a number of witnesses to support his case: Mr Birt (Chief Mate), Mr Hawley (2nd Mate), Mr Chambers (Midshipman), Feltham (Steward), together with the apprentices Barrett, Lambert, Flude and Darnell.

The first three were questioned by the Captain's solicitor, Mr Corde, and then cross-examined by Dr Coleman. Captain Mills felt the blood rising to his cheeks with fury as the witnesses would not back up his story, but instead seemed to side with the Doctor. He rose from his seat before the fourth witness was brought in and made the following declaration to the Court.

'I do not wish or intend to examine any more witnesses. I am afraid that they cannot be relied upon to tell the truth of these matters. The three who have already spoken have uttered falsehoods that do them and me no credit at all.'

He sat back down with a scowl on his face, and Mr Lowther requested Dr Coleman to call his own witnesses to give evidence.

The first to be called for the Defence was Lambert. Captain Mills blustered indignantly when he heard his own witness summoned to give evidence for the opposing side, but powerless to intercede he satisfied himself for the moment by staring hard at the lad all the time, hoping to put him out of countenance.

Lambert proved to be a very poor witness, but in effect his evidence supported the Doctor's case and not that of his captain. Matters not being moved on much more, and the hour growing close to lunchtime, the Court adjourned until the next day.

*

Thursday 22nd December. Captain Mills arrived at the Consulate in the blackest of moods, but, knowing he must appear calm, restrained himself from making a scene. Instead, he presented to the Court a paper which he had written in consultation with his solicitor, stating that, since the charge could not be proved, he wished to abandon the case. The panel discussed this among themselves for quarter of an hour, before deciding that they could not reach any decision until they had heard more evidence. As a result, Dr Coleman had his witnesses brought in and they told their stories. Despite the best efforts of the Captain's solicitor, Mr Corde, nothing was said under cross-examination which contradicted the Doctor's denial of the charges against him; at that impasse, the Court adjourned once more.

Once back on board the *Colinda*, the Doctor was besieged by passengers complaining that the little food there was on board was bad and could not be eaten. Wearily, he made his way to the Captain to report this, fully expecting a rebuff. He was not disappointed.

'What is that to me?' Captain Mills uttered icily, turning his back on the Doctor to indicate that the interview was at an end.

Dr Coleman was not going to stand for that, and he arranged to be rowed ashore whether the Captain would give permission or not. He arrived back on board the *Colinda* two hours later with a letter from the Consul to Captain Mills, instructing the latter to arrange for supplies without delay. Upon being given this document, the Captain smiled most politely, while at the same time calmly ripping it into small shreds and scattering them onto the table.

'It is not my business to find food for these …' but his last word was said to empty air, for the Doctor had left the room.

27
Mills complains

The weather continued fine during the days of the trial. It had begun on December 21st and ended on the 27th. Christmas Day was a Sunday. None of the passengers or crew of the *Colinda* felt much inclined to celebration; the Captain and Dr Coleman kept to themselves. All on the *Colinda* but the children felt depressed, and even they were barely permitted much expression of joy.

Dr Coleman continued to minister to the sick, but nervous tension made him short-tempered, even with Miss Forsyth, and she felt helpless.

Finally, on the Tuesday after Christmas Day, the Court assembled to give its verdict. Captain Mills sat stony-faced, his gaze fixed on Dr Coleman as it was read out by Mr Taylor.

*

The verdict of this court is as follows: After hearing the evidence given, and inquiring, investigating and fully understanding the complaint, and after hearing the response of those complained of (through the Surgeon, Mr Coleman and Mr Robert Ewart, deputised by the rest to conduct the defence) it manifestly appears to the Court: Firstly, that this Court does not find that the Master of the *Colinda* Mr John Mills has made good his complaint. Secondly, the Court has observed with regret a very evident want of disposition on the part of some of the Witnesses to give evidence which might establish the Masters complaint, though this did not necessitate the censure of the Court. Thirdly, that during the course of these proceedings the Court has daily been importuned by complaints made to it by the Passengers to the effect that inadequate provisions, food and water were supplied to them by the Master, and the Court has found justification of this complaint and that food supplied was so totally unfit for the Passengers needs that the Court feels a duty to remonstrate with the Master on the subject and to recommend that he should pay greater attention to the health and comfort of the people under his charge. Fourthly, the Court does declare and certify and order that the necessary reasonable and proper Costs and Expenses of the present proceedings be paid by the Master of the *Colinda*. This report being clearly read to all parties by the Clerk of the Court, the President does declare the proceedings terminated and the court does dissolve.

Signed, Henry William Rouse Esq, Her Royal Majesty's Consul at Valparaiso, Lieutenant Marcus Southen, Her Majesty's Ship Portland, Mr Robert Cumming, Master of the British Ship Briganza, and Robert Taylor (Clerk of the Court). Given this day, the twenty-seventh of December, 1853.

*

Captain Mills heard this with stifled fury, but he held his own counsel for the moment, for he had already decided on a course of action.

*

Once again, John Powell Mills found himself in need of raising funds quickly. It was no use this time to pretend he was suffering from influenza. As part owner of *Colinda*, he sold much of the cargo, though it was the property of the Hudson's Bay Company, for a low price to pay the costs of the case, paid the court costs and pocketed the money left over. He was, though, unsuccessful in his attempt to mortgage the *Colinda* and all her contents for 6,000 Chilean pesos.

On 19 February 1854, the *Colinda* finally left Valparaiso for Vancouver's Island with Mills still in charge, but with an almost entirely new crew, for the others had abandoned the ship. Only seventeen of the original passengers remained on board—all Norwegian. Those left behind were seen on the streets of Valparaiso in a destitute state. They said they would not travel on the boat with Captain Mills but would to travel to Vancouver's Island with another captain. Eventually, most of the men were hired by Matias Cousino & Thomas Bland Garland to work in the mines at Lota. The old crew worked their way back to London where they sued in the Courts of Admiralty for the nonpayment of wages.

On 17 April 1854 the *Colinda* arrived at Fort Victoria, Vancouver's Island. The authorities had been worried by her nonarrival. Mills was arrested upon landing by John Hall, the Constable there. Upon the non-delivery of the *Colinda's* passengers and cargo, the Hudson's Bay Company applied for redress to the Vice-Admiralty Court of Vancouver's Island, and obtained an injunction against the ship and Mills for his failure to properly execute the charter and for selling their property. Mills was tried, convicted and given into the custody of Constable Hall for imprisonment in the Bastion Prison. He was allowed out on parole on certain days, returning at a stated hour for incarceration. One day he was quite late; Hall became impatient, and, when Mills turned up, told him if was late again he would lock him out. He was imprisoned for 4 months, two of them in solitary confinement, and not released till late August 1854.

The Governor of Vancouver's Island, James Douglas received a Power of Attorney from James Tomlin of London, owner of the *Colinda* to place a new captain in charge and supply him with capital. She sailed from Victoria on 16 March 1855 for London via San Francisco under James M. Reid, and arrived in London on 7 July.

Some of the emigrants who did not continue on the *Colinda*, including Mrs. Leigh and her family, finally reached Vancouver's Island months later. Dr Coleman and Miss Forsyth stayed in Valparaiso.

After his release, Mills made his way back home, arriving in London late November 1854.

28
The Colonial Office, London

John Powell Mills was tired and ill. At home Rachel endured his presence with unusual fortitude, though she had no respect for him. He spent much of his time in the China Hall Public House writing letters complaining of his treatment to anyone who might have influence in compensating him for his great troubles.

Sir George Grey, Colonial Secretary, was, as yet, unaware of the trouble on the *Colinda*. The early afternoon of Tuesday 9 January 1855 found him going through correspondence received that morning. Among the letters was one which caused him to raise his eyebrows and sigh with irritation. It was from John Powell Mills.

*

To The Right Honourable Sir George Grey Colonial Secretary
Tuesday 9th January 1855

Honourable Sir,
I have recently arrived from Victoria, Vancouver's Island, where I was most
maliciously and cruelly persecuted. I assure you, Honourable Sir, this Colony is far worse than any other foreign Port for

British subjects to go to for trade, on account of the most despotic, arbitrary power the authorities there have been given.

I am Master and part owner of a beautiful new ship '*Colinda*'. I was chartered by the Hudson Bay Company to proceed from London to Victoria with passengers and merchandise. The loose manner of the Company's servants on departure, and promises made to the passengers by them created a tissue of grievances which was out of my power to control—it finally produced mutiny. On my arrival at Victoria my ship was taken in a very illegal manner from me—I was cast into a den of a Prison, not fit for a dog kennel, and kept there 4 months and 9 days. At their mock courts I was interrogated privately, no person being admitted. I was kept in solitary confinement 2 months, while Mr Douglas, the Governor, seized the *Colinda* in the Queen's name, also seizing all my own effects, instruments, vouchers and every article belonging to me, leaving me perfectly destitute—the ship was converted into a brothel for prostitutes and drunkards—and they made use of her to convey coals to California.

I have therefore humbly petitioned to you, Right Honourable Sir, in hopes that you may take a consideration of the usage I have had to endure, and will be the instigation of having a Public Investigation at which I shall be most happy to attend before any tribunal to answer all things—the best of British subjects are driven to leave their Country by such lawless actions from large companies.

I have the &c
(signed) John Powell Mills
Master of the Barque 'Colinda' of London. 581 tons register.
direct opposite the Entrance of Her Majesty's Victualling Yard, Deptford, Kent'

*

Sir George wrote to the Governor of Vancouver's Island a few days later, enclosing Mill's letter and asking him what he knew about the *Colinda*. James Douglas wrote back to Grey, but by the time his answer arrived, George Grey had become Home Secretary, and the matter was dealt with by one of his successors at the Colonial Office, Sir William Molesworth.

*

James Douglas to The Right Honourable Sir George Grey
Victoria Vancouver's Island
13th May 1855 —received 23 July by Sir William Molesworth, Colonial Secretary.

Sir,

I have the honour to acknowledge your Despatch of the 16th January 1855, transmitting a copy of a letter from Mr John Powell Mills, Master of the Barque *Colinda*, complaining of proceedings taken against him by the authorities on Vancouver's Island, and desiring me to cause enquiries to be made into the facts of the case, and to furnish you with a report on his allegations. I therefore wrote to the Supreme Court of Civil Justice; and their reply indicates that the Magistrates appear to have acted with fairness and impartiality towards all the parties concerned, and there is no reason to suppose that they were influenced by any ill-feeling towards Captain Mills, who was unknown to them except as a person charged with an offence against the Laws of his Country.

After losing his case in Valparaiso, Captain Mills sold off a large portion of the *Colinda's* cargo, the property of the Hudson's Bay Company. He then advertised in the *Echo del Pais,* a Valparaiso Paper, announcing the approaching departure of the *Colinda*, for the Port of San Francisco and offering to take goods and passengers for that port, at the lowest rates. That plan does not, however, appear to have been carried into effect.

Captain Mills finally arrived off the Port of Victoria on the 17th April, and the few able seamen on board deserted the *Colinda*, and fled to the American side of the mainland in course of the following night, leaving the ship with the Master, mates, apprentices, cook and steward. She was towed into the Port of Victoria by a Steam vessel, sent out to her assistance.

Captain Mills produced an account of the Goods sold by him at Valparaiso and a statement of his expenses on the ship's account leaving a balance unaccounted for of £700 Sterling, which he refused to surrender, as required by Law. Therefore, an action for embezzlement was taken against Captain Mills and after some litigation the money was finally recovered. The Process was in itself strictly proper and was conducted in all respects, according to the directions of the statute in such case provided.

In reply to the only allegation in Mr Mills's letter, which remains unanswered I will state that the *Colinda* was not made use of as he asserts by the Hudson's Bay Company to convey coals to California, nor employed by them in any other manner; she lay idle in this Port until chartered for the delivery on her way to London of a cargo of coal at San Francisco.

I have the honour to be Sir
Your most obedient humble Servant
James Douglas, Governor.

*

Back in London Douglas's answer was discussed by the civil servants in the Colonial Office. A certain Mr Merivale wrote a memorandum to his associate, Mr Ball.

*

23 July
This appears to be a very sufficient explanation of the charge made by the late Master of the *Colinda* against the Authorities at Vancouver's Island. Should he be so told—or would you send him a copy of the despatch.

*

Mr Ball responded:

24 July
It certainly appears so. I see no necessity for sending a copy of the despatch to Capt. Mills. It would be sufficient, I think, to inform him that an explanation has been received from the Governor from which it appears that the proceedings taken against him were in course of law, with which Government cannot interfere.

*

On 3 August 1855 a reply was finally sent to Mills stating that nothing could be done for his case as the proceedings taken against him were deemed to be 'in the course of law.' Mills then wrote the following letter of appeal to Sir William Molesworth.

*

To The Right Honourable, Sir William Molesworth, Secretary of State for the Colonies
6th August 1855

Honoured Sir,

I beg to acknowledge your reply to a letter I addressed to Sir George Grey, of the 9th January last. I feel extremely thankful for it; but feel extremely pained to hear the Government can do nothing in the Case.

Honoured Sir, I am not writing again to solicit the aid of Government in righting a most sorely persecuted British subject. Your answer, Yes, or No, was all I required, but more to acknowledge the receipt of your letter.

Honoured Sir. Knowing your uprightness and the great Interest you take in the affairs of the Colonies belonging to Great Britain, I feel certain you will forgive me for stating a few incidents in respect of my cruel treatment at Vancouver's Island, You, Honoured Sir, have heard one side of the story from His Excellency Governor Douglas, but the said Gentleman is also the Head & Chief Factor of the Honourable Hudson Bay Company, he was also my Agent for the ship, and my ship was employed by the said Company, so I will ask you to judge of what redress, or justice, I could obtain there. Governor Douglas did not make an Investigation of all the proceedings of the ship's passage before casting me into that vile place not fit for a poor dog, and keeping me there four sittings and a half of their supreme courts, without even noticing me—was there not unmerciful persecution in this? Is this the Law of our Land? Does it not state, Honourable Sir, that a subject shall not be any unnecessary time in prison before being brought to trial neither is he guilty until found so by his countrymen? I was treated as guilty from the first day of my incarceration, fed upon a dog's portions of food and was also suffering from a disease, which my surgeon tells me is incurable.

When His Excellency thought fit to bring on my Case I was acquitted. He knew it must fall to the ground, had there been any person there in the shape of a Lawyer it could never have taken place. Even after acquittal by the Jurors, I was most spitefully sent to prison again, and was released 9 days later after the judge left a message with the sheriff to set me free. The charge against me was trumpery. The Honourable Hudson's Bay Company owed me near £1,400, but they would not pay me. I therefore did as the Law allows, detain a portion of their chattels amounting to £700 and certainly should have detained more had the Cargo not been perishable. I had lost 5 months valuable earnings, and was put to enormous expense & trouble and mental anxiety through their brutal and mutinous passengers compelling me to go into port under the plea of having bad provisions which the company procured. And here Honoured Sir, I state on my solemn Oath, and my good conscience and before the Almighty God, I did strenuously strive to do that which was right & just.

I may say, Sir, in Vancouver's Island is a splendid Island where many thousands of our countrymen might find a comfortable home under proper Legislation, but many settlers are there living in a great state of dissatisfaction, there is plenty of Law such as it is without any justice the Rule is most despotic in the extreme.

Trusting, Sir, I have not trespassed
I have the Honour to remain Honourable Sir Your most obedient Humble Servant
John Powell Mills of Swansea Sth Wales,
Opposite H.M. Victualling Yard Entrance, Deptford

*

This letter was ignored. Mills never received an answer to it, and he spent many of his waking hours drinking away his resentment at the China Hall Public House while holding forth on the great injustices life had dealt him to any who would listen.

29
Alex and Mina

If the second part of this tale should seem to betray partiality for the character of Dr Coleman, I ask your indulgence. He was my friend for five years, and the remainder of his story bears some telling.

It is true that his relationship with Miss Forsyth had become closer than they were prepared to admit while on the *Colinda*. Perhaps it was their dealings with Captain Mills which pushed them closer together.

On 26 March 1855 Dr Henry William Alexander Coleman married Williamina Manson Forsyth in Valparaiso. He loved her with all his heart, and she loved him, but their happiness was not to last. Less than sixteen weeks after their marriage she died. My good friend Henry could hardly bear to speak of her when I knew him, so choked with emotion did he become. I had supposed that her death was due to yellow fever or some other tropical disease, but eventually, he confessed to me that she had died of complications during childbirth, to which both she and the child had succumbed.

Inconsolable, and shattered beyond all measure, he made his way to Peru, where he remained for some years practising medicine, and becoming an expert in unusual diseases. But life became a little easier for him after a while, and he met a lady there who comforted him. Charlotte Sophia had been born in India in 1835 and there was a placidity about her which pleased his senses and charmed him. They married in Peru, and then travelled to London for an extended honeymoon where their first child, Catherine Sophy Babington Coleman was born. On their return to Peru, he continued to work hard while his wife kept a jealous watch over him. In 1866 a second daughter, Marian Agnes was born. Shortly after this they returned again to England, this time for good. He set up in practice in Lutterworth, Leicestershire, and it was a few years after that I met the family.

It happened thus: Catherine, the elder daughter, was a happy but sickly child, whereas Marian was a healthy but unhappy girl given to strange moods and fancies. Shortly after the birth of their brother, Henry Wycliffe Coleman in 1872, Marian, then only six years old, began to exhibit a most strange behaviour that troubled her parents greatly. The girl was unusually secretive and suffered from kleptomania in so great a degree that no one's possessions were deemed safe from being stolen. Her father was so concerned that he arranged to take her to London in order to consult with me. My experience dealing with criminals, he felt, might cast some light on the matter, for I had recently published a paper on the origins of criminal behaviour, tracing it back to childhood.

I had not heard of Dr Coleman before, but his letter interested me, and so I agreed to interview him and Marion in my surgery. I took an instant liking to him, and our association continued long after I had done all I could to reassure him that there was nothing wrong with the child.

He had become Medical Officer at the Lutterworth Union Workhouse, and his experiences with the inmates of that institution were of great interest. We spent a number of useful evenings discussing the behaviour of the criminal and the proto-criminal whenever he travelled down to London, and we corresponded on these matters in some detail.

One evening, as we sat discussing past times, he told me of his travels on the *Colinda*, I listened with interest, for he was an interesting speaker. When he told me the name of the ship's captain, I was astounded, and so it was that I heard much of the tale I have recounted in the second half of this book.

By 1877 he was not in the best of health, and had been diagnosed with Phthisis of the lungs. His marriage had not been happy for some years; his wife, Charlotte was suspicious of everyone and everything, and was something of a spendthrift who continually worried him over their lack of money.

That year he died, leaving his estate to be divided between his children. His wife left the household and went to live in France, declining to have anything to do with the upbringing of her own children, who went to live with their father's widowed mother in London. His logbook from his time on the *Colinda* was naturally in the keeping of the Hudson's Bay Company in Vancouver. However, he had kept a carefully written copy and this, together with a slim volume of notes and memoirs, was bequeathed to me as a gesture of gratitude for my help in easing his worries about his younger daughter.

Eighteen days after his death, his older daughter, Catherine, who was visiting her mother in Dieppe, suddenly and mysteriously died.

That is the last I heard of the Coleman family. I trust that the two living children are healthy and well.

30
Dr Gover lays down his pen

And what of Captain Mills? For that, we must go back a few years.

He died aged forty-nine in 1866 of heart disease and cirrhosis of the liver caused by his alcoholism. He had been found unconscious, face down on a table at the China Hall Public House among empty tankards and carried back home where he never woke. Rachel was not sorry to see the back of him; his last days had been burdensome to them both. She went to live with her brother William.

What had made Mills travel the world? If it was part of a boyish dream to make his fortune, then he lost sight of that goal early on. If it was to get away from an intolerable life at home, he succeeded only to find an intolerable life at sea. What made him behave as he did? Was it a need for power over others that drove him, a need to impose his will on others because he felt unappreciated? His world was his ship—whichever ship was that of the moment. There he could be master of a world, though that world be a microcosm of reality. He wished to be a hero, but ultimately was doomed to disappointment and failure, becoming bitter as he grew older.

And yet, there may be a twist to this tale which must be mentioned. For another interpretation can be placed on all these events. It could be that Captain John Powell Mills was, after all, misunderstood; that he was truly acting for the best at all times and was merely unfortunate in his associates and in the circumstances that surrounded him. Should we give credence to Dr Coleman's version of what happened on the *Colinda*, or was Mills the victim of an unjustified mutiny? And what of Dorcas Newman who met such an unfortunate end on the *Subraon*? Might Mills have been unaware of what was going on beneath his very nose? The sinking of that ship points, perhaps, more to his incompetence than to intent. Was he merely one who spent his life trying to cover up ineptitude, in the full knowledge that he never should have been allowed to captain a ship? Did he bluff his way into positions of command, and, if so, what does that say about those who were fooled by Captain Mills into placing him in positions of authority, for his reputation as captain was not good?

*

There may be a lesson to learn about mankind from this narrative, though I have no intention to moralise. I leave you, reader, to form your own conclusions about the life and doings of Captain Mills. I have largely left myself out of the second half of the narrative, though my researches were as meticulous regarding the *Colinda* as they were about the *Subraon*. Please be aware that I am not a sea-faring man, and that the sailor language I have used is my own impression of their talk.

It has taken me some time to put this narrative together; I was a single man when I began these researches, and now, though in the Autumn of my life, I have married and have a wife and a stepdaughter to look after. I can hear little Maudie calling me now, just back from a walk with my sister Rebecca.

I have written here about people whose lives were far more difficult than mine, my life has been a happy one. It is my hope that you who read these pages have as happy and fulfilled a life as I, and that you never know the privations of those unfortunates who travelled in appalling conditions as emigrants to new worlds.

Signed: Robert Mundy Gover
Kensington 1891

AFTERWORD

Many of the events you have read about in this book really did happen, and the following is a guide to some of the incidents you have read.

1. There really was a Medical Inspector of Her Majesty's Prisons called Robert Mundy Gover, but his visit to Northallerton Gaol is my invention. John Powell Mills Jnr was a prisoner there in 1867, and for the reasons stated.

2. All journal entries, letters and diaries are my own creations, written to help propel the narrative, though Dr Coleman really did keep a detailed journal of the voyage of the *Colinda*.

3. Though many of the actions of the passengers on the *Colinda* really did happen, those on the *Subraon* are an invention. However, there really were eleven girls from the Dublin Orphan Institution on board, and Dorcas Newman's story is as faithfully recounted as a work of historical fiction will allow.

4. One of the sailors uses the word *campusments*. The phrase he was trying to say was *compos mentis*.

5. The 3rd Earl Grey devised a scheme to convey emigrants to Australia. Earl Grey tea is named after his father, the 2nd Earl Grey.

6. Dr Coleman's surviving children both found themselves briefly in the workhouse. In 1919 Marian, who had worked as a hospital nurse, was admitted with mental disorders to the Northumberland Street Workhouse, London, where she stayed for a month before being transferred to the Claybury Asylum in Essex. After working as a farmer and as a clerk, Henry Wycliffe Coleman spent a brief time in the City of Westminster Union Workhouse in 1922.

7. All legal proceedings mentioned and described really did take place.

8. John Mills (a cooper) son of John Mills (coal dealer) married Ann Shaw (a minor) daughter of John Shaw (shoemaker) with her father's consent in 1844 in Rotherhithe. Their son John Powell Mills b.1848, imprisoned in 1867 at Northallerton Prison, was no relation to the ship's captain, the subject of this story, though details of his crime are correctly reported, and therefore Captain Mills' wife Rachel was not in reality unfaithful to him.

9. Doctors Coleman and Gover never met, and their association with each other is fiction.

10. The cover illustration *The Emigrants* is from the Illustrated London News (June 1850).

Bound for Australia

1. I have not seen my home For ma - ny a day, I've
2. I was down on my luck With no - thing to do, Had

left it be - hind And I'm sail - ing a - way, To
not a po - ta - to To put in a stew, A

come on this voy - age I spent all my pay, Now we're
babe on the way: In three months it's due, So we're

bound for Aus - tra - li - a.
bound for Aus - tra - li - a.

Here up on deck, When the sun's shin - ing bright,

Hope - ful and hap - py, Though land's out of sight, We for -

get all our cares Till the cold of the night, While we're

bound for Aus - tra - li - a.

Words and Music: Bryan Kesselman © 2016

About the Author

Bryan Kesselman's first book, *Paddington Pollaky Private Detective* (a biography of a Victorian private investigator) was published in 2015. This book, *The Madness of Captain Mills* , is based on real events, and like the first book, involved extensive research involving contact with archives in several countries. Bryan is a composer, musical director, and opera singer, and lives in the UK. Works include music and lyrics for an opera based on the Dreyfus Affair, first performed in 1998, and Zimbabwe Suite for choir and orchestra, commissioned for performances in Zimbabwe and London.

If you enjoyed this book, please consider leaving an online review. The author would appreciate reading your thoughts.

http://www.madnessofcaptainmills.co.uk/
http://www.paddingtonpollaky.co.uk/
http://www.kesselmanmusic.co.uk/

You can also follow the author on Twitter: https://twitter.com/bryankesselman

About the Publisher

Sulis International Press publishes select fiction and nonfiction in a variety of genres under four imprints: Riversong Books, Sulis Academic Press, Sulis Press, and Keledei Publications.

For more, visit the website at
https://sulisinternational.com

Subscribe to the newsletter at
https://sulisinternational.com/subscribe/

Follow on social media
https://www.facebook.com/SulisInternational
https://twitter.com/Sulis_Intl
https://www.pinterest.com/Sulis_Intl/
https://www.instagram.com/sulis_international/

Printed in Great Britain
by Amazon